STUMBLING TOWARDS SALVATION

STUMBLING TOWARDS SALVATION

▼

Mechel Cisco

Writers Club Press
San Jose New York Lincoln Shanghai

Stumbling Towards Salvation

Writers Club Press
an imprint of iUniverse.com, Inc.

For information address:
iUniverse.com, Inc.
620 North 48th Street, Suite 201
Lincoln, NE 68504-3467
www.iuniverse.com

ISBN: 0-595-14439-X

Printed in the United States of America

DEDICATION

To my mother who is long since passed. Nevertheless, I
know is smiling down on me with great pride.

EPIGRAPH

She took the beast's hand and kissed it, and smelled the forest. She felt the coarse fur and the sharp claws. "I am ugly," he said. "I am a beast and a fool. But Beauty, my heart is good."

Beauty and the Beast

ACKNOWLEDGEMENTS

Special Thanks to my husband Neff for all his support, encouragement and understanding the importance of my long absences needed to write this book.

INTRODUCTION

"Look at me Gillian and tell me you could be happy married to someone else." Aidan paused. She could not look at him or answer. "Could you live with the thought of another woman in my bed?" He suddenly got her attention. Gillian did not answer, she was silent as she walked over to her dressing table and sat down. Aidan moved up behind her and watched her reflection in the mirror. Her breast rose and fell rapidly with each breath. He laid his hands on her shoulders. She closed her eyes; all resistance began to melt with his touch. He lowered his lips to her ear and took her lobe into his warm mouth.

She fought within herself. "No Aidan, stop." She stood to walk away from him. He caught her and spun her around, pushing her against the wall. His warm breath brushed her cheek. "Please Aidan." She sighed. He turned her face up with his finger, her lips parted and he kissed her pushing her mouth wider with his tongue. The roar in her head drowned out all rational thought. She swallowed hard when his lips left hers. Her gaze drifted down to his mouth. "Please do not do that again." She said breathless.

"My God, your beautiful. I have such need of you." He softly groaned. The sound he made was primeval like some ancient creature in agony. Her innocence was all that protected her from his mounting hunger.

CHAPTER 1

▼

Cardoness, Darnaway Estate

Gillian lay doglike by a fire of peat and ancient tree root far out in the empty grounds of Cardoness as the day slid on into the eve; laid and dreamed waking scenes of the great forest just beyond the valley.

There on a cool night three thousand years before; people humbered in the same shudder of the flame light, ever aware of the vastness of the dark, encircling wood where the bear and boar, the wolverine and the hunting packs wailed.

Gillian rested her back against an old tree trunk, twisting her fingers in her long Auburn curly locks while staring into the small flame that had all but exhausted. Her brown doe eyes twinkled as she imagined freedom, knowing one day it would come; freedom from her life and domain. She felt sure it would come, but what day; how long would she have to wait?

"Gillian!" An angry voice thundered out of the darkness from the main house. Sudden dread invaded Gillian's body. She anticipated with horror at having to answer that call. And for a brief moment, pretended she did not have to. "Gillian!" Diaspad, Gillian's husband, shouted again.

Gillian jumped to her feet this time, knowing well the indignation if she did not come when called.

She hated to see his face; with his caved-in features and the way his skin hung on his bones like loose fitting attire. The foul smell of whiskey permeated not only his breath but his skin as well, as if he had been marinated in it. The smell of liquor was a constant reminder of her imprisonment. Trap of self and nightmare of alienation.

Gillian rushed up to the bottom of the step of the back porch, where Diaspad stood, like a master summoning his dog.

"Yes, Diaspad, you called?" Gillian asked, out of breath. She had hoped his drunken anger might have softened this time, being that she answered so obediently.

"Where have you been wench!?" His anger grew, rather than disbursed itself.

Gillian armed her fears. "I took a stroll, and did not realize the time."

"Come here witch!" Gillian reluctantly took one step toward Diaspad. "Who do you think you are? You may have my name but you will never be Lady of this manor to do as you please! No one will ever take my Nottie's place!" Diaspad reached out, grabbed a handful of Gillian's fiery tresses, and drug her into the house, kicking and screaming.

Nottie was Diaspad's first wife. She had become pregnant by another man and in a jealous rage; Diaspad accidentally knocked her down a flight of stairs, killing her and the unborn child. Diaspad drank to drown his guilt.

Diaspad flung Gillian into a corner of the parlor. She kept still thinking the less she moved, the less he would remember she was in the room. Gillian curled herself into a tight ball as tight as she could. She remained, still like death, with her knees pressed up against the wall and its mockery of soothing warm colors.

The housemaid, Adelaide entered the parlor. "Can I fix you a bite to eat Lord Darnaway?"

"Come here, give us a kiss." He sloppily groped Adelaide. She giggled, cutting her eyes in Gillian's direction and giving her a smirk.

Gillian began to unfold herself now that Diaspad's attention was focused elsewhere. It made no difference to Gillian that her husband spent most of his time in Adelaide's bed. She thanked God; better Adelaide's bed than her own.

Adelaide did not mind the strange request asked of her by Diaspad. His sexual appetites were perverse and indecent by common standards. He liked for Adelaide to lay in a bath of freezing water till she was chilled to the bone, and then she would have to lie very still like a corpse, before he could make love to her. Something he must have taken a liking to after years spent after school in his father's mortuary.

Gillian crawled toward the door slowly and had almost made it out into the hallway when Diaspad caught her shadow from the corner of his eye. He quickly let go of Adelaide and with one hand grabbed Gillian by the hair again. He yanked her to her feet and threw her hard up against the old flowered pattern wall. Her arms caught the brunt of her weight. She remained silent, trying to become one of those big dingy flowers.

"I did not tell you to leave!" Diaspad screamed.

Gillian buried her face into the wall and folded her arms against her chest, bracing herself for what was to come. "Please Diaspad, let me go." She said in a faint cry.

Diaspad jerked her around, curled his fingers into a fist, and hit her hard across the face. Gillian reeled, putting a hand to the livid red welt that marred the high arch of her cheekbone.

Normally, he never hit her on the face. Could not have The Lady Darnaway walking around with bruises about the face.

"A drink is what I need. Keep my dinner warm," he said to Adelaide; "I'll be at the pub." Gillian stepped clear out of his way as he stumbled out of the house.

Gillian retired to her room, she could relax now that Diaspad had left and knowing he would not return until the wee hours. Her room was simple, so simple it was more fitting for a poor farm hand than a Lady. It sat attached to the side of the main house and looked like something that would have been used for storage. A small hearth provided Gillian with heat and it was away from Diaspad, which made the lack of conveniences tolerable.

The wind blew in through the cracks of the old-boarded walls making the tiny room very drafty. Gillian would often have to wrap herself in three blankets to keep warm.

Gillian did not mind the harshness of her life; she chose to look upon it as a temporary inconvenience. Her father, a doctor, had given her hand to Diaspad before he died, with the intentions that Gillian would be well cared for and kept from poverty. He had no knowledge of Diaspad's habits.

Though Gillian's surroundings were unsophisticated and modest at best, she was at least alone. Any place away from Diaspad was wonderful. Any hovel, any site, any space, any domain or corner of the world, as long as there was no Diaspad. Her own little domain to read and study all her father's medical books and notes. To enter the pages and become part of the words. The books kept part of her father alive for her; it was the only thing he left Gillian when he died.

Gillian tucked herself beneath her many blankets, as she did every night, with one of her books to help her fall asleep. She had diligently studied her books, like a student, until the pages were worn and tattered. It did not matter that she knew each page by heart or that she had exhausted all the knowledge the books had to give; she never tired of reading and studying.

Gillian's heavy lids fluttered; the end of another day was here and the abode of sleep was near, there in the deep valley where the sun never shines and the dusky twilight wraps all things in shadows. No cock crows, no watchdog breaks the silence; no branches rustle in the breeze and no clamor of tongues to disturb the peace. The only sound comes from the gentle flowing stream near by. The river of forgetfulness where the waters murmuring entice sleep. Gillian lay floating in the darkness like a soup bone.

CHAPTER 2

▼

Gillian began her day in the usual manner. Diaspad had made his way home again sometime in the night and as usual, found his way into Adelaide's bed. And as usual, he would sleep until late in the afternoon.

Gillian attended to her daily chores out side the house. She fed and watered all the animals and tended to their daily needs, although this was unheard of for a Lady of her means to do such work. Diaspad could well afford to hire hands to work the estate, but seem to find joy in demeaning Gillian at every chance.

Gillian did not mind, she rather enjoyed it, at least it kept her out of the house most of the day, away from Diaspad's reach. She preferred the livestock anyway to Diaspad, they had more class.

The sky was heavy with dark clouds threatening rain, reflecting Gillian's inner despair. She shoveled the hay with forceful jabs of the pitchfork, imagining Diaspad impaled on the other end. It was the little joys that got her through the day.

The day dragged on as a dampened breeze blew in through the opened old doors of the barn. Gillian's skirt twisted around her legs from a strong gust of wind, revealing her alabaster knees. She scanned the horizon just outside the barn doors to a cloud as pitch as a raven's feather. She squinted her eyes as the rain fell like tears from the dark veil of the sky.

There was something riding on the wind, an alien feeling that Gillian had not felt in a long time. What was it? The rousing breeze tousled her hair as the corner of her lips

arched it upward, slightly. Her fingertips examined the strangely familiar gesture her mouth made. What is this? A smile?

But there were no smiles here. No laughter. No reason to hope. But Hope it was, and Hope she felt. But where, where could it have come from?

It was out there somewhere, and it lingered on the wind, invading Gillian's senses like a delicious smell.

Gillian wrapped her shawl tighter around her bosom as the wind began to blow colder. She made herself a cozy warm nest out of hay to wait out the storm.

"Gillian! Where are you wench!" Diaspad bellowed out from the main house. He was awake. Awakened no doubt from the loud thunderclaps. Gillian pretended not to hear; sure he would not come out in the rain to look for her. She snuggled tighter underneath her shawl, it was old and full of holes and just barely served its purpose, but it was all she had. "Gillian!" His voice was more demanding, then silent. Diaspad appeared without warning in the doorway of the barn, dripping wet, and very angry that he was so. Gillian sat up straight, and braced herself. "Why did you not answer me wench!"

"I did not hear you milord, till just now. The thunder was so loud." She made her excuses with no intentions of him accepting them.

"Look at me! I'm all wet on the count of you!" Gillian remained seated in the hay.

"I am sorry Milord, I would have surely came with haste if I had heard you call."

"Get up. Adelaide needs you to gather some vegetables from the garden." He ordered.

"But Milord, there is a storm raging as we speak." Gillian said standing to her feet. "Is that not Adelaide's duty?"

"Do you dare disobey me?" Diaspad balled his fist.

Gillian stared at his ready fist. "No Diaspad, not at all. It's just...."

"Just what?" He said in a mocking tone.

"I am your wife and Adelaide is the housemaid." Gillian said, only as a reminder. She refused to cower at his feet; some dignity must remain.

"Wife?" He mocked her again. "Adelaide is more of a wife than you will ever be!" Gillian lowered her eyes. "Do as you were told!" Gillian said nothing, lifting her eyes to him. A look of scorn filled her eyes as she started to pass him. Diaspad grabbed her by the arm, yanking her to his side. He pulled her close with a tight grip on her arm, squeezing his bony fingers into the soft flesh of her arm. The fresh scent of her hair caught his attention. "Do you have something you wish to say to me, wench!"? He gritted his teeth and tried to ignore her pleasant aroma. Gillian said nothing and turned her eyes away from his gaze. He pulled her tighter into his groin; something he had never done before. "Why have I not bedded you, wench?" He sniffed her hair.

Gillian tried to pull away from the foul stench of his breath. The long abuse of liqueur had begun to eat away at his insides like rotting meat left out in the sun. Breath from the mouth of hell it was. She managed to pull free from Diaspad and ran out into the cleansing rain.

Gillian entered the house, soaked to the bone, with her apron full of freshly picked vegetables. She unloaded them onto the kitchen counter, splashing Adelaide with rain droplets and giving her an evil eye.

Adelaide gave her a smirk, feeling superior in rank, feeling sure within her that one day she would replace Gillian. However, Diaspad would never lower himself to marry a servant; he was after all, the King's cousin.

Gillian cleaned the mud from off the vegetables while staring out the window. The rain had now let up but the clouds still lingered dark and heavy, too full to move.

Diaspad sat at the kitchen table, sorting through the mail mumbling disgruntled remarks. He sipped on a glass of bourbon as he often did; it seemed to help him tolerate the debts he owed. He stopped on a letter and for a moment, and stared at it. "Well now, would you look at this."? He said with a grin.

"What is it, Milord?" Adelaide asked with a smile.

"I don't believe my eyes. It's an invitation to Castle Aberdour, and from my cousin, the King himself."

Gillian turned around and gleamed at the invitation in Diaspad's hand. She stepped a little closer, not taking her eyes off the piece of paper as if it came from another world. To Gillian it did, anything outside of Cardoness was another world.

"Invitation?" Adelaide's face lit up as she gasped with excitement. "A ball, a banquet.... what?"

"It doesn't say. It requests the Darnaway family and household to be at Castle Aberdour before sun down tomorrow. Strange."

Adelaide clapped her hands together, happily. "I can't wait!"

"Well Gillian you have a lot of packing to do. Pack my best clothes and Adelaide will show you what of hers to pack. And Gillian, try to look presentable. You will put on a decent dress, won't you?"

"But Diaspad, I don't own a dress that isn't tattered or torn. You refused me the last time I wanted to buy a dress." Remarked Gillian.

"Well then, maybe you can borrow something of Adelaide's. You will find her something, won't you Adelaide?" Diaspad asked, but with insistence. Adelaide gritted her teeth and nodded.

"You know Milord, I could do with a new frock. I know a shop that is still open." Adelaide gave him a slow smile and batted her eyes. Diaspad reached in his pocket, pulled out some money, and handed it to Adelaide. Diaspad slapped her on her rear as she took the money from his hand. She gave him a sultry smirk, and then looked at Gillian throwing her nose up at her.

Gillian said nothing; not even an emotion crossed her face. She wouldn't bother with wasting it on Adelaide. "Diaspad, may I see the invitation?"

"Why?" He gave her a stern look and moved it further from her reach.

"I have never seen a royal invitation." Gillian explained.

"And it is likely you never will." He chuckled. "Look at your hands, they're filthy, you will soil it!" He slipped the paper into his vest pocket. Gillian returned to her duties and did not press the matter any further.

After dinner, Diaspad sat by the fire, dozing, and full of spirits as Gillian folded the laundry to take upstairs to be packed.

She tipped-toed up the squeaky wooden staircase as so not to wake Diaspad. Gillian entered his bedroom and placed his perfectly folded clothes into a travel tote.

Gillian made sure there were no wrinkles and that each item was placed neatly and the same distance apart from the rest.

As Gillian was opening a wardrobe drawer, her eye spotted the invitation sitting on the wardrobe. She stood still looking at it, trying to read it without actually touching it. It was written in a beautiful hand with letters that flowed and curled.

Gillian scanned the room behind her, making sure she was alone. The piece of paper taunted her, begging her to lift it from its perch. Slowly, she reached her hand out and gently picked up the invitation with care. She rubbed her finger lightly across the fine white paper. "Beautiful." Gillian raised the paper to her nose, trying to capture any remaining scent that may still be lingering within its folds.

Gillian closed her eyes and held the paper to her breast. She imagined the Castle from whom the small piece of paper came, the people, the smells, and the grounds. She imagined freedom.

"How dare you!" Gillian's eyes flew open. Diaspad entered the room without warning. "You wench! Who do you think you are snooping through my things?"

"Diaspad!" She uttered with surprise. "I...." Gillian began to explain but before she could, Diaspad grabbed her wrist and twisted it, sending the provocateur to the floor. Diaspad let go of her wrist, but only to reach for his leather whip he kept at his bedside.

Gillian took a step back, pleading with her eyes. Diaspad slapped the leather thongs into his open palm. "Come here Gillian." He said calmly through gritted teeth. "I'll soon exercise that willful demon from you!"

"Please Milord." Gillian took another step back away from him. But his hand shot out and grabbed her shoulder with fingers of steel. She twisted away from his grasp, almost wrenching her arm from its socket. With his hand now free, Diaspad slammed bedroom door shut.

Gillian ran toward the bed, stumbling against an oak table and falling to her knees. Quicker than a blink of an eye, he was beside her. She tried to crawl under the table, but his black booted foot barred her way. Diaspad hoisted her up by the arm like a sack of potatoes and threw her back onto the bed. He pounced on top of her and unleashed the back of his hand across her face.

Gillian looked at him with no emotion, not even a tear did she lend him. "You wicked, wicked imp. Your big brown eyes won't work their magic on me." Nevertheless, he avoided her eyes and instead gazed down upon her heaving chest. Gillian tried to push him off, not liking the look in his eyes.

Diaspad grabbed her small hands and held them above her head with just one of his large paws. He was like a cannibal ready to feast from a hidden place. A sudden storm rose up. From the flashes of lightning, Gillian could make out brief moments of the sky from the corner of her eye.

He groped at her breasts with his free hand. Gillian gritted her teeth and pinched her eyes shut. Her entire body ached as if she had been flung from a great height. It would do no good to plead, all she could do was lay there spread-eagle, powerless on her back hoping he wouldn't smash her face in when he was done.

Gillian saw Diaspad's hand move down to his pants. Again, a flash of sky. Gillian held on to it. That's the sky, she says to herself. That's the sky and that's a tree limb. She heard his zipper unzip. Diaspad tore at her under garment, ripping it to shreds.

There again, she tells herself, there's the sky and there's the tree. He released his penis to the open. His touch was no longer human. Gillian tightened her thighs and body in refusal. There again, a piece of sky. She clung to the sky with her eye.

Diaspad had never tried such an act with her; in all the time they had been married. Why he chose to now was beyond her understanding.

Gillian pinched her eyes, clinched her teeth, and waited. No screams, no begging. She felt as if she were going to die. Die looking at the sky. Hold on to the sky; hold on to the sky!

Still she waited. His weight was suffocating, she couldn't breathe. She thought she was going to be sick. Where was the sky? Where was the tree? She had to see the sky. There, there it is. Gillian hid in the sky.

Diaspad tried to imagine Gillian dead and cold, her eyelids turning blue, as well as the flesh on her bones. Cold and still. Oh so still. However, Gillian was warm, her blood pumped vigorously through her veins. Warm and alive.

The weight lifted from Gillian's rigid body. Slowly, she opened her eyes. Diaspad stood over her, putting his soft penis back in his pants with an accusing eye.

Gillian got a glimpse of the shriveled pink thing. His frustration turned to anger. "You witch! You can't do anything right, not even arouse me!" Terror gripped her like a virus, she began to sweat, fevered, trying to burn it out.

Diaspad picked up the whip and lifted it in a menacing manner. Gillian covered her face and curled her body like a fetus. She heard the sound of the whip whistle through the air as Diaspad's hand descended. She soon felt the stinging pain as the leather thongs bit into her back.

Gillian took a chance, jumped from the bed, and ran for the door as Diaspad repositioned his arm in the air to strike again. He leaped at her and barred the door with his arm, managing to get another blow to her back. Her body slid down the door and she sagged forward on her knees. Gillian bit her lip, drawing blood, to keep from making an outcry.

"Go clean yourself up, you are a mess! And finish packing. You better not make us late in the morning!" Diaspad pushed her aside with his boot to open the door.

Gillian crept back to her room feeling all loss of dignity and laid down on her bed as tears rolled down her face. Beds were not made to feel comfortable on, not to lie on in sickness, and not to dream sweet dreams upon.

Gillian thought of the moon. The moon survives, draws herself out crescent thin, a curved woman. Untouchable, she bends around the shadow that pushes against her, and she waits. Gillian knew, she too, must learn to draw her life out like the moon.

CHAPTER 3

▼

Gillian awoke early and dressed in a meager dress that Adelaide had thrown her way. It was big on such a slip of a girl, but at least it was clean and free of holes. Gillian was all ready to go after having packed the few personals that she owned in a small bag. No clothes, just the ones on her back.

Diaspad ordered a coach to come around early. The driver loaded the luggage on the carriage as Diaspad helped Adelaide inside the compartment. Adelaide sported a fine new dress and hat to match her inner excitement. Diaspad entered and took a seat next to Adelaide. Gillian helped herself into the closed compartment and took a seat across from Diaspad and Adelaide. Though the seats were padded and soft, Gillian had to lean slightly forward to keep her back off the seat from last night's wrath unleashed on her back. She made no grimace of discomfort or let on she was in any pain.

Gillian sat quietly as the carriage pulled away from Cardoness. She chose the scenery outside her window as opposed to having to look at Diaspad and Adelaide. Diaspad watched her closely, but Gillian chose to ignore him pretending she could not feel his stares upon her.

Though Gillian was dressed in sparse attire, she had an aire of elegance about her. A potato sack still would not have marred her opulence. Maybe this is what Diaspad noticed.

The horse drawn carriage swept along the track that cut across a heath in the village of Aberconway, curling around shinning lakes and winding toward dark pine forest where wolves sang out from distant shadows.

The road was a river of early sunlight over the purple moor damp with mists; an unworldly blend of sight and sound. The fields harvested on each side of the road stretched as far as the eye could see over greenish-brown hills. Castle Aberdour sat ahead, gray and majestic.

Gillian's heart lit up. She had never seen such beauty. From the rear of the carriage, she could see curling plumes of smoke above the chimneys of the village that now sat lower in the protective shadow of the castle. Gillian felt an inexpressible relief, a soothing conviction, and security.

Water welled in puddles in the deep ruts of the road as they neared Castle Aberdour. A row of trees grew on each side of the road stretched out toward the castle, guiding the way. Bright blue and white banners flew from every turret of the great castle, waving a welcome.

Gillian smiled with glee like a child. The coach entered the castle gates where an older man full of vigor met it. He was broad shouldered, steady and clear-eyed. He waved the carriage to a stop just outside the castle courtyard. Diaspad stuck his head out the window of the compartment.

"May I help you sir? Do you have business here?" The old man asked Diaspad in a polite manner.

"Indeed I do!" Diaspad said with a loud smug tone as he handed the man his invitation.

The old gent looked at Diaspad and gave him a smile. "Of course. Please, wont you follow me." He opened the door of the coach. Diaspad stepped down first, and then helped Adelaide. The old gent offered his hand to Gillian as she gave him a kind smile.

"My name is Beechim, I am the King's chamberlain." Beechim led them up a pathway and through an ornately carved gate. The air was crisp and clean, like first spring morning. Beechim opened the gate for the visitors to enter the main courtyard, which was the entrance to the castle.

King Gododdin, Gody as his friends called him, and Prince Aidan watched from a window, not expecting any guests. The King realized it was Diaspad and he and the Prince went down to greet Diaspad and his family. King Gody opened the Castle's huge doors. "Cousin Diaspad!" He smiled. "What brings you so far from home? Why it's been years!"

Diaspad gave him a strange look. "You did." He said showing him the invitation.

King Gody reached in his breast pocket for his specs as Diaspad handed him the piece of paper. He read it with confusion. "Well, I don't know anything about this, but you and yours are welcome nevertheless." Gody never cared too much for Diaspad, but being the kind man he was, he was not one to turn away family. "Oh, forgive me...you remember Aidan? He was but a lad when you last saw him." Gody laughed.

"Welcome." Prince Aidan said in a low voice with a bow of his head and his eyes on Gillian. Prince Aidan was half Felidacephales, "lion head" and half human. They were a race of people that existed on a nearby island until the church ended up wiping out the race. Prince Aidan and his mother the Queen, who died when he was a boy, were the last of the race. The Felidacephales people were human like in every respect except for having the facial features of a cat and possessing the Keene senses of a cat. Since the Prince was only half, his features were mostly human except for the end of his nose, which had a crease as cats do to the lip.

Gillian stood in the background, waiting to be spoken to. "Ah, and this must be your lovely wife." Gody said, taking Adelaide's hand and kissing it. Adelaide giggled behind her hand covering her mouth.

"Actually, no." Diaspad turned and looked at Gillian. "Adelaide is my house maid. And this…." He grabbed Gillian by the arm and pulled her from the shadows. "My wife, Gillian." He said with little enthusiasm.

The King was confused, given the way Gillian was dressed as compared to Adelaide. He gave her a smile and kissed her hand. "Welcome my child."

Prince Aidan took a step closer. Honey colored waves of hair spilled out from under his scarlet cloak perched jauntily on his head. Dazzling green eyes flecked with gold, cat's eyes, met Gillian's brown orbs in a long curious stare. These eyes were a blessing, Gillian thought. A smile played upon her lips as he bowed his head to her. Gillian curtsied gracefully as a wave of emotion she could not identify washed over her.

"Gillian!" Snapped Diaspad. The misery again settled over her like a dark shroud. Her eyes still locked on Aidan; he saw the smile slide from Gillian's face.

Aidan merely peered into her eyes that were fixed on him with a glassy curiosity, and then traced the curves of her face to her voluptuous mouth. However, for Gillian, it was not just curiosity that made her stare, oh no. He was simply the most beautiful creature she had ever seen.

Gillian followed in behind Adelaide after another roar from Diaspad. The entrance was large as most castles. Adjacent to the entrance stood a grand staircase with a gold banister and deep blue carpet trailing up its steps that forked in its middle and lead off in two different directions.

Huge portraits of royal ancestors hugged the stone walls. High above the gigantic doorways stood royal arms emblazoned on gold plagues. In every room, huge fireplaces sat demanding undivided attention in exchange for warmth.

A round plump woman joined them with rosy cheeks and a friendly smile. "This is Aggie." King Gody said. "She pretty much runs this place and everyone in it, including me." He laughed. "She will see you to your chambers. Aggie, why not put Lord and Lady Darnaway in the West wing."

"If it is not too much trouble…." Diaspad spoke up. "I prefer my own room. I snore rather loud and keep Lady Darnaway awake." Gillian looked at him; amazed he was so quick on his feet. She sighed in relief.

Aidan stood beside Gillian; his keen hearing heard her sigh. Gillian could feel the warmth emanating from Prince Aidan's body. The hairs on the back of her neck stood up; she could almost feel his breath on her skin.

"Come Gillian." Diaspad ordered as if he were talking to a dog.

Aggie led them up the grand staircase to their chambers. Diaspad and Adelaide in one wing and Gillian in the wing where Prince Aidan resided.

"This is a beautiful room, thank you Aggie." Gillian said, throwing her cloak upon the bed.

"Oh yer a welcome lass. Oh, forgive me...Lady Darnaway." Aggie put her hand to her cheek, realizing her mistake.

Gillian smiled. "Please, call me Gillian." Gillian said, reaching out and lightly touched Aggie's hand.

Aggie saw how genuine and sweet Gillian was. "Aye lass. Gillian twill be." She smiled. "I will send Beechim ta build ya a fire in ya grate."

"Oh, don't bother. I can do it myself."

"Nay, I won't eare of sooch. He hasta bring yer bags oop inna-way." Aggie said, hanging Gillian's cloak in the wardrobe.

"I have no other bags. Just the small one I brought up with me."

"Ya oonly hove tha woon? Boot lass, whot of yer clothes?"

Gillian smiled. She loved Aggie's mixture of dialects. She walked over to the large full-length mirror. "I know it's not much, but I'm afraid it's all I have." Gillian lifted the fabric of the dress and swung from side to side. She stopped. "It's hideous, isn't it? I imagine the King and the Prince found me uncouth."

"Ya ar a loovfly woman. A Lady. I doot they nooticed anythin boot." Aggie smiled at her with a moment of silence. "If ya will forgive an auld carlin." Old woman. I con see yer a cannie woman. And I ded nootist tha maid, in-er braw dress, I ded. Outspeckle she ded. Tis ashaime yer guidman "Husband" treats ya in sooch a way."

"It is a long story. One that is not interesting to tell."

"I hove a gooda mind ta tell-em a thin-ar two. And I donna care ifin he tis aLord." Aggie spoke like the mother hen she was.

"Oh no! Please, you must not say a word. For my sake please." Gillian gripped her hand tightly.

"There, there lass. Nay, I wonna. Joost an auld carlin speken alaud." Aggie said, with concern.

Gillian smiled. "I'm sorry, I didn't mean to make such a fuss. I'm a stranger to you and you have been very kind to care so."

Meanwhile, in the drawing room, the King and the Prince were discussing their unexpected guests. "What do you make of this father?"

"I'm not sure. I know I sent no invitation.Strange, strange indeed." Gody rubbed his chin.

"A joke perhaps?" Aidan fished for reasons.

"Perhaps. But I don't find it amusing." Gody said.

"Did you not find the relationship between the three a bit strange?" Aidan asked, as he joined his father in front of the fire.

"Indeed I did. It was obvious Diaspad preferred the maid to his wife. Poor child."

"I do not see why. Lady Darnaway is breath taking. Any man would be proud to have such a woman." Aidan smiled.

"Mind your tongue. A handsome woman though she may be, she is also a married woman." Gody smiled as he shook his finger at Aidan.

"I have no intentions but showing the lovely lady respect." He smiled back at his father. Aidan had known a few women in the biblical sense, but only the kind that one pays for. He had never known a woman of such grace and beauty. He had always considered himself a hideous beast in eyes of most women.

Aggie entered the room, breaking Aidan's thoughts. "Sire."

"Yes Aggie. What is it, you look worried?" Gody asked.

"May I spek freely?"

Gody smiled. "Don't you always? Please, tell us what's on your mind."

"Well, I'm a bit worried aboot tha Lady."

"Lady Darnaway?" Prince Aidan asked.

"Aye Sire. The cannie woman, she hoz cume aloong way, and noot a stitch of clothing doz tha woman oon. Noothin boot tha dress oon-er bock."

Gody was silent for a moment. "I have noticed the treatment Lady Darnaway receives, Aidan has as well. What is it you wish us to do? It really is of no concern to us."

"But father, should we not show her some kindness? It is all too apparent the Lady Darnaway is not treated as well as the housemaid. You saw the way she was dressed." Aidan said, with enthusiasm.

"I see I am being out numbered. Tell me Aggie what it is you wish me to do and I will do it." Gody said, defeated.

"Well Sire, ya know I luvfed tha Queen dearly, and wood never do anythin ta disrespect her memory."

"Yes, I know this. Go on." Gody instructed.

"I wuz thinkin tha lass might coold wear sum of the Queens auld clothes. Knowin tha Queen az I ded, her heart woold hov went ooout to-er."

"Aggie's right father. I think it's a wonderful idea Aggie." Aidan said.

Gody paused and looked at Aidan. "Yes, I guess you are right. By all means Aggie, give her whatever she needs." Aggie smiled and scurried off. Gody looked at Aidan warmly and smiled. "You are so much like your mother. You have such a big heart."

CHAPTER 4

───────────▼───────────

All the trees among the hills were burned with topaz and emerald. Far out, toward the Loch, a glimpse of painted sunset sky shone like a great amber window at the end of a cathedral. It was comforting somehow to Gillian, a comfort no human could give.

A cool crisp breeze rolled in through Gillian's bath window, as she lay soaking. She imagined the garden just beneath her window and how beautiful it must be in full bloom. The golden warmth of the sun nourishing each blossom. But everything was beautiful at Aberdour, quite the opposite of Cardoness where everything lay in shadows.

Dawn and dusk were magical times, for they divided the fundamental elements of existence. Night from day, darkness from light. Gillian let out a peaceful sigh, as she relaxed in her warm bath. The simple luxury of relaxing in the tub was something she had not had in some time. There was peace here, and love. She could feel it all around. No fear, no dark shadows lurking about, and no fists raised in anger. There was no evil here to banish to its secret sanctuaries.

Aggie entered Gillian's room and laid out an assortment of beautiful dresses on the bed for her to choose from. "Is that you Aggie?" Gillian yelled out from her bath.

"Aye, Milady. Do ya ned any hep?"

"No thank you, I'm coming out now." Gillian entered wrapped in a towel.

"Let me git-ya a roob before ya chill yer bum." Aggie pulled out a warm soft robe from the large ornate wardrobe.

"Oh thank you." Gillian smiled.

"Eare ya-ar lass. This be kepin ya nice and woom." Gillian turned her back to Aggie and dropped her towel as Aggie draped the robe over her shoulders. "Oh dear lass!" Aggie was startled by the deep red marks on Gillian's back. The bath had soothed her pain, she had almost forgotten. "Ded yer huzbund do this?"

Gillian snuggled under her robe. "It's alright. Just forget you saw anything. Please, for my sake?" Aggie reluctantly nodded, seeing the seriousness in Gillian's eyes. Gillian noticed the dresses on the bed. "What's this?" She traced her fingers on the hem of one of the dresses.

"Ya neded sum thins to wear." Aggie said simply.

"Oh Aggie, they're all so beautiful! I couldn't…. I just couldn't. Could I?"

"Why noot?" Aggie smiled.

"You are so sweet to do this. They are all beautiful." Gillian paused as she stared out over the dresses. "But I'm afraid I just can not accept your kindness."

"And why noot? I donna oonderstond?"

"Lord Darnaway, that's why NOOT." Gillian smiled. "I don't think he would be too happy about this. I would have to ask him."

"Ask if ya con dress for dinner? Why I never herd sooch a-thin! Moost huzbunds woold want their wif ta look as butiful as poosibul."

Aggie stood too. "She never sad sooch, boot she's a-lady and wooldn't. Boot I saw tha fear in-her eyes when I mad mentshoon. She's a kind soul. Boot donna you be gettin all oopset! Makin a rutcuss conna oonly git-her inta trooble."

Aidan nodded. "I understand this must be handled with care. You did the right thing in coming to me with this." Aidan gently put his hand on her shoulder. "Don't worry, I will take care of this. Lady Darnaway will come to no harm and Lord Darnaway will not be the wiser." He smiled. "Now, let us pay a call on Lord Darnaway, shall we?" Aggie gave him a look out the corner of one eye, not sure what he was up to.

The two walked up the corridor and a flight of stairs toward the North wing. Aggie had intentionally put Diaspad and Igraine in the North wing, it being the furthest away from everyone else.

Aidan knocked at the door three times as Aggie stood just behind him. A female voice called out from behind the door. Aidan looked at Aggie. Aggie raised her eyebrows and gave him a nod. "I bet it's tha maid." Aggie whispered.

"It's Prince Aidan. I would like to speak with Lord Darnaway, if I may." Aidan stood waiting and could hear rustling from behind the door.

After keeping Aidan waiting a few minutes, the door opened just enough for Diaspad to poke his face through. "Yes?"

A strange odor seeped through the opening, but Aidan was so annoyed by the wait, he paid little attention to it. "Lord Darnaway, it has come to my attention that Lady Darnaway lost all her belongings on your trip here. I will send someone to go and look for them at once. In the

mean time, Aggie will find your wife some suitable cloth-
ing until her things are found." Aidan smiled graciously.
Diaspad shut the door without as much as a thank you.
Aidan looked at Aggie. "Not very friendly is he."

"They're a strange lot, inded." Aggie said, as they
walked back down the corridor.

"Now, we have The lovely Lady Darnaway to contend
with." Aidan grinned.

"I conna see you donna ned my hep." Aggie smiled. "I
hove work ta doo, anyway."

Aidan and Aggie parted before Aidan reached the West
wing. From the West wing the empurpling dye of sunset
stained the sky. It was the most scenic of all the wings of
the castle, over looking the gardens and Loch Leven
beyond.

Aidan approached Gillian's door and paused for a deep
breath before knocking. He rapped firmly on the door.

Gillian came to the door in her robe, surprised when she
saw Aidan standing there. "Oh, Prince Aidan." Gillian
clinched her robe together, embarrassed by her appearance.

"May I come in for a moment?"

"Yes, of course." Gillian bowed her head and stepped
aside for him to enter. "Please excuse my manner of dress,
I just assumed the knock at the door was Aggie."

"No, I am the one who is intruding on you." Aidan
smiled warmly. "Please, I hope you won't find my intrusion improper."

Gillian returned the smile. "No, of course not your
highness, what can I do for you?"

Aidan walked over to Gillian's bed where the dresses
still lay. "You can start by wearing one of these dresses to
supper." He grinned at her. "Aggie tells me all your

belongings were lost on the trip here."

"Oh, she did?" Gillian played along.

"Yes, I am sending someone to search for your things." Aidan walked over to where she was standing. He tried to keep himself from smelling the fresh scent of her just bathed skin.

"His highness is very kind. Thank you." Gillian smiled, smitten from the sound of his deep voice alone. How wonderfully mellow and whispery it was. Comforting somehow, like a soft warm blanket. His mere presence was intoxicating.

"Are these clothes to your liking?"

"Oh yes, Sire. They are beautiful! But...." Gillian paused.

"I think they will fit, you look to be the same size as my mother." He scanned her body.

Gillian walked over to the dresses and looked at them as if now they had taken on a different appearance. "These were your mother's dresses?" Gillian looked at Aidan, her mouth wide open. "Oh Sire, I could not wear these dresses! Not the Queen's dresses."

"Why not?"

"I couldn't disgrace the Queen's memory or your father. It is a kind gesture, but I would feel as if I were dishonoring the Queen." Gillian walked back over to the Prince.

"Nonsense, it would not be a disgrace. My mother would want me to offer the dresses to you, as well as my father. Besides, you are a member of the Royal family as well." Aidan took a step closer. Gillian's heart was pounding so hard; she thought it might pop out of her chest at any moment. "A woman as beautiful as yourself should wear beautiful clothes. Although, the dress could never compare only enhance."

Gillian felt her face flush with heat. She felt silly. "His highness is too kind." She lowered her head.

With his finger under her chin, Aidan gently tilted her head back up to meet his gaze. He looked deep into her big brown eyes, wanting desperately to feel the fullness of her lips. " You deserve only kindness, Milady. Will you please accept these dresses in the name of friendship?" He smiled.

Gillian paused, then smiled. "If you truly insist."

"I do." Aidan placed his hand over his heart and gave her a bow. Gillian giggled, flirtatiously. "Now, I will leave you to dress. Until tonight, Milady." He said, in his luscious low voice, then took her hand and lightly kissed it. Gillian blushed again, as she watched him exit her room, and reminded herself to take a breath.

Gillian stood in front of a freestanding full-length mirror that sat majestically framed inside fine mahogany. It had been a very long time since she had seen her own full-length image. So much time had passed; she almost did not recognize herself.

Gillian loosened her robe, freeing her naked body to the mirror. She stared at her body for a moment, accepting herself. To simply be introduced, to make acquaintance, to see the body in which she lived.

Gillian traced the angle of her neck and collarbone lightly with her fingers. Guiding her hand down to her breast, gently she circled each one. She wondered how she compared to other women. She cupped her breast in her hands and felt it this time. She felt her touch from the inside out and not just from the outside. Her heartbeat was real and strong, she felt it. It was nice to fully be inside her body with wants, passion and desires. A need for simple happiness, just like other women. " Am I anything anyone would want?" She whispered.

A knock came at the door. Never had Gillian encountered so many people in such a short time. Nevertheless, she welcomed the intrusions. "Come in." She said, aloud.

As she placed one of the many dresses up to her in front of the mirror.

A young blonde hair, blue-eyed chambermaid entered. "Good eve, Milady."

Gillian turned around. She had once again expected Aggie. "My name is Anne. I brought you some fresh towels."

"Thank you. You can put them in the bath, if you please." Gillian continued debating over each dress.

"Can I get you anything, or do anything for you Milady?"

"Yes you can. You can tell me which dress suits me." Gillian turned around toward Anne and held up a different dress.

The girl looked flabbergasted. "YOU want my opinion Milady?"

"Yes, I do. Now, do you like this one...or this one?" Gillian held up two dresses.

Anne smiled, honored that a Lady would even want the suggestion of a simple chambermaid. "Well Milady, with your beautiful red hair.... I think the sheer black one. It is very elegant."

Gillian gave her a smile. "Good choice. The black one it will be." Gillian held the gown against her as she looked in the mirror.

"Will there be anything else, Milady."? Anne asked.

"Nothing I can think of." Anne nodded and walked toward the door. "Oh, Anne."

Anne stopped and turned to see what her mistress wanted. "Thank you for your help."

Anne gave her a big smile, feeling appreciated. "You're very welcome Milady."

CHAPTER 5

▼

Everyone was gathering downstairs in the parlor waiting to go in for supper. Diaspad was already downstairs; he had not bothered to wait for Gillian or to escort her downstairs. Adelaide was in the kitchen with the rest of the servants, angry that she was not invited to attend supper with the Royal family. Gody exchanged small talk with Diaspad and tried to make up for lost time, as Aidan entered the parlor.

"Good eve, everyone." Aidan said. "And where is your lovely wife?" Aidan directed his question at Diaspad.

"Don't know. Guess she is still up stairs." Diaspad said with little concern as he took a gulp of wine.

King Gody looked at his pocket watch then returned it to his watch pocket. "Ranulf should be arriving soon now. You remember Ranulf?" Gody looked at Diaspad.

Diaspad swallowed the last of his wine. "How could I forget."?

"Ranulf can't resist being fashionably late." Aidan chuckled.

"Did I hear my name?" Count Ranulf entered and gave Gody a big hug. "Cousin, how are you?" He asked, giving Aidan a pat on the back. Ranulf was very handsome with brown hair, cobalt blue eyes and muscular build. A charmer and a known ladies man. He possessed all the attributes a woman could want but one, commitment. "Diaspad." Ranulf said, with little emotion, merely to recognize his presence.

The tension was broken by Gillian's entrance. Gillian appeared like an apparition in all her eloquence. She was statuesque in her sheer black gown with hair piled neatly on her head and cascading ringlets caressing her bare shoulders. "I hope I haven't kept you all waiting." She smiled apologetically.

All the men's voices were mute, even Diaspad, from the vision before them. "No, no dear," Gody was the first to speak, "not at all."

Aidan was struck in the heart by the creature in font of him; he could not move or speak. If he had been taken by her before, he was even more so now. There she was. There was Gillian, her auburn hair all a flame beneath the chandelier. Her delicate song-like voice. And oh, the sweetness of her face, her skin so delicate, so delicious in her sheer dress, and her sex, he could smell her scent throbbing, like a flower she was, opening.

Aidan could only watch her from a respectable distance. Humankind, not his kind had kept him there, at a distance. She was lovely, not a distorted creature like himself. Oh what a splendid, eloquent creature she was. Did she know? Did she know how exquisite she was? No. Humble, humble she was.

"You are a vision, my dear!" Gody replied. Gillian smiled and gave him a gracious nod.

"Quick! Someone introduce me to this fascinating creature." Ranulf made a leap toward Gillian and took her hand.

"Lady Darnaway, this is Count Ranulf. Ranulf...Lady Darnaway." Gody made the introductions.

"No! Say it isn't so! You can't be married to Diaspad?" Ranulf kissed her hand slowly without taking his eyes off her. You could almost see the indecent thoughts rolling about in his head. "Diaspad, how do you do it?" He smirked and made no attempt to hide his dislike for Diaspad. "What a lucky dog you are." He said to Diaspad, without taking his eyes off Gillian.

Gillian smiled politely, not knowing what to say. She had never had so much male attention. Diplomatically, she removed her hand from Ranulf's clutches.

"Come Ranulf, stop hovering over the girl and let us go in for supper." The King said. Ranulf offered his arm to Gillian, to escort her in to the dining hall, beating out Aidan, who had hoped to have the honor.

Diaspad jumped ahead of the others, without offering to escort Gillian into the dining room. Needless to say, the gentlemen found this behavior odd and rude.

In the middle of the dining hall sat a long wooden table surrounded by gold damask chairs. At the head sat a throne-like chair in which the King always sat. The windows were arched and cut high into the walls for emitting light. At the far end of the room stood a fireplace that was large enough to be a small room on its own. Two musicians entered the dining hall, one with a violin and the other a flute.

"Come Lady Darnaway, you sit next to me." The king smiled as his chair welcomed his portly frame onto the cushion. Gillian sat at the King's right, Ranulf next to her, Diaspad to the king's left and Aidan next to Diaspad.

Servants began to stream in the dining hall carrying platters of roast duck, fish, vegetables, fresh bread, wine, cheese and pastries of all shapes and sizes.

Diaspad kept a close eye on Gillian. Silent as he watched her, waiting for her to make a mistake, waiting for an excuse.

"Well, I'm starved." Ranulf commented. "What more could one want, good food and lovely company to share it with." He smiled at Gillian. Gillian smiled and lowered her head slightly embarrassed by Ranulf's tentative attention. Gillian raised her eyes to find Diaspad glaring at her. The meal began.

"Lady Darnaway, since you are new to this family, we must have a party to introduce you to society." King Gody suggested, after pressing his napkin to his mouth.

"Is that not why we were invited in the first place? A party of sorts?" Diaspad gulped down his wine, hardly touching his food.

"To be honest Diaspad, I never sent an invitation. But you and your lovely wife are welcome nevertheless, for as long as you like."

"His highness is very kind. And please, wont you call me Gillian?" She smiled.

"If you insist." Gody smiled.

"I don't understand." Diaspad said as he poured himself another glass of wine. "If you didn't, then who did?"

"It is a puzzlement." Gody replied.

"Well who the hell cares!" Ranulf replied.

"Please cousin, your language." Aidan reminded him a lady was present.

"Excuse me. We'll have to have a party anyway!" Ranulf grinned.

"Any excuse, hey Ranulf?" Aidan smirked at him.

"I doubt if we will be staying long enough." Diaspad spoke as if purposely to dampen the mood. "Gillian's not a party girl....are you, MY DEAR?" He said with sarcasm as he pushed his plate away.

"Don't be so selfish!" Ranulf spoke up. "What other miserable thing could you possibly have to do in your miserable life that was so important!"?

"Ranulf!" Aidan scolded a warning to be on his best behavior.

Gillian became very uneasy. "Please, don't go to any trouble on my account. Diaspad is right, I'm not much of a party go-er." She smiled, nervously as she looked at Diaspad to see if he showed any inclination of anger coming her way later.

Aidan right away noticed her nervous fidgeting. He could see she felt right in the middle of a possible plight. "Let us take advantage of this opportunity. We have not had a celebration in some time. It will do us all good. Everyone can be invited. I'm sure Adelaide as well as Lady Darnaway will enjoy one of our parties."

"Sure, sure. What ever." Diaspad said with little emotion as he opened another bottle of wine.

"Asshole." Ranulf said under his breath. "Well then, it's settled." Ranulf patted Gillian's hand that was resting on the table, stretching the moment out as if he forgot to remove his hand. Aidan noticed this, and though he loved Ranulf, he resented the fact that Ranulf had already assumed Gillian would be just another one of his tryst.

"Isn't there anything stronger in this place? This wine tastes more like water." Diaspad set the bottle down hard on the table.

"Don't you think you have had enough? What do you think this is, the local pub?" Ranulf remarked. "Save some for the rest of us."

"And who do you think you are, my wife? The two of you have a lot in common, she's uninteresting beneath the sheets and you manage to be uninteresting most of the time." Diaspad smirked.

Aidan jumped to his feet, and this time it was Ranulf who had to remind him to be calm. "How dare you!" Aidan gritted his teeth. Gillian wanted to crawl under the table. This was just simply one more humiliation to add to the others she had indured. Bitterness twisted inside her like an adder. Gody immediately stepped in between Aidan and Diaspad. Ranulf joined Aidan and held him back by the arm.

"I will handle this. Calm yourself." Gody said, giving Aidan a soft pat on his shoulder. Gody took the drunken Diaspad by the arm and escorted him out of the dining hall. A few minutes passed when the king returned, alone. "Now, shall we finish our meal?" He said, seating himself and trying to smile.

Gillian was utterly embarrassed; she could hardly lift her eyes to meet anyone's gaze.

Ranulf started a story to try and lift the tension. Aidan glanced over to Gillian who could only return a tiny smile as a thank you for coming to her defense. She could still feel Aidan's eyes upon her; she shifted her eyes to him once again. Their eyes met, each looked away, feeling found out by the other.

Ranulf leaned over to whisper in Gillian's ear, placing his hand on top of hers. "Are you alright?"

She smiled; his breath tickled her ear. "Yes, I'm fine thank you." She whispered in a delicate voice. Gillian sat there wondering during her entire inner struggle, after the horrible life with Diaspad, why she could not simply imagine just getting up and walking out.

"Has everyone finished? Shall we retire to the parlor for brandy?" The king suggested.

"Good idea!" Ranulf jumped to his feet. And once again, Aidan was prevailed over by Ranulf for Gillian's hand. Gillian was still shaken from Diaspad's cruel remark, but tried to hide her emotions. Aidan kept an attentive eye on Gillian, sensing her distress. He admired the way she carried herself, a Lady she truly was.

CHAPTER 6

▼

Gillian stood in front of a roaring fire as the men sipped brandy from snifters. Ranulf remained attentive to Gillian, not straying far from her side. Aidan wanted a chance to apologize for his outburst, but Ranulf was like a dog in heat.

"Ranulf, are you staying at Aberdour or do you plan to go home?" Aidan asked with a little witticism in his voice.

"Well cousin, I would hate for you to go too long once again without my company." He looked at Gillian. "I think I will stay, most definitely."

Gillian gave him a faint smile, not wanting to encourage him any further with more emotion. She was out of practice, as far as reading the intentions of the male persuasion, but Ranulf's feelings were very apparent.

"Hmm. How fortunate for us." Aidan smirked at Ranulf. Gillian covered her mouth to smother her giggle.

Aidan left Ranulf to hover over Gillian for the moment, to have a word with his father. "Tell me father," he spoke softly, "what did you say to Diaspad?"

"I simply gave him what he wanted. I told him where he could find a bottle of my best brandy if he would return to his chambers with it." Gody looked over at Gillian, who was enduring Ranulf's charms. "It's a shame, isn't it? Such a lovely girl."

"Diaspad is sick father, and his kind of sickness doesn't discriminate among who it spreads. Not even the most fair." He paused and looked in Gillian's direction. "Now if you will excuse me, I think the lady has been saturated long enough in Ranulf's intoxicating charms."

Gody laughed. "Yes, I believe she does look as if she needs a rescue."

Aidan walked casually over to Ranulf and Gillian with his hands placed behind his back. "Ranulf, if you will excuse us, I promised to show Lady Darnaway some of the families history after we had supped." Aidan offered his arm to Gillian. "Shall we go to the library?" Gillian nodded happily with a smile. Finally, Aidan had stolen a moment.

He escorted Gillian out of the parlor and toward the grand staircase. "I hope I wasn't too presumptuous in assuming you needed a recess from Ranulf's cavorting?"

Gillian laughed. "No, not at all. Your cousin is quite the charmer."

"I hope he wasn't too overwhelming. He can be." Aidan said as he led her down a corridor.

"Maybe a bit at first." She laughed. "I found him sweetly pathetic."

Aidan laughed. "Yes, that does describe him." He said looking at her. "I never noticed, what a joyous laugh you have."

Gillian stopped laughing and her smile turned to shyness. "Well, thank you for stealing me away when you did. It has been some time since I have had the attention of a handsome man at my disposal. I think I was dumb struck by the undivided attention."

Aidan opened the large wooden door to the library and waited for Gillian to enter. "I would think you would be used to it. I can't imagine a man not laying eyes on you and falling hopelessly in love." Aidan led her over near the fire.

Gillian blushed bright red. "I think that is the sweetest compliment anyone has ever gave me."

"By the way, I did not get a chance to tell you how lovely you look in that dress. It suits you well." He grinned.

"Thank you."

"I must be honest with you. I intentionally brought you up here to give you a brandy to calm your nerves after your husband's…"

"Cruel outburst?" Gillian finished his sentence. Aidan nodded.

"I thought a drink would help. However, I see you do not need it. My mistake." Aidan gave her a slight bow of his head. "You seem to be a woman in control of your emotions."

"Only because I've had a lot of practice." Gillian walked over to one of the large windows. "So tell me, what grand things would I see out this window if it were light?"

Aidan paused to admire her, then walked over to her. "From this window, you can see the Loch and to the right, Ardchattan Chapel."

"I would like to see the chapel, I imagine it's lovely." She smiled at him.

"I would be honored to show it to you tomorrow, if you like."

"His highness is very kind." Gillian bowed her head. "You and your family have been very kind to me, I feel I must apologize for my husband's behavior tonight."

"No please. You must not fret. We all understand."

"It is a wonder you did not ask us to leave. You are very gracious people." She smiled warmly. "You came to my defense, like the gentleman you are. No one has ever done such a thing. You made me feel as if I had some worth for the first time in a very long time."

Aidan's heart was breaking for her; it was evident that Diaspad's cruelty had worked its damage over the years. However, it was also apparent to him the warm lively woman underneath waiting to be reborn. "If you will forgive me for being so bold…your husband does not deserve the gift's God has granted him."

"Diaspad is a lost soul. He did not use to be as bad as he is now, not in the beginning. The more he drowned himself, the worse his behavior came. I do not know what has eaten at him the worse, the drinking or the guilt. I am not excusing his behavior, but I don't think he knows what he does anymore." Gillian paused with a slight simper. "Once I thought I saw a glimmer of human decency in his eyes."

Aidan watched the smile play about her lips as a sinking feeling settled down in the pit of his stomach. "Forgive me." He bowed his head to Gillian. "I did not realize…I mean…you have a forgiving heart to love a man so hurtful." He said with disappointment.

Gillian laughed lightly. "Love? I could never love a man such as Diaspad. I loathe him if anything. Nevertheless, I try to pity him. He must have loved his first wife very much to be reduced to such a horrible beast." Gillian smiled at Aidan. "Listen to me, going on so. I think I have said too much."

"No. Not at all. Friends open up to each other and I hope that we are becoming good friends." He smiled.

"Your highness is once again very kind."

"If we are to be friends, you must please call me Aidan."

"Only, if you agree to call me Gillian. I'm not sure I know who Lady Darnaway is." She returned the smile.

"Agreed."

Gillian held out her hand. "Shall we shake on it?" Aidan reached out and took her tiny hand in his with some reluctance. Most people did not want to touch him after the first time. Maybe because he was only half-human, maybe from fear. Gillian felt tongue-tied with the admiration reflected in his eyes. All too aware of his large soft hand still holding hers. A spark seemed to travel from his palm to hers. The air pulsed between them, the feeling new and intense.

Gillian pulled her hand away, but not from wanting too, severing their connection. "Well, it is getting late, I think I will retire for the evening it has been a long day. Until tomorrow?" She smiled.

"The night is sure to be too long." Aidan shot a predatory look. "Let me walk you to your chamber." Aidan opened the library door and waited for her to pass through. "Is there anything you need before you retire?"

"No. I will be fine." Gillian smiled warmly, as Aidan escorted her down the corridor to her chamber.

"I'm sure tomorrow will be a pleasant day to give you a tour around the grounds."

"Yes, I hope so. I look forward to it." Gillian had almost forgotten about Diaspad, for the first time she felt a moment of freedom.

They reached Gillian's chambers. Aidan opened the door for her but stood respectfully outside the threshold. "I'm sure Beechim stoked the fire for you, it should last all night. If you should need anything, just ring." He smiled, feeling he should say more.

"Yes, I will." She smiled, feeling a bit awkward.

"My chambers are just down the corridor if you should need me." He smiled, now too feeling bungling.

"I feel safe knowing you are so near." She said gracefully.

"Well then, I will bid you sweet dreams." Aidan wanted very much to kiss her goodnight.

"Goodnight." Gillian stepped through the threshold and slowly closed the door after waiting for Aidan to make the first move toward departure.

Aidan retired to his chamber closing the door with force as if trying to keep something out. He collapsed heavily on his bed hearing nothing but the pounding of his heart. He breathed in Gillian's scent as it emanated through thick castle walls, out of seams and cracks around and through glass, seeping in from God knows where, stirring a passion within and between his legs. He wanted to run to her, to hold her, protect her but was utterly immovable.

Gillian dressed for bed and slid under the big feather comforter. It was heaven. Like sleeping on a cloud. She plumped the pillow beneath her head as the entire bed sweet and soft caught her and turned her in downward toward sleep. In her dreams she saw Aidan's eyes, magnetic eyes and in those eyes a heavy power that lay hold of her entire being.

CHAPTER 7

▼

Gillian opened her eyes on the first morning at Castle Aberdour. There was a refreshing chill to the morning air. She felt more like she was coming to life than waking up. Gillian walked shivering across the cold floor to the window where she could hear bells ringing in the distance. The morning shone through the windows like a bright morning star beckoning to Gillian to take part. Gillian opened the window; the air was sweet with the breath of early spring. The trees were all crowned with newborn leaves; promise of spring. Gillian knelt sweetly by her open window in a warm stream of sunshine and whispered a prayer of gratitude that came straight from her heart.

A knock came at the door. "It's joost me dear."

"Come in Aggie." Gillian called out across the room.

Aggie waddled in with a full grin on her face. "Good morn, dear. Ded ya slip well?"

Gillian smiled. "The best nights sleep I ever had."

"Oh that's woonderful dear." Aggie said as she opened the drapes on the remaining windows. "It's gonna be a beautiful day. Ya ned any hep with dressin before breakfast?"

"No thank you."

"Igraine is oon her way oop ta tidy oop a bit."

"Igraine?" Gillian asked as she seated herself at the vanity and began to brush her hair.

"Oh, I plum forgot ya hoven't met her yate. She's tha other chamber maid." A knock came at the door. "Cume." Aggie yelled. A stout woman with dark hair, plain looks and a scowl on her face entered. "Milady this is Igraine."

Gillian smiled and walked over to meet her. "Nice to meet you." Gillian extended her hand.

"Miss." Igraine said, acknowledging Gillian, but that was all. Gillian lowered her hand after it was not accepted.

"Igraine hoz joost returned froom a visit with her kin." Aggie tried to make small talk.

"Oh, how nice." Gillian smiled. "Do you see your family often?"

"No." Igraine said in an unfriendly manner.

"Lady Darnaway, Igraine cumes froom a small village near here." Aggie said.

"Darnaway?" Igraine seemed to come alive.

Gillian smiled. "Yes. Do you know my husband, Diaspad?"

Igraine's face became a little pinched. "No." She began to roughly make the bed, thrashing the covers and pillows around as if she were in a wrestling match. Gillian looked at Aggie. Aggie shrugged her shoulders then left the room.

Breakfast was being served buffet style, in the dining hall. Ranulf was the last to enter and serve himself. "Good morn! Good morn to all!" He hurriedly plopped spoonfuls of food on his plate. "And a special good morning to you." He said, sitting down beside Gillian, taking her hand and kissing it.

"And a good morn to you Ranulf." Gillian smiled.

"You are in bright spirits for one who normally does not wake till much later." Aidan commented.

"I was simply famished! And besides, when one has such loveliness to wake up to," he smiled at Gillian, "how could one possibly sleep."

Gillian laughed. "You should make the beauty of the day or the sun your reason to wake."

"But dear lady, the warmth of the sun or the beauty of the day could never compare to your smile." Ranulf beamed a smile her way. Gillian blushed and took a sip of her juice.

Aidan gave Ranulf a scoffer look. "Getting a early start, are we cousin?"

Ranulf smirked. "You know what they say cousin…the early bird…"

From the end of the table, King Gody cleared his throat loudly. He meant it as a warning for the two to shut up. "Has anyone seen our sleeping beauty today?" Ranulf said just before taking a sip of his coffee.

Gody wiped the crumbs from his mouth and returned the napkin to his lap. "If you are referring to Diaspad…no. Do you know if he will be joining us for breakfast, Lady Darnaway? I mean Gillian?"

Gillian smiled and wiped her mouth before answering. "No Sire, I do not know. But he is a late sleeper, I would-n't expect him."

Ranulf leaned over closer to Gillian. "Can I interest you in a carriage ride after breakfast?"

"Oh, that would be nice but Aidan has offered to show me around Aberdour." Gillian smiled graciously.

Ranulf cut his eyes over at Aidan who was smiling back smugly. "Oh he did, did he?"

"Another time?" Gillian said to be polite.

Ranulf didn't take his eyes off Aidan. "Yes, of course."

Everyone had a peaceful breakfast without Diaspad's presence.Aidan stood when he saw that Gillian was finished. "Well then, why don't we get started. Are you ready?"

"Yes!" Gillian said with excitement, wiping her mouth one last time.

Aidan escorted Gillian out of the dining hall with his hand respectfully placed on the small of her back. "Would you like to see the chapel first?"

"Yes. Oh, let me run up and get my shawl. Do you mind?" Gillian smiled sweetly.

"No. I will wait right here for you." He smiled.

"I won't be but a minute." Gillian yelled as she reached the top of the stairs. Aidan waited patiently at the foot of the stairs.

Gillian dashed in, grabbed her shawl and was on her way back out when an arm came out of no where and slung her against the corridor wall. "Hello. Dear."

"Diaspad! I thought you were asleep." Diaspad held her in place against the wall by her throat.

"You mean you hoped I was. Where do you think you are off to?" He gritted his teeth.

"Aidan has been kind enough to give me a tour around Aberdour." She explained.

"Aidan! Getting ahead of yourself aren't we? You will address him as his highness or Prince! Don't embarrass me wench!"

"Yes Diaspad. Please let me go. I don't want to keep the Prince waiting." Diaspad released her throat but took hold of her wrist and twisted it behind her back.

"Don't you forget who is master." Spittle splashed in her eye as he twisted her wrist even harder. Gillian gritted her teeth shut to keep from crying out.

"Is there a problem?" Aidan stood at the end of the corridor. Diaspad quickly let go of Gillian when he heard Aidan's voice. Aidan slowly approached them.

Gillian tried to smile but her wrist was hurting. "No. Diaspad was just asking me where I was going in such a hurry."

Aidan was fully aware of what had just taken place but made no confrontations for Gillian's sake. "I was going to show Lady Darnaway around Aberdour. Would you like to join us?" He remained calm.

"No." Diaspad answered.

"Shall we, Lady Darnaway?" Aidan waited for Gillian to proceed in front of him then gave Diaspad a hard stare.

Gillian said nothing for a few minutes nor did she try to explain the incident. Just outside the castle, Gillian paused to feel the warmth of the sun on her face. "What a nice day this is turning out to be." She tried to put all thoughts of Diaspad out of her mind but her wrist was red and beginning to swell. Gillian kept her wrist hid behind her back not wanting Aidan to know she was hurt.

"The chapel is up this path here." Aidan pointed to the stone path just ahead of them.

Within the precincts of Aberdour on the highest point of a great rock overlooking the village, stands Ardchattan chapel, consisting of a nave that holds no more than forty people. At the East End, stands a semi-circular apse divided from the nave by a typical Romanesque arch. In full summer, the warm stone walls become a backdrop to roses, wisteria, and all sorts of evergreen.

Gillian stood in humble admiration of the flying buttresses that framed the ceiling. In front of her and Aidan stood the Virgin Mary that was placed behind the high alter and decorated in the most feminine taste. Soften colors, and dimly lit, it enabled the worshiper to commune in silence and to feel her presence and sympathy.

The old chapel still had the scent of pure beeswax candles and the incense that lingered forever in any church where the Monstrance had been held.

"My mother resurrected this chapel. She and my father were married here. She loved it very much. Beechim takes care of it in her memory." Aidan spoke with a tender voice.

"It's beautiful, I see why she loved it so." Gillian took a seat on the first pew and placed her wounded wrist in her lap, covering it with her shawl. "Beechim was close to your mother?"

"Everyone adored her. She was very giving, caring almost to a fault." Aidan took a seat beside her.

"My mother died when I was young also. How old were you when your mother died?" Gillian asked in a soft tone.

"I was a young man of fourteen. She went to help care for the sick in her homeland and in return became ill herself." Aidan looked up at the Virgin

"I'm sorry. It doesn't seem fair sometimes, we loose the good too soon." Gillian gave him a warm smile, which he returned as she placed her hand on his.

Aidan was silent for a moment, taken back by the strong emotion that came from the simple touch of Gillian's hand and too embarrassed by the depth of his desire for her.

He reached out and gently pulled her hand out from underneath her shawl. "I noticed you favoring this hand." Aidan delicately held her wrist in his large hand to get a better look at it. "It is swollen. Does it hurt much?"

Gillian felt very little pain the moment Aidan touched her. "No, not much."

"Come, we must go back to the castle and take care of your wrist." Aidan said with concern.

"No. Please. I want to see everything you have to show me today. Please don't let Diaspad's actions spoil this day too." Gillian pleaded. "If it starts to cause me much pain, I promise I will let you know."

Aidan could not refuse those big brown eyes. Lovely brown eyes with thick black lashes; and the pure sweetness of her mouth when she spoke. "Alright." Aidan pulled out his handkerchief from his breast pocket and walked over to the basin of holy water. He submerged the cloth in the cool water, then wrung it out. "Here, at least let me wrap your wrist to help the swelling. The coolness of the water should help and it doesn't hurt that it's holy water." He smiled.

Gillian watched his face as he attentively wrapped the cloth around her wrist. He was even more beautiful in the dim light of the church. "You have a gentle touch." She said softly.

He smiled. "How does that feel?" He asked still holding her wrist. Gillian nodded still focused on his face. Aidan bent over and kissed her wrist then placed it softly back in her lap.

Gillian felt flushed. She stared at his smooth lips. "Yes. That feels much better." She was utterly enthralled, and couldn't stop studying him; the way his green eyes sharpened then softened with his thoughts. The gentle way he looked at her and held her with his eyes.

Aidan knew if he didn't say or do something right at that moment he would find himself taking her in his arms. "Well…as much as I would like to remain here alone with you, I did promise you a tour." He grinned. "Would you like to see the stables next?"

"Yes." Gillian smiled.

"Do you ride?" Aidan asked as they made their way out of the chapel.

"Yes, but it has been some time. I miss it very much."

CHAPTER 8

▼

The sky stretched radiant and warm in all directions. Gillian and Aidan walked past uneven sidewalks and moss covered stones on the way to the stables. In the near distance lay loch Laven. The loch waters were blue, a magnificent blue; not the blue of spring nor the soft azure of autumn, but a clear resolute tranquil blue, as if the water were past all emotions and had settled down to serenity.

In the other direction were mountains covered in thick rich woods, which seemed to contain every conceivable shade of green. The trees were tender with newborn baby leaves. The air was faintly charged with an aroma of pine balsam and the sky above crystal clear blue. One might have expected Pan to come piping a tune from around any bush at any moment.

The stables housed many fine horses that were taken care of as only the herd of royalty would be. Everything was immaculate and well cared for right down to the dirt that made up the floor. A small quaint cottage sat near the stables where the stable hand lived.

Gillian and Aidan entered and was met by a young man. "Lady Darnaway, I would like for you to meet Lan." Aidan made the introductions. "He is the mar'shal." Handler.

Lan smiled with his perfect pearly teeth and took Gillian's hand and kissed it. "I am honored to make your acquaintance." He said with his charismatic French accent. And gleamed with abounding charm for a stable hand. Lan was the epitome of tall, dark and handsome. Polite but straightforward, clean and orderly like the stables he kept.

"You have some beautiful horses here." Gillian gleamed back.

"I can not take credit for their beauty, I merely take care of them, but on behalf of the horses, I thank you for the compliment." He smiled with an agreeable fascination. Gillian gave him a slight bow of her head. She instantly liked him. "Darnaway?" He paused. "Any relation to Diaspad Darnaway?"

"My husband. Do you know him?" She smiled.

Lan glanced at Aidan. "Yes, I have met him." He said with little emotion. Gillian could see there was more to the story. "And may I say, I pity you Madame." Gillian was about to ask how the two knew each other when Beechim entered the stables out of breath.

Beechim took a deep breath, having caught everyone's attention. "Excuse me, Milady...Milord, the king would like to see you, it's of the utmost important."

Aidan looked confused. "Yes, of course Beechim." Aidan took Gillian's hand. "I am sorry. Do you mind?"

Gillian smiled. "No, not at all. I will wait for you."

"Lan, would you keep Lady Darnaway company until I return?" Aidan asked.

"Yes, of course." He smiled.

"I will make this as quick as I can." Aidan said, then kissed her hand. Gillian smiled as she watched him leave the stables with Beechim. Lan took the opportunity to study her from head to toe.

"You and Aidan are good friends?" Lan inquired.

Gillian turned her attention back to Lan. "Yes, I like to think so."

"Aidan is a kind and gentle soul. I would not like to see him hurt."

"Nor I." Gillian said with firmness.

Lan was quiet while he studied her further. "Gillian. That is a nice name."

"Thank you." She said.

"It suits you." He smiled "Much better than Lady Darnaway."

"Well if you think so, feel free to use it." She smiled.

He grinned, flashing his pearly whites. "Alright, Gillian."

"You are educated?" Gillian inquired.

"Yes. Why? Do you feel it a waste on a stable boy?" He asked with a note of armament.

"No. Not at all, just uncommon. You carry yourself like…"

"A pretentious peasant?" Lan finished the sentence for her.

Gillian leered at him. "Like a refined gentleman." Lan smiled. "Before you rudely interrupt someone, you should hear what they have to say. It may surprise you." Gillian smirked.

Lan smiled into her eyes. "Yes. You are right." He paused. "The king had pity on me and took me in when I was young. He saw to it I had the same education and upbringing as Aidan."

Gillian nodded. "You love Aidan very much, don't you?" She smiled.

"Yes. He is like the big brother I never had." Lan turned his head away from Gillian.

"If I am not being too personal, where is your family?" Gillian asked.

Lan turned around and looked at her but was silent for a moment. "This is my family now. My father did not accept us. My mother took me and we moved to Paris soon after I was born. We returned here when I was ten and the rest is history."

"I see, I am sorry." Gillian lowered her eyes.

"No need. King Gody has been a wonderful father to me. He has provided for me and saw to it that I needed for nothing. Never has he treated me less than a son."

Gillian looked at him and studied him for a moment. "Then why…"

"Why do I live here and not the castle?" Gillian nodded. Lan laughed. "It is my choice. I love horses. This is all I ever wanted. Common work does not make the man common-place." He said with the same note of fortification.

"And having a title of nobility does not necessarily make a Lady impudent and uppity." Gillian defended herself.

Lan smiled to see she was nothing like most of aristocracy he had come into contact with. "Touché. No, it doesn't."

Gillian returned the smile, now that they understood each other. "You are not fond of the blue-bloods are you?"

Lan laughed. "I could never see myself as one of those fellows that wear fancy clean shirts-guilty of a proper education and suspected of fat purses." Lan leaned against one of the stalls as he stared at Gillian.

"Why do you look at me that way." Gillian smiled, blushing just a little bit.

"I was just wondering…wondering why a intelligent woman like yourself would marry a man such as Diaspad?" Lan cocked his head to the side, studying her more intensely. "You don't seem like the type to marry for money or position. In addition, you do not seem naive or stupid. Pity was it?"

"And how do you know what kind of woman I am." She smiled flirtatiously. "We have just met sir. Maybe I married for love."

"Love? Quelle idée!" Lan shook his head. "Love and Diaspad do not exist together." Gillian was surprised; Lan seemed to know Diaspad well.

"So tell me, how do you know Diaspad?" Gillian folded her arms.

"It's a long story, maybe I will tell you one day, but for now it would only bore you." He grinned. "I like you Gillian, you are one I could call friend."

"Hmm. You seem to distrust nobility, how do you know you can trust me?" She grinned.

Lan pushed himself away from the stable stall and walked toward her. "Because Aidan likes you. A blind man could see that. I trust Aidan and Aidan is a good judge of character." He stepped a little closer. "A beauty though you may be, it takes more to win Aidan over. It takes kindness, compassionate big heart. If you had not these things, he could not call you friend." He walked around her and sat on a bale of hay. "So, you did not answer my question. What made you marry Diaspad?"

Gillian spun around to face him. "Don't you think that is a bit personal? I mean, we hardly know each other."

"Well now, that is something we will have to work on. Let me guess, you come from wealth, big house, good education, trained in all the proper etiquette's the social graces. All your friends had married and you thought how wonderful married life would be; to love and take care of someone. Being so anxious, you married the first man to ask you, thinking love would come later." He smiled. "So how far off was I?"

"Very. You are too bold sir."

"Alright, so why don't you tell me the right story." Lan leaned back against the wall and waited.

Gillian folded her arms again. "It's a long story, maybe one day I will tell it to you, but for now it would only bore you." She smirked.

Lan smiled and pulled out a long piece of hay and stuck it in the corner of his mouth. "I see. It is you who do not trust me. All the more for us to become friends confidants even."

"And what makes you think I need a confidant?"

"Because you are married to Diaspad and I know Diaspad. Being a new bride, I am sure you must be disillusioned by now. Even lonely, I suspect."

Gillian cut her eyes at him. "Do you always speak your mind?"

"I tell the truth, nothing more, nothing less." He smiled, holding the piece of straw in his teeth. "Do you ride?" Gillian nodded. "Then I will have to pick you out a horse. One to match your qualities."

Gillian smiled. "And what type of horse might that be?"

Lan stood to his feet. "Let me see." He paused, as he thought about each horse. "Come with me." Gillian followed him over to the first stall. "This one might suit you…" He moved on to the next horse. "Now, this is the horse for you." He said looking at Gillian.

"And what makes this horse so right for me?" She grinned.

"This is Mirage." Lan patted an Arabian filly firmly on the neck. "This horse is much like yourself. She is much more than what you see. Beautiful, yes. However, even more beautiful is her spirit. She is young and has never mated; her passion untamed." Gillian raised an eyebrow. "Her heart is warm, courageous and loyal. She is not afraid to give her all, heart and soul."

Gillian rubbed the horse on her muzzle. "Now how do you know I possess any of these qualities?" Gillian smirked.

Lan smiled a sheepish grin and led Gillian back over to the bail of hay where she sat down. "Madame, I know horses and I know women." He said as he sat down next to her.

"Do you now?" Gillian said with sarcasm

"Yes." He took Gillian's hand and turned it palm side up, tracing the lines of her palm with his finger. "You see, women are like horses." Gillian looked at him strangely then at her hand. "Not that women are like animals. Horses are a gift from God, like women. The two are unique to mankind. If you treat a horse with love, tenderness and respect they respond to you in the same way. I know when a horse has been treated unfairly, or a woman for that matter. There is something in the body language, something in the eyes." Gillian felt herself being drawn into his smoldering dark eyes. Everything about him was dark, his eyes, his hair, and his features; almost as if he were always present in a shadow. "When one does not receive the love and care one deserves, it is hard for one to shine to their full potential." Gillian held her breath, he was awfully close. Too close. Gillian quickly stood to her feet, feeling he was going to kiss her, pulling her hand away. "I see I must have struck a nerve. Too close to the truth?" He grinned.

Gillian held her head high. "Too close for such new acquaintances."

"I have offended you, I apologize." He smiled and gently tugged at her hand, pulling it near and gave it a kiss.

Gillian's resolve melted, but she did not show it. "Though titles have no regard with you, I do deserve a little more respect. I'm sure your sweet nothings whispered in a innocent mademoiselle's ear may admit you certain liberties but I assure you sir, I am neither innocent nor lenient."

Lan quickly stood to his feet. "You are right and I meant no disrespect. A Lady you are indeed." He bowed his head. "Am I forgiven?" He looked up at her with big puppy eyes. Gillian gave him a short nod. "It is good to see Diaspad has not managed to strip away the respect that you would demand for yourself." Gillian said nothing but looked at him as if he had once again found her out. "I must remind you, that though you wear your title of Ladyship with honor, your role of woman is the most important of the two." Gillian found his boldness unending.

Aidan soon returned with a grave look about his face. Gillian turned around instantly, sensing Aidan approaching behind her.

His serious expression gave her concern. "Aidan, are you alright? What's wrong?"

Aidan was silent as he took Gillian's hand and seated her on the bale of hay. "I'm afraid I have some bad news." He paused to select his words.

"Please Aidan, you're scaring me. Don't keep us in suspense." Gillian pleaded.

"Shall I leave?" Lan asked.

"No, that isn't necessary. You may be needed as well. I'm not sure how to put this Gillian." Aidan struggled.

"Just come out with it." Gillian brushed his hand lightly with hers.

"It's your maid, Adelaide." He paused. Gillian waited. "I'm afraid she's dead."

"Dead?!" Gillian's eyes jolted wider.

"What happened?" Lan asked.

"No one knows at the moment. She was found a little more than an hour ago." Gillian was silent, giving Aidan concern. "Gillian, are you alright?"

"Yes. Not to worry, I am fine. Where is Diaspad?" Gillian's first thought was to blame Diaspad.

"I don't know." Aidan answered, he also, had the same thought.

"I think we should return to the castle." Gillian said.

"I will join you, in case I am needed." Lan said.

Aidan, Gillian and Lan returned to the castle where Beechim met them just inside.

"Sire, we can't seem to locate Lord Darnaway anywhere." Beechim said.

"I'm sure he will turn up Beechim. Where is father?" Aidan asked.

"He is waiting for you and Milady outside Lord Darnaway's chambers."

"Thank you Beechim. Let us know when Lord Darnaway returns won't you?" Aidan and Lan escorted Gillian upstairs where the king was pacing frantically.

"Oh good, there you are. I am sorry my dear." Gody took Gillian's hand. "Such an awful, awful tragedy." Gillian gave him a warm smile. "By any chance do you know where your husband might be?"

"No sire, I'm sorry. I don't. The last I saw him was this morning on our way out." Gillian replied.

"Dear, would it be too much of an upset if I asked you some questions about Adelaide?" Gody asked, still holding her hand.

"No sire. I will answer to the best of my knowledge. But first, may I ask, how did she pass?" Gillian was sure Diaspad's sex play must have gotten out of hand.

"It looks as if she drowned in the bath. Do you know of any reasons why she might take her own life?" Had she been upset?"

It was evident to Gillian some ugly secrets were soon to be revealed. They weren't her secrets and she would be the last one to protect Diaspad. "No sire, Adelaide was not the type. She had too many plans for the future." Gillian paused. It was apparent that everyone had Diaspad in mind. "May I see the body now?"

"Oh my dear, are you sure you want to do that? A horrible sight it is." Gody warned.

"With all due respect sire, I have learned much from my father and his travels and my never ending studies. I may be of some help. I assure you this is not the first dead body I have seen." Lan smiled at her, thoroughly impressed.

Gody looked at Aidan for his approval. Aidan gave him a nod. "Very well." Gody opened the door for Gillian to enter.

Gillian walked into the chamber taking a good look around at the room as everyone else followed in behind her. "Please, no one touch anything." Gillian instructed. Adelaide's wet body lay on the bed wrapped in white sheets. Gillian stepped closer and pulled back the sheet from Adelaide's face and shoulders. The brown strands of her hair were beginning to dry. Her face-now calm and peaceful, different from the expressions Gillian was use to seeing.

"Poor, poor woman." Gillian heard Gody say in a soft voice.

"Who found her?" Gillian asked, still looking at the body.

"Igraine." Gody answered.

"And was this the way she was found, nude I mean?"

"Yes." Gody said.

"I doubt that she took her life." Gillian explained, turning around to face them.

"How can you tell?" Aidan asked.

"Was a note found?" Gillian asked.

"Not to my knowledge." Gody replied.

"Well, in most cases, people who drown themselves usually are dressed, not wanting to be found nude. And there is usually a note of some sort." Gillian explained.

"Brilliant deduction." Lan replied with a smile. Aidan and Gody turned to look at him.

"I'm going to examine her body, if you should like to leave." Gillian said, giving them the opportunity.

"We will wait out in the corridor." Gody said.

Gillian walked over to the window and pulled the heavy drapes back to admit more light into the dimly lit room. The white light poured in through the glass, shining on Adelaide's body like a beacon.

Gillian removed the sheet from Adelaide's body to better examine her. Adelaide's spiritless body had taken on a waxy blue-gray color; her lips and nails now pale replaced the rosy pink of vitality. The eyes that had once looked down upon Gillian with arrogance, now had begun to flatten, loosing their spherical appearance from loss of fluid.

Gillian examined her arms and legs, finding nothing out of the ordinary. Adelaide had some old scars on her wrists that Gillian knew for a fact was from Diaspad's twisted sex games.

However, on Adelaide's neck were marks that told a different story. No doubt they had gone unnoticed from Adelaide's long wet hair covering her neck when she was pulled from the bath. Gillian pulled the hair to the side to reveal both sides of Adelaide's neck. She turned Adelaide's head from side to side to study the numerous small bruises, then felt around her throat and neck.

Gillian covered the body back up except for the shoulders and head. "Sire." She called out to let them know it was all right to return. The three men entered the room and stood next to Adelaide's body on the bed. Gillian walked around to the other side of the bed. "Look here, at her neck." Gillian showed them the bruises then began to palpate Adelaide's neck. "Her windpipe had been crushed."

"Strangled?" Aidan was the first to speak up.

"Yes, exactly. If you look closer you can see the position of the fingers that left the bruises." Gillian explained.

"The body is still fairly warm and no rigor has set in yet, I would guess she has been dead no more than three hours."

"Who would do such a thing?" Gody asked. Everyone looked at each other, but no one said a word.

"I would like to talk with Igraine if I may. She may be able to shed more light on all of this." Gillian said, covering the rest of Adelaide's body with the sheet.

"Why don't we use the library." Gody suggested.

"I will tell Igraine you would like to see her in the library on my way out." Lan said.

"You're not going to join us?" Aidan asked.

"I will catch up with you later and you can fill me in." Lan smiled and left the room.

CHAPTER 9

Gillian stood looking out the library window as everyone waited for Igraine. Gillian thought back to the way Adelaide's body looked lying there so still. Still and cold just the way Diaspad liked his women. Where could he be? Moreover, what would life be like at Darnaway estate now that Adelaide was dead? Gillian felt bad for thinking about herself at a time like this, but she could not help it. Could Diaspad have done this? Did he have it within him to do such a thing?

The door opened and Igraine entered to find all eyes upon her. Nervously, she fused with the lace trim around her sleeve, tugging at it.

"Please Igraine, be seated." Aidan said, with a smile to calm her. "We would like to ask you some questions."

Igraine nodded and took a seat. Aidan gave a look at Gillian to begin. Gillian took a few steps toward Igraine with a soft smile. "Igraine, why don't you just start from the beginning. Tell us how it came to be that you found Adelaide."

Igraine took a deep breath, a little irritated. "Same as I said before." She looked at Gillian with a slight sneer.

Aidan took a step and stood next to Igraine's chair. "But neither I, nor Lady Darnaway were here to hear it. Please tell it again." Aidan politely insisted.

Igraine took another deep breath and exhaled very annoyed. "Well, I entered the chamber to gather the dirty laundry. I did so, then went into the bath for the towels and that is when I saw the woman under the water. I called for Beechim and the two of us pulled her from the tub and onto the floor. Beechim went to fetch the king. When his highness entered, he told Beechim to go and fetch the prince." Just then Ranulf entered quietly after being informed by Beechim of Adelaide's death. He folded his arms and stood next to Gody and listened.

"And what were you doing while Beechim was going after the prince?" Gillian asked.

"I took one of the dirty towels, no use using one of the clean ones and laid it over the body, she was dripping all over the floor. Then I took another towel and tried to dry up the water on the floor; I did not want the water to reach the rugs. The late mistress picked those rugs out and I did not want them to be ruined by too much water. I try to keep things just the way the mistress would have wanted it."

"Yes, I'm sure you do a fine job." Gillian said, noticing Igraine's indifference to Adelaide's death. "Then what happened?"

"The prince came in, him and Beechim lifted the body and carried it to the bed. I rolled the spread off the bed so it would not get wet, then pulled the sheet over the woman's body. Then the king asked if I would go look for Lord Darnaway." Igraine squeezed the round carved ends of the armchair unconsciously under Gillian's watchful eye.

Gillian nodded and paused with a moment of silence. "I see. Did you notice anything different about the room? Anything out of place?"

"No milady."

Gillian circled around her slowly. "Any strange smells?"

"Nothing."

Aidan stepped in front of Igraine. "Did the room look as if there might have been a struggle, before you started picking up the laundry?"

"No sire."

Ranulf unfolded his arms. "Why are you two even questioning this woman? It's all too apparent who killed this poor woman!" He could keep quiet no longer.

"No one is being accused. We are just trying to get all the facts straight." Aidan said.

"May I go now, I have work to do?" Igraine asked.

"Yes Igraine, thank you for your patience." Aidan said, as he walked over to the door to let Igraine out.

Gillian stood staring out the window again, deep in thought. "Gillian." Gody called out to her. Gillian turned around. "Would you like for me to make arrangements for Adelaide?"

Gillian smiled. "Yes sire, that would be nice. She has no family that I know of, so what ever you feel is fitting."

I will ride into town and set everything up with the undertaker. Ranulf, why don't you join me." Gody said.

Ranulf walked over to Gillian and gently wrapped his arm around her pulling her close. "I would hate to leave Gillian at a time like this. This is a time when she most needs her friends." Aidan rolled his eyes at his father.

"Aidan can handle things until you return Ranulf, now come along." Gody spoke as if he was speaking to a child. Aidan smirked at Ranulf.

"Yes, that's what I'm afraid of." Ranulf said in a whisper. Ranulf took Gillian's hand. "Can you manage without me for awhile?"

"I will try." Gillian said with seriousness, trying not to laugh.

He kissed her hand. "Till I return milady." He held on to her hand, and gazed into her eyes.

"Ranulf, for God's sake!" Gody scolded. "We aren't leaving the country you know. We are coming back."

Aidan and Gillian were left alone. Aidan approached Gillian at the window and stood behind her. Gillian could feel the nearness of him without a single touch. "Won't you share your thoughts?" Gillian turned around to face him. His closeness made her thoughts stray. "Please, let me in?" She smiled. His deep green eyes looking down on her. "You know something, don't you?" Gillian watched his lips.

It was inevitable that secrets about Diaspad would be told. No one, other than Ranulf, had so much as said it but everything pointed to Diaspad. Everyone had witnessed Diaspad's temper but only Gillian knew of his deviant behavior.

Gillian took a deep breath and released it slowly. "I don't know where to begin."

"Come." Aidan gently took her hand and led her to the sofa and sat down beside her. Gillian looked down at his large soft hand still cradling hers. For the moment, all she could concentrate on was his hand. His breath was warm and sweet, like honey; she could feel it on her cheek. "If we are to get to the bottom of this, we must share our thoughts." He said in a soft, tender voice. "Start where ever you would like." Gillian looked up at him and gave him a nod.

"I know that everyone believes Diaspad killed Adelaide." She paused.

"You don't. Do you?" Aidan asked.

"No. I don't. Not that it didn't cross my mind." Gillian said.

"Tell me why you have come to this conclusion." Gillian took another deep breath. Aidan waited patiently.

"To tell you that, I would have to reveal things, horrible things about my life." Gillian pulled her hand from Aidan's warm caress. She stood and stepped over to the fire. "I couldn't bare it if you were to be revolted by what I know I must reveal. It offends good taste and moral senses."

Aidan was silent as he stood and joined her. "What ever it is that you have to tell me, it could never affect our friendship." Aidan took her hand again for support. "Would these things vindicate Diaspad?"

"They may as far as murder is concerned." She answered.

Aidan lifted her chin with his finger to meet his gaze. "What you reveal to me in confidence will go no further than this room if you like." His voice was soft and soothing.

"I would like that, but the king will have to know to understand my course of thinking. And if I should be thought less of, then so be it." She paused. "I know all too well Diaspad's appetites. From liquor to women. He has a depraved fetish that I became aware of shortly after we were married. I was disgusted and horrified when he made known to me what my wifely duties were to be in the bedroom." Gillian turned her face away from Aidan with shame.

Aidan touched her lightly on the shoulder. "Please, go on. Take your time."

"As you may know, Diaspad worked in a funeral parlor when he was younger." Aidan nodded. "He seems to have a morbid taste for death. He can function as a man only if his partner lays in ice cold water; cold as a dead body would be." Aidan was not expecting a story such as this, but he showed no appearance of shock as so not to upset Gillian. "I refused him, so Adelaide has been his lover since we have been married. He has never shown any physical abuse toward her, maybe because she was always willing to do what ever he asked of her." Aidan's silence made Gillian uneasy. She could not look at him for fear of seeing disgust in his eyes.

Aidan sensed this. "Gillian." He took her by the hand and the two sat back down on the sofa. "I am glad you shared this with me. I understand a lot more things now." He brushed the side of her cheek with his hand. "I feel no less for you now that you have told me about Diaspad, if anything I feel closer to you." Gillian smiled, relieved. She stared up into his eyes again, drinking in their pacifying quality. For a moment she thought he might kiss her. "Knowing all this, what are your thoughts as far as Diaspad's innocence is concerned?"

"Motive. Why would he kill her, after all she was willing to do what ever was asked of her."

"Maybe things got a little out of hand." Aidan searched for answers.

Gillian shook her head. "It is possible, but not likely. After all this time, not once had their activities gone too far. He was not brutal with Adelaide he saved all that for me. I don't claim to be an expert but there were things about the room that just didn't fit."

"You asked Igraine about a smell?" Aidan remembered. "I thought that strange but I knew you had your reasons."

"Yes, that is one of the things I noticed missing from the room. Diaspad liked the smell of formaldehyde. I do not think he could fully function without it. He would always have it on a cloth placed near the bed. I have cleaned up the next morning after their nights of…whatever, enough to know what was commonplace. Formaldehyde has a distinct odor, anyone entering the room would be sure to have smelled it. I noticed another thing. The bed had been neatly slept in. Diaspad was a tormented sleeper. Those linens would have been disarrayed if Diaspad had slept in that bed."

Knowing that Gillian knew the sleeping habits of Diaspad did not set well with him. If Diaspad had Adelaide as his lover, he wondered how Gillian fit in to all this as Diaspad's wife. A rage grew inside him to think of the heinous acts Diaspad must have forced Gillian to be a part of. He wanted to ask, but did not for the fear of embarrassing her. Moreover, part of him did not want to know for fear of going mad from the images in his mind.

"I can see now why you have your doubts. Though I must be honest and say I have no more respect for your husband." Aidan commented, trying to keep his anger in tact.

"One more thing. The marks on Adelaide's neck look to have been done by smaller hands. If you look at Diaspad's hands you will see they are quite large." Gillian pointed out.

"Adelaide must have been alive this morning when I approached you and Diaspad in the corridor, assuming he had just come from his wing of the castle." Aidan said.

"He had changed his clothes. He might not have slept in his chamber, but he did change his clothes. So Adelaide must have been killed after we left the castle and I'm assuming after Diaspad had left also."

Aidan nodded. "So it is possible we are looking for a female."

Gillian nodded. "What do you know about Igraine?"

Aidan looked at her. "You don't think?"

"I think we have to look at everyone and especially any females living here. I have no doubts that some will accuse me giving the situation." Gillian said.

"Yes, but your where a bouts can be accounted for. You were with me all day." Aidan said.

"But what if I am wrong about the time of death? What if she was killed last night? We said goodnight around ten o'clock. If that is the case, maybe Diaspad was so drunk he didn't notice Adelaide was dead this morning. Then that would make me a suspect as well." Gillian said.

Aidan smiled. "I have faith in you. You seem to be well educated in these matters. I think your father taught you well and would be proud." Gillian smiled up at him. "Now, you were asking me about Igraine? My father could tell you more details than I, but I will tell you what I do know. Igraine came to work here when I was a boy; she was my mother's personal maid. After my mother died, she moved to France for awhile then returned with a boy and she and Lan have been here ever since."

"Lan?" Gillian said with surprise.

"Oh, I guess I forgot to mention it. Igraine is Lan's mother." Aidan said.

"I see. So where is Lan's father?"

"I don't know. I'm not even sure who the father is, but I believe Lan knows though he doesn't like to talk about it." Aidan said. "My father has been a substitute father for him."

"Yes. He mentioned that. He loves you both very much." Gillian smiled.

"Yes, we feel the same for him. He has been the little brother I never had. Although we are close, there is still a part of him we have never been able to be a part of. I think a lot of those feelings deal with his father."

"So was Igraine always so friendly?" Gillian said with sarcasm.

Aidan laughed. "There was a time, before my mother died, when Igraine was pleasant, warm and friendly even. Something happened before she left, I assume with Lan's father, she was never the same after that."

"So she was pregnant before leaving for France." Gillian began to put pieces together in her head.

"Yes. Diaspad might be able to tell you." Aidan said.

"Diaspad?" Gillian looked confused.

"Didn't you know? Igraine worked for Diaspad for a short time, but that was so long ago, I guess you wouldn't know."

"When was this?"

"Well, I must have been no more than four or five." Aidan explained. "Of course I don't remember any of this, it's something I guess I heard mention when I was older."

The giant grandfather clock pounded out the time with four long pongs. Aggie entered with a large tray of tea and cakes. "Ya dears hov ben cot oop in tis mess, I betya forgoot all boot lunch or tea time."

Aidan realized the time. "I'm sorry Gillian, you must be famished."

"Actually, I haven't given it a second thought. But now that you mention it, I could do with a bite." Gillian smiled looking at the tray.

"Ya poor lass, ya ben threw so mooch, anow tis. Con I do anythin for ya?" Aggie asked with sympathy.

"No Aggie, I'm fine really. Thank you for being so kind." Gillian took Aggie's hands into hers and gave her a warm smile.

CHAPTER 10

Aidan met Gody as he was returning from making arrangements with the under taker. "Is everything taken care of father?"

"Yes. I made all the arrangements." Gody replied as Beechim took his coat. "Beechim, how about a spot of tea to warm my bones. There's a storm brewing."

"Father, I must speak with you." Aidan said in a serious tone.

"Come let's go into the parlor." They entered the parlor. Gody stood against the fire to warm his backside. "Alright son, you have my attention."

"Father, Gillian has told me some things that has led me to believe that Diaspad had nothing to do with Adelaide's death."

"Really. What sort of things." Gody's interest was peaked.

"She has told me in confidence. Personal things that would only cause her embarrassment. Horrible twisted behavior from Diaspad against Gillian and Adelaide." Aidan tried to explain.

Gody nodded. "I understand. I believe we are all aware that Adelaide and Diaspad were lovers. And we have all witnessed his abuse toward Gillian first hand."

"There is no motive for Diaspad to kill Adelaide. She was probably the only person who actually liked him or at least tolerated him." Aidan explained.

"Here's your tea uncle." Ranulf entered with a cup and saucer in hand. "We are in for a storm tonight. Did I miss anything?"

"Aidan was just telling me that he and Gillian have strong doubts that Diaspad had anything to do with Adelaide's death." Gody explained.

"What?" Ranulf almost spilled the tea as he handed it to Gody. "You must be mad!"

"Motive and evidence. It all points in another direction." Aidan explained.

"What on earth would make the two of you not suspect Diaspad?" Ranulf asked.

"He simply has no motive." Aidan answered.

"But we have witnessed the man out of control on numerous occasions. You've seen the way he treats Gillian." Ranulf pointed out.

"Yes, but Gillian has informed me his anger is always directed at her and never at Adelaide. Never has he raised a hand to Adelaide or spoken a harsh word. She did anything the man asked of her." Aidan said.

"So it is as we suspected, Adelaide was Diaspad's lover." Ranulf stated.

Aidan nodded. "Gillian has shared some horrible secrets, ones that I do not wish to repeat. Everything she has told me now makes sense."

"Think what you like cousin, I'm not so easily convinced." Ranulf said. "Where is our lovely Gillian, by the way?"

"She is dressing." Aidan said.

"And how is she holding up? Lan tells me she is quite the little sleuth. I must say I was impressed with what Lan told me. The way she examined the body and all. Most women are squeamish about that sort of thing, you know. There's just no end to the little surprises we keep discovering about our faire young lady." Ranulf grinned at Aidan as he began to pour him a drink. "And the more I discover, the more intrigued I am."

"Careful cousin. Don't play your little games on this one." Aidan warned. "She has suffered things we can't imagine. Gillian needs our care and support."

"Aidan's right Ranulf. I won't have you playing with this girl's head." Gody scolded.

"Who said I was playing a game? Did it ever occur to the both of you I might be falling for this woman? That Gillian might have truly captured my heart?" Ranulf looked at the two of them.

Aidan and Gody looked at each other and answered at the same time. "No."

"Did I hear my name?" Gillian entered with a beaming smile and again taking hold of all the consciousness that existed in the room. She had a way of sucking a man's breath right out of him if not forewarned.

"How fetching you look." Ranulf said making a leap toward Gillian. He took her hand and kissed it.

"Thank you." Gillian said as she politely tried to pull her hand from Ranulf's clutches.

Aidan stood just a few feet away from her smiling. He was radiant to Gillian, in his bright blue surcoat. She admired his well-formed muscles of his legs in his long tight pants. She glanced his way in a short stare.

He joined her, took her hand, turned it palm side up, and laid a long warm kiss to her small hand. Gillian held her breath; his lips were almost scorching. She folded her palm, when his lips left her hand, wanting to keep his kiss always. "You look lovely as always."

Gillian blushed. "His highness is too kind."

"My dear Gillian." Gody said. "With the dark tragedy that has fallen over this castle, you are most definitely the bright light behind the cloud!"

Gillian giggled. "My! I think I will go out and come in again. All of you certainly have a way of boosting a girl's ego."

Gody laughed. "Walk with me my dear." Gillian walked with the king over to the doorway that led out onto the veranda. "I wanted to have a word with you in private."

"Yes sire?" Gillian looked concerned.

Gody gave her a warm smile to ease the look on her face. "I have been talking with Aidan. Is it true that you do not believe your husband to have any part in Adelaide's death?"

"Yes. This is true sire."

Gody smiled at her. "You are an amazing woman, my dear."

Gillian smiled. "Why do you say that sire?"

"I know you have lived a tormented life with Diaspad. A life I would not wish upon my worst enemy. You could easily have him put to death, but you defend him. That was a very honorable thing to do." Gody smiled.

"It is simply the truth sire, nothing more." Gillian smiled.

Gody grinned. "I see why my son admires you so."

Gillian glanced over in Aidan's direction, her cheeks flushed. "And I him. Your son has been a good friend to me. I trust him. I cannot say that about most men."

"Neither can I." He smiled at her. "You are wise to trust Aidan. And I do not say this because he is my son. We all need someone to rely on at times, I know Aidan would not let you down."

Ranulf openly admired Gillian as she continued talking with Gody. He drank in her mountain scenery of her well-filled bodice. "How I would like to get my hands on both of them." He said, nudging Aidan. Then continued to picture her divested of skirt and undergarments.

Aidan smirked at him. "I believe you want this woman so, because she has not given in to your charms. Men want most what they can't have."

"Save your deductions for the murder that has happened here, cousin." Ranulf released his gaze on Gillian long enough to cut his eyes at Aidan. "You admire mother nature's handy work, don't you cousin?" He returned his eyes to Gillian.

"Yes. But if you don't respect the flower, you don't deserve a garden." Aidan smiled.

CHAPTER 11

▼

Night had fallen with incredible swiftness. One moment there had been eerie twilight, a quickly gathering dusk, and the next there was blackness in which not even the surrounding woods could be seen.

Dinner had begun at the usual time. The conversation was light, out of respect for the dead.

Aggie entered and brought in an extra basket of bread. "I gave Lan your message sire. He turned down the invitation, but sent his thanks."

Gody nodded. "Thank you Aggie." He dabbed his mouth with his napkin and turned his attention to Gillian. "I invited Lan to dine with us, but as you heard he refused. Normally, he eats most of his meals with us."

"But not since Diaspad arrived." Ranulf added.

Aidan smiled. "You might say, the two do not get along."

Ranulf chuckled. "That is an understatement."

"I see." Gillian smiled, but left the matter alone.

The storm clouds were now boiling in the sky, low and ominous. The distant rumble of thunder could be heard. The wind had fallen asleep in the woodlands and the veins of lightning flickered across the sky, then the rain fell.

A commotion in the corridor brought an interruption to the evening meal.

"Sire, let me take your wet things." They all heard Beechim say rather loudly, as if trying to announce someone's arrival.

Diaspad entered the dining hall, slicking back his wet hair with his hand. No one said a word at first; they just stared at him. "What?" Diaspad asked looking back at all of them. "The look on your faces." Diaspad took a seat and began to fill his plate. "You look as if you are all at a funeral." He chortled.

"How fitting you should say so." Ranulf remarked.

Diaspad gave Ranulf a go-to-hell look then shoveled some potatoes in his mouth. "What do you mean?" Diaspad asked, with a mouth full of food.

"Where have you been Diaspad?" Gody asked. "We have been looking all over for you."

"At the pub. It's the only place to get a decent drink." He answered, spitting out pieces of food.

"We should have known." Ranulf said in a sarcastic tone.

"How long have you been there?" Gody asked.

Diaspad looked at Gody, confused. "Why is everyone so concerned about my where-a bouts?"

"Answer the question!" Ranulf raised his voice. "How long have you been there?"

"Who are you, my mother?" Diaspad roared. Gillian looked over at Aidan who was very quiet, but she could see the anger building inside him. "What are you looking at him for?" Diaspad bellowed at Gillian startling her. Gillian immediately lowered her eyes. "Get up! Get me some wine!"

Angrily, Aidan hit the table with his fist quaking the table and everything on it. "Gillian is not your servant." He said in a low calm voice. Though his voice seemed calm, the intense anger in it might have crumbled stone.

Diaspad looked at Aidan surprised he would defend Gillian with such earnest. "Alright, fine. Adelaide! Adelaide, get in here!"

"She wont be answering you tonight or any other night." Ranulf spoke up.

"What do you mean? Where is she?" Annie entered and poured Diaspad some wine. He gulped the wine while admiring Annie. "Now, what have we here?" Diaspad groped her with his eyes.

"Adelaide is dead." Aidan answered.

"What?" Diaspad laughed. "You're joking." Diaspad looked around at the serious faces looking back at him. "I saw her just this morning." The smile slid from his face.

"Are you sure it was this morning you saw her?" Gillian asked.

"Alive?" Ranulf added.

"Yes, of course. Just before I saw Aidan and Gillian about to take off on their little excursion." Diaspad mocked them. Gillian and Aidan looked at each other again. "Is anyone going to tell me what the bloody hell is going on?"

"Adelaide was found dead this morning, in the bath." Gody answered.

"Any idea how she got that way?" Ranulf spoke with contempt.

Diaspad took another look at the faces staring back at him. "You all think I did it?"

"You were the last to see her, were you not?" Ranulf questioned.

Diaspad emptied the wine left in his glass, then filled it again. He looked at Gillian with scorn. "What kind of lies have you been filling everyone's head with?" Gillian shook her head as Diaspad rose from his chair. Aidan caught him by his collar and pulled him back in his chair with one yank.

"Gillian was the first to come to your defense. You owe her gratitude. If it wasn't for her knowledge you might be accused." Aidan enlightened him, but he offered no thanks.

Diaspad glanced at Gillian surprised she of all people would be the first to defend him. He took another gulp of wine and stood up. "Get your things Gillian, we are leaving at once!" Gillian's heart jumped up in her throat. "I won't stay here and be accused." Gillian could not move, her legs were so cold. "Get up I say!" She rose slowly as if pulled by some invisible string. Gillian looked at Aidan without a word as her senses were all swept away. Despair flooded over her with the thought of returning to hell with Diaspad. Tears began to well in her eyes as she felt anguish and a cold demented rage. First it burned her then it numbed her.

Diaspad noticed the two with their eyes locked on each other. "Sit down Diaspad!" Gody spoke with authority. "No one is going anywhere until this matter is solved."

Gillian's eyes released their tears in relief. Aidan lent her a warm smile, wanting to comfort her. All the while Diaspad watched. Gillian took a deep breath and sat back down, wiping her face with her napkin.

"Come, come my dear, dry your eyes lest everyone here should think you do not wish to return home with me." Diaspad smiled mockingly. Gillian looked at him then glanced at Aidan before lowering her eyes. "Well then, since we are forced to remain here, Gillian, why don't you tell me just how close you and Aidan have become?"

"Quiet Diaspad! Can we not manage to have one pleasant dinner without your nonsense?" Gody scolded.

"I am just inquiring about how my wife has been spending all her free time. The two of them seem to be very cozy." Diaspad filled his wineglass again.

"Be quiet Diaspad! Before you say something you will regret!" Ranulf sneered.

"I assure you your wife's virtue is still intact!" Aidan came quick to her defense.

"I am not stupid nor blind." Diaspad said to Gillian. "I have seen the looks you give him. I know what is on your mind!"

Gillian's mouth fell open. "Diaspad please. You have had much to drink."

"You want him to bed you! Do you? Is that what you want?" Again Gillian's mouth fell open, but she could not speak from embarrassment. Ranulf stood, ready to pounce. "Answer me!"

"No!" She all too quickly shouted. Aidan stood quickly, he seemed poised on the edge of violence like a hound awaiting the release of his leach. The candlelight flickered from all the sudden movements, shadowing Gillian's face. She blushed a pink hue to her cheeks and her bosom rose and fell rapidly under her lace bodice.

"How can you speak in such a manner?" Thundered Aidan. "Your mad to speak so!" Diaspad remained seated as he continued to flirt with danger. Aidan hovered over him, his breathing heavy and low. Horrifically beautiful in his rage.

Gillian gave Diaspad a look that penetrated him to the core. It was the icy look of absolute contempt. Diaspad's cruelness sounded like a demon, some loathsome thing for which the voice was an imitation of human.

Gody stood from his chair. "That will be quite enough! Everyone, please, sit down! Let us please try to finish dinner in peace."

Everyone sat back down as the king suggested. Silence took hold of the room as everyone finished with the evening meal. Gillian did not dare take her eyes off her plate as she quietly sipped her glass of water.

Gillian padded her napkin against her lips and made the mistake of glancing up to find Diaspad sadistically watching her. He mocked her with a smile. She knew then the silence would not last. "So Ranulf, you're a ladies man, what do you think of my wife's bosoms?" Gillian could see Aidan's rage begin to boil. "I ask you, have you ever seen the like? They're larger than your best milker uncle." Everyone was now on the edge of his or her seat. "And those thighs…show Aidan your thighs Gillian. Soft and white. Show him what he's missed. Why they're right for keeping a man's ears warm!"

Gillian's eyes grew large. In one swift swoop, Aidan leaped from his chair, grabbed Diaspad by the throat with one hand and pinned him a foot off the floor against the wall. Ranulf leaped over chairs to Aidan's side. Gody jumped up and tried to pull Aidan's grip loose from Diaspad's throat.

"Aidan don't be rash! Let him go." Gody tried to calm him, but Aidan squeezed all the more tighter.

"Go ahead." Diaspad said with air he managed to gather into a whispery voice. "You will never have her. I will never let her go."

"Aidan, this is what he wants you to do." Gillian's voice came from across the table. "He wants you to end his suffering, but it will be you who pays for it. He is not worth it." Her sweet voice began to melt his rage as he released his grip, sending Diaspad crashing to the floor.

Aidan stood looming over him. "Once again, Gillian saves you." Aidan turned to leave, when Diaspad threw back his head and babbled forth with laughter. A devastatingly scornful sound. "Your heart is written on your face. Lie to yourself and others if you will. How Gillian must laugh at you behind your back. Do you think a hideous creature; a monster like yourself would be looked upon in favor? Do you think she would want those hairy paws of yours on her delicate body?" Aidan continued out of the room. Gillian wanted to run to him but didn't want to give Diaspad the satisfaction. The malice now returned to her face as she stared down at Diaspad.

Ranulf stepped up and took a hard swing at Diaspad, knocking him out cold. "I like him better this way." He said looking down at Diaspad's unconscious body. "Don't you think?" He looked at Gillian and smiled.

Aidan caught his reflection passing by a corridor mirror. He stopped to study his image and thought back on Diaspad's hateful words. Could he really expect for beautiful Gillian, perfect Gillian, to see him for more than the creature that stared back at him?

CHAPTER 12

▼

Gillian retired to the parlor along with Gody and Ranulf, she had hoped to find Aidan waiting there, but he was nowhere in sight. The king's guards picked up Diaspad's lifeless body and hauled him up to his chambers to sleep another one off.

No one knew quite what to say especially Gillian. It seemed simpler to just pretend it never happened.

Gillian approached the parlor hearth; the expression on her face seemed disturbed and anxious. Her lips were half asunder, as if she meant to speak, she drew a breath; but it escaped in a sigh instead of words.

Ranulf could see her uneasiness. He poured her a drink and handed it to her. "Here, drink this. It will calm you."

"What is it?"

"Brandy. It will do you wonders." Ranulf smiled.

Gillian smiled and took a sip. "Thank you."

"Well, if the two of you don't mind, I will take my brandy and turn in with a good book. Ranulf, you'll keep Gillian company wont you?" Gody asked.

"Yes, of course uncle." Ranulf smiled.

"Sweet dreams sire." Gillian smiled.

Gody felt saddened for Gillian knowing all that she had indured. He felt he should offer her some encouraging words. "Sweet dreams for you as well my dear. Don't you fret; I promise all will turn out well. Oh Ranulf, you will mind your manners?"

"Yes uncle." He smirked. "Here, let me refresh your drink." Ranulf offered.

"Oh, no. I am fine. It did help thank you." She smiled warmly.

"Come, sit by the fire with me. There's a chill in the air tonight." Ranulf threw two large pillows on the floor next to the fire and took a seat on one and patted the other with his hand. Gillian reluctantly took a seat. "Now, isn't that better?"

Gillian nodded with a smile, wondering the whole time where Aidan must have been. "Yes, this is nice."

Ranulf gazed into her eyes. "You look beautiful in the fire light."

"Thank you." Gillian said softly, trying not to look too long into his eyes.

"I have wanted a few moments alone with you, but something is always getting in the way." Ranulf said, still gazing in her eyes.

"Oh really, why?" Gillian asked, simply.

"I know that you and Aidan are fast becoming friends. I wanted you to know that I am also your friend." He said with sincerity.

Gillian touched his hand. "That is comforting to know. One can always use friends."

Ranulf placed his hand on top of Gillian's. "Let me take you away from here."

Gillian looked at him strangely. "Excuse me?"

Ranulf laughed. "I mean just for an evening. Into town, for dinner and dancing. You need a break away from this dreary old castle."

Gillian laughed. "That sounds nice, but Diaspad would never approve."

"Well maybe we could work around that. Give him a bottle and he'll never be the wiser. Besides, when was the last time he took you dancing?"

Gillian laughed. "Never."

"You're even more beautiful when you laugh." Ranulf said with a serious look. "You should laugh more often. Though I doubt there is much laughter in your household." His gaze deepened.

Gillian smiled, not so afraid to look longer into his eyes, sensing his sincerity. "Do you ever get lonely Ranulf? I mean, I know you are never at a loss from female companionship but what about a true mate?"

Ranulf paused and looked into the flames of the fire. "Yes, I am lonely sometimes. I guess we all are at times."

"Why have you not married? Too picky?" She smiled. "Surely you have loved?"

Ranulf turned his eyes back to the fire. "Yes, I have loved. A long, long time ago."

"What happened?" Gillian asked.

Ranulf took a deep breath. "She died."

"Oh Ranulf, I'm sorry..." she placed her hand on his again, "if I had known, I wouldn't have brought it up."

He offered her a smile. "It's alright, it was a long time ago. You might say I haven't allowed myself to love since."

"You blame yourself somehow." Gillian said. Ranulf looked at her as if she somehow read his thoughts. "Why else would you not allow yourself love. You know, friendship goes both ways."

He paused, remembering. "Jullian was her name, I was the only one to call her by her given name. She was beautiful like you, but in a different way, more of a quiet kind of beauty, one you would not necessarily notice at first. The gentlest person I ever knew. She never asked anything of me, I should have married her, but I waited and waited, then it was too late. She met with an accident, carrying my unborn child."

"Ranulf, I am so so sorry." Gillian said with tears in her eyes.

"Well, like I said it was a long time ago. I didn't mean to burden you. You have your own trails to attend to." He smiled.

"No. I am honored." She smiled as he wiped the tears from her cheek. "It's not too late for you, you can love again."

"I have never met another woman like Jullian until you. The two of you share many of the same qualities, but are separate still. I have become accustom to a certain type of woman, one that is not available or one that is not the marrying kind."

"I see. Those are types of women you feel safe with. You don't have to worry about falling in love. Either they are married or not the sort you marry, so you're safe."

Ranulf laughed. "Yes, I guess your right."

"Seems to me, you need to look elsewhere. Broaden your horizons. Allow yourself to fall in love. I imagine it's wonderful." She gleamed.

Ranulf took her hand and kissed it. "And what if I were to fall in love with you?"

Gillian laughed. "Then once again you choose one who is not available." Gillian placed her hand gently on the side of his face. "Dear sweet Ranulf, maybe love will choose you when you least expect." Gillian stood and offered her hand. "Come, walk me to my chamber."

Gillian and Ranulf stood outside her chamber door. Ranulf took her hand. "I guess I will bid you goodnight, milady." He rubbed his lips gently across her hand. "If you should have need, you know where my chambers are don't you?"

"Yes. Thank you, but I will be fine. I will make sure to lock the door."

Ranulf caught her hand as she opened the door. He drew her into him swiftly, as if to kiss her. He gave her a mischievous little smile. "You know, if you don't wish to be alone tonight, I don't mind keeping you company."

Gillian grinned and pushed some space between them. "Say goodnight, Ranulf."

"Goodnight, Ranulf."

Gillian drifted through the motions of brushing her hair, of undressing and putting on her nightclothes. She slipped into her robe and stepped out onto her covered private balcony. The rain was beating down over Aberdour. The haunted wood was full of the groans of mighty trees wrung in the tempest and the air throbbed with thunderous crashes in the darkness of the heavens.

Gillian could see Aidan's chambers from her terrace. She could just make out a dim light coming from his window. A sudden flash of lightning revealed Aidan standing out on his large veranda. She felt she needed to see him, to talk to him. There was no sleep while the storm raged.

Gillian left the safety of her chamber and found herself outside Aidan's chamber door. She knocked three times,

firmly. She had not expected Aidan to hear her knocking
from his veranda. She waited patiently, a sufficient
amount of time; she turned to leave when the door
opened.

"Gillian." Aidan was surprised.

"I'm sorry, do I disturb you?" She asked softly.

He smiled. "Never. Please, come in." Aidan closed the
door behind her. "Is anything wrong?"

"Oh no. I couldn't sleep. I saw you from my balcony, I
thought you might not be able to sleep either." Gillian
looked around the room, which was a large drawing room
and dining room combined.

"Let's go into the next room, there is no fire in the grate
in this room, I don't want you to get cold." Gillian followed Aidan into the bedchamber. It was pleasantly warm
and dimly lit by the glow of a fire in the large fireplace.
The amber tones dancing about the room provided a sense
of security. A massive canopy bed of deep rich reds and
gold commanded attention. To Gillian's far right sat a
huge fireplace with sofa, chairs and large overstuffed pillows on which to sit and enjoy the warmth.

Gillian was quiet as she stood next to the open glass
doors that led out onto the veranda. The rain was still
coming down. Gillian seemed in a wet world, wet but safe
and warm. She turned and looked at Aidan, who was quietly watching her, and gave him a smile. "I'm sorry, I must
seem very distant. The rain has a calming effect on me, I
guess."

"Yes, it is the same with me." He said softly. "I love to
just sit and listen."

"I was looking for you earlier." She said, still standing
next to the open door.

"You were?"

"Yes, but I thought you might need some time alone. I wanted to apologize for the things Diaspad said tonight."

"It was not your fault." He gave her a slight smile.

"Diaspad can sound very cruel if you are not use to hearing it all the time. I am deeply sorry. You did not deserve any of his abuse. I hope he did not hurt you?" Gillian touched him with her sincerity.

Aidan's heart had been breaking for her all along and here was dear sweet Gillian concerned about his feelings. "I am fine...now." He smiled at her tenderly. "I am also sorry for the horrible things Diaspad said to you."

Gillian paused in silence and looked out at the rain, then laughed. "Look at us. We are both apologizing for Diaspad's verbal lashings."

Aidan stepped closer and leaned against the opposite side of the doorframe. "Gillian, how have you managed to live with such a monster? How have you remained the kind-hearted person that you are?"

"Diaspad can't hurt me with his words, not anymore. I learn to put up a wall to keep him out some time ago. It's simple survival." She smiled. "I hate that your family has to witness Diaspad's behavior. He seems to get worse with each passing week."

Gillian rubbed her arms briskly and walked over to the fire. The light revealed the sheerness of her nightgown that clung to her gently. Aidan's face was still. His cat eyes moved searchingly over her, as if he could discover in all the unimportant details of her appearance some crucial secret.

Gillian sat down on the floor next to the fire; Aidan followed and sat next to her. "Why don't you leave him?" Aidan asked without taking his eyes off the flame.

Gillian looked at him taken by surprise at his question. She paused before answering. "It is what my father wanted. He never asked anything of me, but that I marry Diaspad. I did so to please him. I can not betray his wishes nor his memory."

Aidan nodded with disappointment. "I see."

"Diaspad is jealous, you know. Of you I mean." Gillian looked at him.

Aidan looked at her confused. "What do you mean?"

Gillian smiled as she looked deeply into his eyes, with no words at first. Aidan's mouth was dry, his heart thumped against his ribs. Her eyes, her big beautiful eyes had the most extraordinary power within them.

"You don't know, do you?" She asked. Aidan slowly shook his head; his eyes fixed on her. Gillian slowly reached up with her hand and gently caressed the side of his face. "You don't know how beautiful you truly are…do you?"

There was an odd, sharp ache in Aidan's chest and a sensation in his stomach as if he had fallen from a great height. "Beautiful?" He couldn't believe her words.

Gillian gleamed a smile at him. "You have an exquisiteness that goes beyond the mere physical. No one has ever told you this?"

Aidan shook his head and was silent as he watched her lips, waiting for her to recant the words she just spoke. None came. All expression left his face. "Do you toy with my emotions?" He asked with all seriousness.

"No Aidan, never." She smiled at him sincerely.

Aidan paused again in silence. "Tell me what you see when you look at my face? Honestly. You can't surely see a man?"

Gillian could see years of pain in this dear, dear man's eyes. Pain that Diaspad knew how to feed on. She smiled warmly. "I see a man. A man who is splendid in his own uniqueness. Mind, body, and soul. Honestly."

Aidan watched her eloquent words spill from her wonderful lips. Words he had never heard. He looked down at his hands. "Look at these hands, are they not the hands of some creature, of some monster?"

Gillian leaned closer and gently took his hand, turning it palm side up. She pulled it to her and pressed her sweet lips into his warm palm. Aidan closed his eyes; he could not recall a pleasure as delicious as this one. Her scent caressed his nose and he inhaled deeply a sweet subtle perfume mixed with rose scent oil of her skin and then felt soft luxuriant hair fall against his arm.

Gillian released her lips and looked deep into his eyes. "I see no monsters here." She said with a serious tone.

Aidan wanted desperately to take her into his arms at that moment, and Gillian could see it in his eyes. Her breath quickened from his stare, her heart pounded. The both of them all too aware of the heat building between them. Be quiet, she said to her body, to her loins, her inner being. She mercifully found herself with a wanting need.

His breath seemed loud against the roar of the rain. The bulge in his pants was aching to be free. Aidan reached up and gently brushed back a strand of hair from her face. What a tender thing to do, she thought.

Aidan stroked her cheek with his finger, then her neck and collarbone ever so gently. He stared at her bare neckline, at the plunging neck of her gown and at the tiny shadow between her breasts. Gillian closed her eyes and dreamed it was his kisses tingling her skin. Her skin anticipated his touch, like when one knows they are about to be tickled.

Gillian suddenly opened her eyes after feeling the absence of his touch. Aidan stood and walked back over to the open door to feel the cool air against his face. Gillian realized the moment was too intense for them both.

Gillian stood, walked past Aidan and stood on the veranda looking out at the rain.

Aidan joined her at the railing. "Gillian." She looked at him. "Did Diaspad make you do horrible acts, like Adelaide?" He asked, but couldn't look at her.

Gillian took a deep breath. "No. I refused him." She did not elaborate, and Aidan was still unaware she had never been with a man.

"Good, I think I would end up killing him if he had." He said calmly. Gillian smiled and without warning, stood on her tiptoes and gave him a slow kiss on the cheek. Aidan touched his cheek as if the keep her kiss from fading. "What did I do to deserve that?" He smiled.

"For being a true and noble prince. And for being my friend." She smiled.

CHAPTER 13

▼

The storm clouds lingered on through the night awakening the morning with their loud rumblings. The heavens were not yet through with emptying their wet bounty onto Aberdour.

Breakfast had begun and all were seated except Gillian and Diaspad. Aggie entered with a hot pot of coffee, filling everyone's cup.

"Aggie have you seen Gillian this morning?" Aidan asked out of concern.

"Oh, I almoost forgoot," she laughed, "aye sire, tha miss iz noot felin well tis morn. I'm aboot ta tak-er oop sum tea-n-biscoots."

Diaspad came stumbling in and took his seat. Ranulf pulled out his pocket watch and gave it a glance. "My, my Diaspad. What do we owe this honor, and before noon?" Ranulf mocked him.

"I have been known to breakfast before noon on occasion." He commented with the same amount of sarcasm. "Coffee!" He yelled, in the direction of the kitchen. "Today!"

"Lower your voice man. There's no need to shout." Gody scolded.

Annie entered this time with the pot of coffee and a friendly smile. "Well now, this is better." Diaspad said, smiling at Annie. Igraine entered with some fresh pastries. "Now, I would much rather be served by this sweet young thing, then to have to look at Igraine's sourpuss." Igraine sneered at him then left the room. Annie poured the coffee delicately with a careful hand. Diaspad reached his hand behind her and gave her bottom a squeeze. "What is your name child?"

"Annie, milord." She giggled innocently.

"That is a fine name child. Just fine." Diaspad gave her another squeeze.

"Go about your chores Annie, thank you." Aidan said, then waited till she was out of the room before turning his attention to Diaspad. "Child is right. You should take care were you place your hands."

"Child? Why that's no child. Did you see how full her hips were? And that ass…tight and firm. Annie, Annie with the terrific fanny."

Aidan stood with force almost knocking his chair over. "Filthy pig!" He said with contempt just before walking out of the room.

"Pig? Was it something I said?" Diaspad laughed.

"You should take care, that mouth of yours might one day get you killed." Ranulf smiled, happy to do the deed himself.

Aidan entered the kitchen where Aggie had just finished preparing Gillian a tray to take to her room. "I will take that to Gillian if you don't mind Aggie." Aidan smiled.

Aggie grinned. "Yer sooch a-dear. Run ya oot ded he?" She asked, referring to Diaspad. "I canna blim tha lass fer noot coomin doon. Eare ya go." She placed the tray in Aidan's hands. "Yer smilin face will doo-er good."

A gentle tap-tap came to Gillian's door. "Come in Aggie." She called out.

Gillian had her back to the door as she slipped into her dressing robe as Aidan entered. Aidan caught a glimpse of the marks, now healing, on her back as she pulled the robe up over her shoulders. Aidan tried to lower his eyes but couldn't. He loudly cleared his throat to make his presence known.

Gillian turned around suddenly. "Aidan!" She smiled.

"I hope you don't mind, I asked to bring your tray."

"No. Please, come in." Gillian stepped closer to him, her hands clasped at the breast of her gown. She stood in front of a window; Aidan could see the silhouette of her perfect body, a shimmering glimmer through the sheer dressing gown. He could make out every detail: the fullness of her breast and the curve of her hips. And there between her legs, where the gown clung just slightly to the shadowy recess at the juncture of her thighs. "I am pleased to see you."

Aidan smiled. "I don't mean to disturb the sanctity of your chambers."

Gillian blushed slightly. "Don't be silly."

"Well then, where would you like your tray, Madame?" He asked, grinning.

"I'm sorry, please set it on the table next to the window." Aidan sat the tray that supported a china tea service emblazoned with pink and yellow roses down where

Gillian had requested. "A few seconds earlier, and you would have caught me at a disadvantage." She teased.

Aidan smiled. "Maybe next time."

"I see Aggie has placed two cups on the tray. She must have read my mind. Please, join me?" Gillian made a motion with her hand at the empty chair as she took a seat.

"I should go and leave you to finish dressing." He remained standing.

"Please? I hate to eat alone. Please don't go." Her eyes spoke with great insistence. "Unless you think it improper?"

Aidan shook his head. "I will join you, if you want." Aidan took a seat. Gillian beamed a smile at him. "Aggie said you were ill?"

Gillian chuckled. "No, I'm fine. I heard Diaspad's voice this morning. I just could not bare whatever humiliation he had to serve me for breakfast. I asked Aggie to make my excuses."

"I am glad you are not ill." Aidan studied her with an intense stare as she poured the tea with a delicate hand. Her fingers were dainty, precise and did not spill a drop. How lovely she looked, just bathed and her hair still piled up and pinned in place. Fresh like the morning's first dew.

"The wonderful thing about tea being poured is the way it shines in the light, the way the brown of the tea becomes amber and gold, the way it twists and turns like a dancer as it fills the cup." Gillian looked up to see his eyes focused on her. She blushed a bit. Aidan allowed his finger to brush lightly against the back of her hand as he took the tea she offered him. "The weather doesn't look as if it will let up any today. I had hoped to take a walk down by the loch." Gillian said looking out the window. She returned her eyes back to Aidan and smiled, finding him still staring at her. "You are very quiet this morn. Anything wrong?"

He smiled. "No. Just thinking." He said, diverted from his reverie.

"About what? Here, have a biscuit." She offered.

"About last night."

Gillian nodded as she swallowed a bite of biscuit. "It was eventful." She said, assuming he was referring to Diaspad's behavior.

A short time had passed from the present moment to the one last night that was still fresh in his mind. It was a strange sensation to still be yearning for that moment. He wanted to touch her again, to slowly slide the hairpins out of her auburn locks. To inhale the fragrance of her curls. To slide the silkiness of her dressing gown along her perfect skin. Aidan looked over at Gillian's bed, not yet made up. He imagined her pinned underneath him to the pink and green garlands on the sheets.

"Aidan?" The sound of Gillian's voice broke his trance. "Is there something on your mind, you seem distant?"

Aidan smiled. "I'm sorry, you must think me rude. I do not mean to seem distant. I assure you, I am very, very near."

Gillian looked up at the thin spattering of rain on the windowpane, and took a deep breath and released it slowly. "I guess I must eventually come face to face with the world outside this room today." She looked at Aidan and smiled. "Though I would prefer to spend it sitting here talking with you."

"Yes, I would like that as well." He grinned. "Father has informed me that the undertaker will be arriving this morning. I thought you might like to meet him and talk with him."

Gillian paused as she watched the droplets of rain on the panes turn into streams of water. "Yes, I do believe I would." She looked at Aidan and smiled. "Will you wait while I dress?"

Aidan nodded, though he preferred her as she was. "Gillian." She turned around just as she was about to enter her dressing room. "I must warn you, Diaspad may still be down stairs."

Gillian nodded. "Yes, well, if I must face him this early in the day, then I must. I feel secure with you there." She smiled a sweet smile at him before entering her dressing room.

Beechim met Gillian and Aidan as they were about to enter the parlor. "Milady, forgive me. I have not yet expressed my condolences for the loss of your maid."

Gillian placed her hand lightly upon his. "Thank you Beechim, you're very kind." Beechim suddenly became distressed and turned his head to release a horrible cough. "Are you alright?" Gillian asked with concern.

Beechim caught his breath and smiled. "Oh, I'm just fine. Don't worry yourself milady, just the malady's of an old man."

"Beechim, why don't you let Aggie fix you one of her concoctions for that cough and maybe some rest would do you good as well." Aidan suggested.

"Yes, sire, that may be just the thing I need." He gave them a smile then left.

"Oh Aidan, Gillian, there you are." Gody replied as they entered the parlor. An older gentleman stood to his feet when they entered. "Lady Darnaway, this is the undertaker, Mr. Tristamm." The man nodded with a warm smile. He was a comely looking man with brilliant blue eyes. They were too close together, those eyes. Nevertheless, he wasn't unattractive, and his face wore a smile of quiet devotion that never seemed to leave his face.

Gillian returned the smile. "How do you do?" She suddenly noticed Diaspad slouched on the sofa. He was quiet, but his gaze never left Gillian. She tried to ignore him; he was staring so hard, she could almost feel his eyes burning right through her.

"It was nice of you to come all this way, and in this weather Mr. Tristamm." Aidan said.

Tristamm smiled. "It is no trouble at all sire. Besides, it is my job." He spoke in a soft voice that one almost had to focus both ears just to catch his words. "His highness has informed me of the details of this poor unfortunate woman's demise. Am I to understand there is no family?"

"Not that I am aware of, but you might ask my husband." Gillian suggested, looking at Diaspad. Tristamm looked over at the silent lump on the sofa and waited for an answer. Diaspad shook his head.

"Well then, you leave everything to me and I will see that this woman receives a proper funeral." Tristamm smiled at Gillian.

"I'm sure you will do a beautiful job." Gillian smiled politely. "When a death does occur in circumstances such as these, you do take extraordinary measures?"

"Oh yes, milady. When there is a question concerning a death, we examine the body very closely." Tristamm spoke with some enthusiasm. "We are very modern. I like to think we keep up with all the new sciences."

Gillian nodded. "You will be sure to clean under her nails and save the findings?"

"Oh yes, milady. Of course." Tristamm replied.

"Ha!" Said the lifeless lump on the sofa. "And who are you now? Madame sleuth?"

Gillian as well as the others ignored Diaspad's remarks. Mr. Tristamm had a strange look on his face, as if he were the only one in the room to have heard Diaspad.

"Oh but Lady Darnaway is wise to ask such questions. Much can be learned from the smallest of details." Tristamm spoke to Diaspad as if his comment needed a reply.

Ranulf entered the parlor bright and cheery. "Oh hello Tristamm, What brings you out on a day like today? Here for Diaspad by any chance?"

"You know bloody well why he's here you fool." Answered the angry lump.

"Diaspad, still with us are you?" Ranulf smirked.

"Forgive my husband, Mr. Tristamm, Adelaide's death has effected us all deeply. We are all a bit on edge. Lord Darnaway was very fond of Adelaide." Gillian spoke up, taking back her dignity. "We will all miss her."

"Yes, please forgive our rudeness." Gody made excuses for everyone else.

"Please, say no more. It is perfectly understandable." Tristamm replied. He noticed two of his men carrying Adelaide's cloth wrapped body up from the bowels of the castle to the covered cart waiting outside. The body had been placed there to keep it cool until Tristamm could collect it. "I see that my men are ready, so I will say goodbye and be in contact with you soon."

"Thank you again, Mr. Tristamm. It was a pleasure to meet you." Gillian smiled.

"The honor was all mine, milady. I will escort myself out." Tristamm gave a nod to the king and Aidan, then left.

Diaspad's eyes were still focused on Gillian. "Quite the little hostess aren't we?"

"Gillian is merely being the Lady that she is, which is more than I can say for you!" Gody scolded.

Ranulf laughed. "You weren't aware your wife possessed more than just beauty, were you?" Aidan slowly made his way behind the sofa, standing guard over Diaspad. Ranulf took Gillian's hand and kissed it. "It seems our lovely Gillian is beginning to bloom before our eyes."

"Yes, bloom." Diaspad sneered.

Aidan placed his hand on Diaspad's shoulder to secure him to the sofa in case he should decide to pounce on Gillian. "All flowers need a little love and care to flourish and grow." Gillian gave Aidan a little smile to simply acknowledge his sweet comment.

Diaspad shifted under the weight of Aidan's hand. "And I wonder who could be providing her with all this love and care. Let me see…how does it go, doesn't the Good Book say thou shall not covet thy neighbor's wife? Or in this case, thy cousin's."

"Well it's obvious you are not to blame. When was the last time you gave anyone love or care, other than your next bottle." Ranulf smirked.

"Please Diaspad, no more. You don't know what you say." Gillian pleaded.

"Now don't I?" Diaspad remarked in a flippant manner.

"Everyone here has been nothing but kind and respectful. Please do not offend them with your fabrications and falsehoods." Gillian spoke with a noticeable pluck.

Diaspad tried to sit up but Aidan pushed him into the sofa. "You dare look me in the eye missy and lie? What man would come to your defense so, as Aidan, unless he had tasted your goods?"

"A gentleman! Something you have yet to know anything about!" Gillian stood firm. All looked at her in amazement and adoration.

"So, you are telling me your virginity remains in tact?" Everyone remained silent. Gillian was so mortified she couldn't move. There came a welcoming rustling in the room, the mere stir of the fire and the creaks and noises in the floor, which can be brought on by a shift of the breeze. The silence was deafening; it came too abruptly and she felt the loneliness and emptiness of the unbearable moment. "So I see. No one was aware that Gillian was still a virgin. Frigid, if you ask me. No blood stains on our vestal sheets as of yet, I'm afraid." Aidan moved away from Diaspad, afraid that he would strangle him at any moment. Diaspad looked at the silent faces. "Or at least, she was a virgin when we arrived."

Aidan wanted to go to Gillian's side and take her hand to show his support but instead stood near the fire, lest he give Diaspad more ammunition. Gillian couldn't raise her eyes to look at anyone; especially not Aidan. Ranulf looked at Aidan with a mischievous grin. Aidan knew something was up. However, he was concerned about Gillian. He had hoped she would just walk out of the room to save face, at least then he could eventually go and find her. However, she was stronger than that; she had yet to run from any humiliation she might have suffered due to Diaspad. Aidan knew this moment would be no different.

"Well, someone has to say something." Ranulf broke the tomblike silence. "I guess it will be me." Ranulf took Gillian's hand again, grinning. "Gillian, may I congratulate you for having such high standards and for not wavering them or reducing them to Diaspad's level." Gillian put her hand over her mouth to hide her smile. Gody and Aidan both smiled at each other, nevertheless, remained silent. "Dear lady, forgive me if I embarrass you with what I am about to say, but if you bare with me I am sure you will benefit." Ranulf paused and turned to his uncle with a smile. "Uncle, is it not written somewhere under the laws of marriage, that if a couple fails to consummate the marriage, it does not exist by law or church?"

Gody remained silent, and then a smile came over his face. "I do believe you are right, Ranulf."

"This is ridiculous! I never heard of that!" Diaspad protested.

"Even so Diaspad, you claim Gillian to be frigid; that is cause enough for divorce. And if the two of you have never been together as man and wife, then the marriage is null." Ranulf folded his arms across his chest, feeling proud. "And not to mention consent. Consent is still one of the legal conditions for marriage. If Gillian's hand had been contracted against her will would that alone not be grounds for annulment?"

"I am afraid he is right Diaspad. That is if Gillian wishes it." Gody said. All eyes turned to Gillian.

Diaspad leered at Gillian. "You ought to be aware, my dear, you are under obligations to me; I keep you. If I were to turn you out, you would have to go to the poor-house."

"Nonsense!" Gody raised his voice. "Gillian would become ward of Aberdour."

"Come now." Aidan spoke up and neared Gillian. "We are all putting Gillian under a lot of pressure and in a confusing position. We know what we want for Gillian, however on her end there is much to think about."

"You are right Aidan. Forgive us Gillian, we are all getting ahead of ourselves. We will talk later about this matter." Gody said.

Gillian nodded. "I think I'll get some air. Will you excuse me?" Gillian left the room alone and that was the way she wanted it, for now.

Gody walked over to Diaspad. "Son, I've known you since you were born. You must be tortured by demons that none of us could possibly imagine. I pray that you find peace somehow and if I were you I would ask God for forgiveness for the hell that you put that poor woman through. You could start by giving her a divorce so that she wouldn't ever have to lay eyes on you again." Gody left the room as well.

Ranulf plopped himself in a chair adjacent from Diaspad. "Well you seem to have a knack for clearing a room. Isn't there a bottle of booze somewhere that you haven't managed to empty?" Diaspad growled and stormed out of the room. Aidan took his seat on the sofa. Ranulf grinned at him. "You're just dying to go after her, aren't you?" Aidan looked at Ranulf, but didn't bother to answer. "So what do you think?"

"About what?" Aidan was coy.

"You know very well, about our lovely lady being untouched, pristine, chaste, immaculate." Ranulf grinned. "I can't recall having ever known a virgin."

"I doubt one would remain a virgin long in your presence." Aidan laughed. "And to answer your question…

Gillian's purity doesn't come as a surprise. In fact, I respect her all the more for not yielding to Diaspad's twisted desires."

"One day you will have to tell me what really went on under Diaspad's roof." Ranulf said. "I dare not ask, for I know you would not betray your lady love's confidence."

"Lady love?" Aidan said with a slight smile.

"Oh don't even try to deny it, not with me cousin. The way you look at her...God man, it's obvious." Ranulf laughed.

"Look who is calling *me* obvious." Aidan grinned.

"Oh I know I'm obvious, but the difference is, I don't care." Ranulf smirked. "Don't get me wrong, I like that you have shown interest in a woman. Now we just have to get her unmarried."

"If Diaspad will agree. In addition, let's not forget there is much more to this than Gillian attaining her freedom. She has nothing, no home, and no money. She doesn't even have clothing for God's sake. We must think about her future as well as her present situation." Aidan said with deep concern. "No one has bothered to ask her if she would even want to be ward here."

Ranulf took a deep breath and let it out slowly. "Yes, I guess your right. However, I don't see any problem with her remaining here. She would be well taken care of and would not want for anything."

Aidan nodded. "Yes, I agree. However, we must consider that Gillian may not want to go from one person's home to another. She may want a home of her own, a life of her own."

"What about a dower? Do you know if there was one on her wedding day?" Ranulf asked.

Aidan shook his head. "No, Gillian has never mentioned one to me. I will have to check with father to see if by law she can still claim a third of Cardoness or any part of the Darnaway estate in case there was no dower."

"With or without a dower, to remain here as the king's ward would be the best thing for Gillian." Ranulf exclaimed.

CHAPTER 14

▼

Gillian reached the top of the stairs, still intent on getting that fresh air that Diaspad had made her in such need of. On the way she met Beechim who was about to retire for a little rest.

"Beechim, can you suggest the best part of the castle to view Loch Leven?" Gillian asked.

Beechim scratched his head as he thought. "Indeed I can. Come, I will show you."

"Please, just direct me, you are in need of some rest. I can find it on my own." Gillian smiled.

"Oh please milady, it would honor me to show you myself. It is not often that an old man like myself gets the privilege of escorting such an lovely lady." He said with insistent smiling eyes.

Gillian smiled. "Are you sure you feel up to it?" He nodded. "Alright, lead the way." Beechim held out his arm to escort Gillian.

Beechim led Gillian up, around and in and out of corridors until they reached the staircase that would take them to the tower room. Beechim entered a small doorway with Gillian following behind. The two climbed stair after stair, higher and higher. Gillian realized they must have been climbing the central tower, the tall one that she saw on her approach to the castle.

As Gillian looked out the narrow-slit windows cut into the stairwell, the landscape at each turn became smaller, more distant and more precious. At last they emerged into a small room. The room was full of gray light. Swallows sailed back and forth past a large window. For the first time, Gillian looked carefully at Beechim's face. He was clearly old, but there was still a Spring light within his eyes. His features were sturdy and well carved. His eyebrows gray and wiry and his forehead free of worry. Gillian found his features well molded and noble like the ones you might find on an ancient coin.

Gillian walked over to the window and tried to open it. "Here, let me help you miss." Beechim put his weight into the window breaking the rust seal. "There we are. I'm afraid it's not a good day for sight seeing, but if you look straight out past the gardens you can manage to see some of the loch."

"The view is lovely. Even more so I imagine, on a sunny day." Gillian said, taking a seat on the wide window casement.

"By the way, I have a book you might be interested in, about the history of Aberdour. There are even some of the old sketches of the building plans and grounds." Beechim suggested.

"Oh yes. I would indeed be interested."

"Fine. I will bring it to your chamber later. Keep it long as you like." Beechim said then began to cough.

"Please, go get some rest. I will be fine by myself." Gillian offered him a smile.

"Are you sure milady?"

Gillian took his hand. "Quite sure. Now, off with you." She smiled.

"You're very kind milady." He smiled. Gillian gave him a bow of her head and watched him leave the room.

There had been a great deal of rain and Gillian loved the newfound place in the tower with its quiet stillness.

Gillian looked out onto wind-swept hills slashed by steep wooded valleys alternate with undulating fields that were patchworks of bright yellow, lavender and fresh green. The seasons pale pink roses drowsy with fragrance lazily climbed a weathered stonewall that lined a path leading down to the stables.

Birds trilled meandering streams burbled and the picture perfect ancient stone village of Aberconway gleamed as silver in the far distance, as a thundercloud unleashed its wetness again blanketing the land. Loch Leven sat under a milky mist as the green fields and hills of Aberdour swept to its banks.

Gillian wanted to stay in that tower forever, not to be disturbed, content just to sit there and gaze out the window. To lock the door and barr herself in the tower. Here, there was no need to hide in the darkness; no need to wait as the darkness bled itself into light. No fists to arm herself against, no steps that had to be taken lightly in fear, and no need to lie like death on the wake of the household abuse and best of all, no Diaspad.

Was it possible? Could her dreams of a life without Diaspad be coming true? It all seemed too simple. Diaspad would not let her go so easily.

Water began to well in her eyes. The colors of the garden became one muddled blur. Her head ached and she felt a tightening in her throat and then a release that was worse than crying. A dark and horrible realization of the life she had led with Diaspad. The dread, the trepidation of having to return to hell once she had seen heaven.

Gillian wanted to yank all the old roots from her chest, like tomatoes left growing until November stalks thick and grounded. In these moments her fears raced like thoroughbreds, asking for more reins. And Gillian, the driver, the only one who knows of the strain to hold them back.

The very thought of returning with Diaspad gripped her like a vice. She sweats, fevered, trying to burn it out. No end in sight and worst of all, no Aidan. No Aidan. How could there ever be no Aidan?

Gillian felt her chest twist like knotted weeds, without precision, with only the primitive knife of need, she hacks a clearing in her heart, a place for Aidan; there he will stay. A place she can run to, where it is always warm and safe and full of light. Just as she imagined Aidan's embrace.

"Aidan, dear sweet Aidan." Gillian whispered to herself. She smiled as she put her hand over her heart to feel the pulse of life beneath her ribs. Her heart was beating strong, but not from fear; not fear this time, something stronger. It was a warm sensation that neither the rain nor even the briskness of the wind could snuff.

The fact that she loved here was as much a miracle as anything that had happened to her. Though she might not have known it yet, or to its furthest extent, it happened in this castle. Gillian felt rooted here, connected in someway she had never felt anywhere else, especially not Cardoness.

CHAPTER 15

▼

Time and day slipped on as Gillian remained in the very spot Beechim had left her. The peacefulness of the little 'corner of the world' Gillian had claimed for herself allowed her to escape her reality momentarily. She had spent the entire day alone with her thoughts and oblivious to time.

The rest of the day had past without any sign of Gillian, giving Aidan cause for worry. He found Beechim still resting in his chambers and inquired about Gillian's where-a bouts. Beechim happily told him, sensing Gillian would not mind Aidan's intrusion.

Aidan stood silent in the threshold of the tower room, watching Gillian in her tranquil silence. Gillian sensed him. "I don't mean to disturb you, but I was worried."

Gillian smiled. "Were you? Please come in."

"Are you alright?" Aidan asked.

"Yes, I'm fine. Come. Sit with me."

Aidan joined her as he studied her face. "You have been up here all day?"

"All day?" Gillian was so absorbed in the view; she had not noticed the growing darkness. "Yes, I guess I have. Time just got away from me. It is so beautiful up here."

Aidan regarded her smooth face for some time. He wondered if she knew how appealing she was. Without thinking he raised her chin with his hand lifting her face to the shimmering light that still lingered. For a moment no words were exchanged, just a fixed gaze from one to the other. Gillian lifted her hand to his brow and traced the curve of his face with light fingertips. She traced every line stopping at his lips, which she parted delicately with her finger. She laid her palm gently against his cheek. "You are so beautiful." She said tenderly. "I can't imagine a sweeter face."

Aidan took her hand, and laid a kiss to the middle of her palm. "Though your hands are the loveliest I have ever seen, your lips are even more so, and if I were not a gentleman…"

Gillian beamed him a smile. "And if you were to forget your place?"

Aidan grinned. "Well dear lady, your lips would succumb to the most sensual kiss, the likes they have never known."

Gillian blushed and made a little giggle. "Now you sound like Ranulf."

A handsome smile lightened his face. "Really? Well, maybe my approach needs work." Aidan paused, turning more serious. "You have been doing some thinking?"

Gillian stared out the window as she took a deep breath and released it. "Yes."

"Share your thoughts?" Aidan tried not to push.

"What is going to become of me Aidan?"

"What do you wish?" He asked.

Gillian looked at him. "Is the choice really mine?"

"Yes." He grinned. "It is your choice. Annulment, divorce. Of course, that is if you want to be free of Diaspad."

"Yes, I do. What would my father say to all this." Gillian lowered her head.

Aidan gently lifted her chin with his finger. "Your father gave your hand to Diaspad so that you would be taken care of financially, yes?" Gillian nodded. "You can remain here, we can take care of you. You can become Ward of Aberdour."

"Ward?" Gillian was a little surprised.

"Yes, why not?" Aidan asked.

"If I become Ward, your father can marry me off as he pleases. Who is to say I would not end up in the same kind of marriage? Is that what you would want for me?"

"No. Of course not. Father would never try to marry you off without your consent. Just think about it. You don't have to worry about that now." Aidan smiled. "Come. Dinner will be ready soon and you haven't eaten all day."

Gillian smiled. "Yes, I guess you're right. I hate to leave, it's so peaceful up here, on top of the world."

"I use to come up here as a child. To get away and hide. No one every discovered my hiding place." Aidan smiled. "I remember I could stay up here all day, and I too, would miss a meal now and then."

"I feel safe up here. I don't know why, I just do." Gillian sat smiling out the window. "The sun is going down, I guess we should go before it gets too dark to see our way."

Aidan stood to his feet and offered his hand. "Come, let's go in to dinner."

CHAPTER 16

▼

Aggie cleared the dinner plates before serving dessert. She picked up Gillian's plate then gave her a once over. "Lass, ya hardly tooched abite. Ar-ya ill?"

Gillian felt all eyes upon her as she pressed her white damask napkin to her lips before replying. "I have a slight headache, that is all." She gave a little smile.

"Aggie, why not give Gillian one of your powders." Gody suggested.

"No thank you, I will be fine. I'm sure its just because I skipped lunch." Gillian smiled at Gody.

"Are you sure?" Gody asked.

"Yes, don't worry about me. Really, I will be fine. Some fresh air maybe."

Ranulf jumped up, wiping his mouth. "Here, let me escort you."

"But you haven't had your dessert. Please, finish your meal, I can manage."

"I couldn't possibly eat another bite." Ranulf said, quickly making his way over to Gillian's side. Everyone stood as Gillian excused herself.

Gillian allowed Ranulf to escort her through the parlor and onto the veranda. It was still raining lightly, but the coolness of the breeze felt good against her aching head.

"All this bloody rain. When will it stop." Ranulf said, looking up at the night sky.

"I enjoy the rain, just as much as sunny days. However, I would like to see more of Aberdour. Some days are perfect for rain and others for the sun I guess. The breeze does feel nice against my head."

"Are you feeling any better?" Ranulf asked.

"Yes, some." Gillian smiled.

"The stress of this morning I imagine. Moreover, if you do not mind me saying, all the more reason to be rid of Diaspad. Have you given divorcing him much thought?" Ranulf blurted out.

Gillian was surprised at his candor. "To be honest, I have thought of little else."

"I'm guessing Aidan must have spoke to you about becoming ward of Aberdour?" Ranulf asked.

"Yes, he did." Gillian stood against the railing facing the rain, not wanting to talk of the matter.

"And what do you think?" Ranulf asked, standing against the railing with his back to the rain and watching Gillian's face.

Gillian took a deep breath then released it. "I don't think I am comfortable with putting my life in the hands of another man to use as he pleases, not even a man as noble as your uncle. If I should ever choose to marry again, I prefer it be my choice."

Ranulf pulled Gillian's hand from the railing and placed her palm on his chest. "Marry me Gillian. I will take care of you. You can rest assure I would never treat you as Diaspad does. And you would not have to worry about being disparaged."

Gillian smiled and let out a little giggle. "You can't be serious. You tease me." She said smiling. Ranulf stared at her deeply. "You are serious." Ranulf nodded. Gillian was silent for a moment as she studied his face. "Oh Ranulf...I don't know what to say."

Ranulf put his finger to her mouth. "No need to say anything now. Just know I made the offer. Think about it. Take all the time you need. I realize you have feelings for Aidan, I can see that. Just how far they go, I will not ask. If you should have any feelings for me, perhaps they would grow into love and if not...then I hope we will remain friends always."

Gillian smiled up at him. "You are very sweet Ranulf. No one has ever proposed to me before. I will always remember it as my first."

Ranulf smiled a handsome smile. "That sounds like a 'no' and I will not accept it until you have given my offer more thought. Agreed?"

"Yes." Gillian humored him and gave him a smile. She rubbed her arms briskly, chilled from the breeze coming off the loch. "Ranulf, would you mind getting me my shawl? I left it in the dining room on my chair."

"No, of course not. I shall return." His footsteps faded as he entered the parlor.

A few seconds had past, when she felt the warmth of her shawl, then a pair of strong hands, light but firm, upon her shoulders.

"You sent Ranulf in for this, I believe." Aidan was behind her, his low soft voice in her ear.

"Aidan, you surprised me."

"Do you mind? That it was I who brought you your shawl?" He asked.

"No, of course not." She smiled.

"How is your head? Better?" Aidan asked.

"Some."

"Let me see if I can give you some relief." Aidan said, as he took a chair from against the wall and placed it just behind Gillian. "Please, have a seat."

Gillian grinned. "What are you doing?"

."Please, trust me." Gillian took a seat and Aidan stood behind her. "Now just relax." He leaned deliberately closer to her, inhaling the sweet fragrance of her hair as his fingertips lightly brushed across the smooth skin of her neck. Aidan began to massage circles on the sides of her head neck with delicate fingers. Gillian relaxed, her eyes drifted shut; her head fell back into the supporting cradle of his hands. Her entire being focused on the soothing sensation of his touch. Ripples of heat radiated down her spine. Deep inside her, something stirred, like a delicate flower unfurling beneath the warmth of the sun's rays.

"Mmm. That feels nice." Gillian moaned. Aidan pulled the pins from her hair and let it fall loose. Something he had always wanted to do.

"Does that feel better?" Aidan asked.

"Much better, thank you." It began to rain harder as the big droplets of rain splattered onto part of the veranda.

"Come sit back here, so you don't get wet." Aidan motioned to a cushion-covered bench.

Gillian kicked off her shoes; her beautiful black shoes with thin heels and thin straps. Aidan watched as she pushed them one at a time off onto the floor. He saw her narrow small feet and the imprint of the strap across her delicate foot. He wanted to touch them, to take her tiny foot into his hand and kiss it.

"I think the wind is picking up." Gillian said.

"Yes, we must be in for more rain. I don't mind the rain, I rather like it. Though I would like to show you more of Aberdour." Aidan looked at her.

Gillian smiled. "Funny, I was just saying the same thing to Ranulf."

"I will make you a promise." Aidan smiled. "If it does not stop raining soon, I will take you on that tour in the middle of a tempest if I must."

Gillian laughed. "Alright, I will hold you to that." All of Aberdour lay in silence. The silence covered the grounds all around the castle. There was not even the bleat of sheep or the lowing of cattle. Just the song of the rain. "I'm tired, I think I will say goodnight."

"You look as if you could use a good night's sleep. Come, I will escort you to your chambers." Aidan stood and offered his hand.

At the threshold of Gillian's room, Aidan pushed open the door, spilling light into that hallway, along with the feminine scent of potpourri. As they stood outside her door, Gillian once again felt the wrenching temptations she must not give in to. Still, despite her inexperience, she was not about to fall into a swoon if he should kiss her.

Aidan stared at Gillian's bare shoulders, at the plunging neckline of her gown and at the tiny shadow between her breasts. Gillian stood silent, giving him the opportunity to kiss her, instead, Aidan took her hand, kissed it and said goodnight.

Gillian smiled and said goodnight taking a step back she closed the door between them.

Aidan closed his eyes as he put his hand on the door, wanting to call her back and kiss her. To intoxicate himself with the smell and taste of her body.

"You're a fool cousin." Ranulf made his presence known with arms folded across his chest, leaning against the corridor wall.

Aidan turned around. "Spying are we?"

"Why in God's name would you turn down the perfect opportunity to kiss a woman like that? She as much offered her lips to you." Ranulf asked as he followed Aidan down the corridor.

"Lower your voice." Aidan insisted.

"She wanted you to kiss her." Ranulf said as they reached the door to Aidan's chamber.

"I saw no such a thing." Aidan said simply.

"No, you probably didn't. You know cousin, its expected of you to wear the hat of a gentleman, but you also must learn when to take it off." Ranulf said as Aidan opened his door. "I can tell you she never looked at me that way, not even when I proposed marriage."

Aidan looked at him, studying his eyes. "What did you say?"

"You heard me. Just tonight I asked Gillian to marry me." Ranulf smiled.

"Ranulf you didn't?" Aidan asked with concern. "What if she were to take you serious?"

"I hope that she does." Ranulf grinned.

"You can't be serious?" Aidan asked.

"Dead serious, cousin. I told her to think the offer over." Ranulf said.

"Why Ranulf? Why would you do such a thing? You are not in love with her."

Ranulf placed his hand on Aidan's shoulder. "I realize you have feelings for this girl. If she should receive an annulment, better that she marries me than someone that may not have her best interest in mind. Unless you plan on making the same offer?"

"Ranulf you know as well as I that father would not just marry her off like that. As ward, Gillian would be allowed to remain here as long as she wished." Aidan said.

"But look how long she has been without a man. Someone to care for her and treat her with love and respect. Don't you think she deserves this?" Ranulf said.

"Of course I do. Nevertheless, how long would it be before you find another young lady just as deserving of your love and respect? I think you should have put more thought into this Ranulf and next time think with the head on your shoulders and less with the one in your pants." Aidan closed the door behind him.

CHAPTER 17

▼

Gillian slept heavily and peacefully until she suddenly awoke in her darkened chamber from a noise. The spluttering fire had lapsed into a dull glow, which threw grotesque shadows on the walls.

It was one of those nights when the storm winds hurtle over the fresh green meadows and black hollows and moans around the eaves like a lost creature.

She was aware of a close darkness, a disturbing absence of light that ought to be there. Then gradually she realized as she became more awake that Diaspad was standing beside her, looking down over her. He was still and quiet as she instantly tried to focus her eyes. In instinctive fear, Gillian lay still, not moving, hoping he would go away. But he didn't, he just stood there with a wicked smile.

Gillian knew she had to do something, anything but lay there and allow what ever was about to happen. She slowly reached for the opposite side of the bed, trying to ease her body to the other side. If she could get to her feet, she would feel she had more of an advantage.

Gillian slowly inched her hand across the sheets; she stopped suddenly. Something wet; warm drenched her fingers, then a solid mass. There was something in the bed with her. Something dreadful. A scream froze in her throat. She slowly pulled the sheet back but could see nothing in the darkness until a flash of lightning lit up the room revealing the bloody head of a pig.

Diaspad let out an evil laugh that would have made the demons in hell shutter. Gillian managed to find the strength to release a piercing scream that woke the entire household.

Aidan instantly bolted from his bed and was the first to reach Gillian's room. He threw open the door, spilling light into the room. He asked no questions and instantly grabbed Diaspad and threw him into the corridor head-first. Ranulf and king Gody were making their way toward Gillian's chambers. Diaspad lay against the wall, laughing in a drunken stupor.

"Aidan!" Gillian screamed. Aidan saw the bloody head lying next to her and pulled her from the bed.

"It's alright. You're safe now, I'm here." Aidan's voice calmed her.

Gody stood just outside the door. "Ranulf, send for two of the mesnie to escort this son-of-a-bitch down to one of the cells in the bowel of the castle!"

Aidan quickly scooped Gillian's trembling body up and carried her off down the corridor to his chambers. He placed her by the fire as he poured her a brandy to calm her nerves. Not even the fire in the grate could warm her.

"Here, drink this." Aidan placed the brandy in her hand. Gillian took small sips trying to hold the glass steady. Aidan sat and watched her attentively. Gillian took the last swallow and gave Aidan a smile.

"I'm better now, thank you." She said, handing him the empty glass.

"Your gown is covered in blood. Feel free to clean yourself off in the bath. There are fresh towels and a robe you can wear." Aidan smiled.

"Alright. Thank you." In the excitement she had not noticed the blood that covered the lower half of her gown. She quickly cleaned up and put on the silky large robe having to roll up the sleeves a few times to make it fit.

Aidan had a blanket waiting for her by the fire when she rejoined him. "Come, sit here." He placed the blanket over her, making sure she was warm and tucked a pillow behind her back. "Let me get you another brandy." He poured her a small brandy and handed it to her. "What else can I do for you?" He asked, feeling the need to comfort and protect her.

"You can stop fusing over me and sit with me." Aidan sat down beside her. "Thank you, you are very kind Aidan." She smiled.

"I'm sorry Gillian. I am sorry that Diaspad treats you so sadistically. I am to blame this time. I lashed out at him and called him a filthy pig the other day."

"No Aidan! I will not let you blame yourself for his evil ways. Let it go." Gillian gripped his hand.

"I can't just let it go. You don't know what it does to me knowing he tortures you so."

Gillian was silent and lowered her head. "I have given this a lot of thought," she raised her eyes to him, "I am going to ask for an annulment. I have seen what it is like for people to treat each other with kindness and respect, I can't go back to that life again."

Aidan smiled, pleased with her answer. "You have made a good decision. We will talk with father in the morning."

Gillian nodded as she yawned. "You need your rest, let me put you to bed."

"But I don't want to take your bed, you need your rest as well." Gillian replied.

Aidan gently pulled her to her feet taking her hand and led her over to the bed. "Now, I will sleep in this chair. It is very comfortable and I have done so on many occasion. You, will sleep in my bed and I won't hear another word about it." He smiled tenderly.

Gillian gave him a smile and a nod. She didn't bother to argue or refuse, she was too tired. Aidan turned back the satiny covers and Gillian climbed in. He tucked her in safely and tenderly, raising all his protective instincts.

Her auburn hair spilled carelessly upon the white mound of his pillow. He sat on the edge of the bed, brushed the strands of hair from her face and waited for her to fall asleep.

CHAPTER 18

▼

Aidan kept his vigil in an over-stuffed chair next to the bed in a light sleep as Gillian slept through much of the night. The rain continued, helping to soothe her into a deep sleep.

Gillian's tossing and moaning suddenly awakened Aidan. Dreams of Diaspad no doubt. Aidan went to her side, to calm her if she should awake.

"Aidan!" Gillian called out. Aidan took her by the shoulders as she awoke with fear in her eyes. She sat up in a panic and grabbed Aidan, hugging him tight.

"It's alright. Just a dream. Your safe, I'm here." His voice calmed her.

Gillian loosened her embrace. "Don't leave me." She looked desperately into his eyes.

Aidan shook his head. "No, I won't leave you. I'm staying right here." His voice was soft and reassuring.

"Hold me Aidan. Tighter, I can't feel you." As Aidan held on to her, Gillian became more awake, more aware. Gillian pulled away slightly, to look at his face. He was so close; she could feel his breath on her skin. She looked into his eyes as she pushed back his honey colored locks of silk with her hand.

Aidan was drunk in the soft white hands that smoothed back his hair and the voice that had called him beautiful. His hands glided softly along her arms until he met her hands and their fingers entwined. Gillian had never felt closer to him than that sweet tortuous moment. She wanted him, the pain, and the pleasure. Gillian could scarcely control her own breathing as he looked into her eyes.

"Kiss me Aidan." She pleaded sweetly.

"It would be my pleasure." He said in his low baritone, releasing her hand and drawing her chin upward. He paused, his lips within a breath of her own. His lips parted with anticipation. "I fear you will not think me a gentleman."

"You don't have to be a gentleman tonight." She whispered.

His mouth came down upon hers fervent, melting away any hesitation he might have had. His lips were hot and soft like velvet. He felt his self-control begin to slip. His whole body was consumed with desire, and he kissed her with less restraint than he would have liked.

She abandoned propriety and decorum as she allowed him to taste her. She had never been kissed in such a way before. Gillian moved her hips closer to him; she could feel his hardness against her thigh.

"No—I must not." Aidan said breathless, as he pulled himself away from her. With a supreme effort he stopped himself from taking her any further.

Gillian was disappointed and wickedly titillated. She was surprised at the power one kiss held. "What's wrong?"

Aidan caught his breath. "I can not allow myself such pleasurable liberties. You have been through a horrible ordeal tonight; I don't want to take advantage of your vulnerable state." He took her hand and raised it to his lips. "As wonderful and delicious as I found your lips, I want to court you as a proper suitor would. Do you understand?"

Gillian smiled. "Yes." She felt both cherished and frustrated. She lay back on the pillow in a half swoon with some disappointment.

"Now, get some sleep." Aidan tucked her in again and kissed her forehead before settling back in the over-stuffed chair.

Gillian awoke again at dawn; the room was full of leaping shadows from the fire. She saw the gleam on the carved posts of the bed and the drapery fallen about in rich colors. She felt animated and rose up from her dream, a pleasant one this time.

Aidan stood by the fire, his hand above resting on the mantle, deep in thought. He was still wearing his brilliant red velvet robe, slightly open, revealing his chest of bronze. Gillian stirred, giving a faint little sigh, waking Aidan from his thoughts. He approached her slowly.

"Have you slept?" Gillian asked with a sleepy smile.

He returned the smile. "Yes, some."

"I have kept you from a good nights sleep by stealing your bed." She rose up on one arm.

"Nonsense. Besides, my bed has never known such a lovely occupant." He smiled. How do you feel?" He sat down on the edge of the bed.

"Fine." She answered, glancing at his beautiful chest through his parted robe. "What time is it?"

"It's still early. Why don't you go back to sleep." Aidan suggested.

"Is it still raining?" She asked as she lay back down on the pillow.

"It has let up some." He glanced out the window.

Gillian took Aidan's hand, pulled it to her and placed his palm against her cheek. "You are a wonderful man Prince Aidan. A truer gentleman I have never met."

"Why? Because I didn't have my way with you last night? If you had known what I was thinking, you wouldn't praise me so."

Gillian laughed. "Because you put my virtue first before desire."

"Do you have any regrets? The liberties I took?" He asked.

"No regrets, and you did not take, I asked you to kiss me. And I would do it again." Gillian felt rather bold.

"And I would fulfill that request were it not you were half clothed and in my bed. I have to be honest with you milady, leaving your side was the hardest thing I have ever had to do. I am flattered and amazed that someone so exquisite would consider being that close to me." He took her hand and brushed his lips gently across her skin.

Aidan and Gillian knocked twice to the door of King Gody's private study. "Come." His muffled cry came from behind the heavy wooden door. Aidan and Gillian entered. "Come in, have a seat."

"Are we disturbing you?" Gillian asked.

"Not at all. Actually, I was doing some reading on the laws of marriage and how property applies." Gody said taking off his specs.

"That is what Gillian wants to talk to you about, Father."

"Alright." Gody smiled.

"I have given this much thought your highness. I am not one to take the vow of marriage lightly." Gillian said.

"We all know that dear." Gody said.

"I want out of this marriage. What ever it takes." Gillian said.

Gody smiled. "Wise decision. You will remain as ward?"

"Yes, but I do ask one thing."

"Yes?" Gody asked.

"If there should come a time when I must marry, I wish that decision to be mine and mine alone." Gillian said firmly.

"I would never force you to marry anyone that was not of your choosing. I will put that in writing if you like." He smiled.

Gillian smiled. "No sire, your word is good enough."

Gody returned the smile. "Well, as I said, I have been doing some reading. Let me tell you what I found. This may not be to your liking and you will have to make the choice." Gody paused.

"What did you find father?" Aidan was curious.

"Am I to understand there was no dower at the time of the marriage?" Gody asked.

"No sire, not to my knowledge." Gillian answered.

Gody nodded as he thought about the situation. "Well, the way I see it is…you can ask for an annulment and receive no money or property since it means the marriage never took place, you are not entitled to any holdings. You would walk away with nothing except what you brought into the household. Or…and I don't mean to be brash, you could consummate then divorce and receive one-third of the estate."

Gillian just looked at him and said nothing for a moment. "I would sooner be a beggar in the streets than give myself to a beast like Diaspad." Gillian was silent. "Unless…you are my king sire and as your ward you have every right to claim what ever dower I might be worth. If this is what you ask of me…"

"No Gillian! Don't think such things." Aidan spoke up. "Tell her father, you would never ask such a thing of her."

"No. No son, I wouldn't." Gody took Gillian by the hand. "Child, I offer you the opportunity to be ward of Aberdour so that your life might once and for all be yours and yours alone to live as you so wish. I talk to you the same way I would if I had a daughter. You are still a young woman and have yet to experience the love and closeness a man and woman can share. My wish for you is to find that special love as I did with Aidan's mother, to truly know happiness in a loving marriage. Now, if you should choose to never marry, then that is your choice to make and I will respect it and Aberdour will still remain your home as long as you like." Gody patted her hand with a warm smile.

Gillian's eyes welled with water. She gave Gody a hug and a kiss on the cheek. "You are such a dear sweet man."

Gody laughed, flattered. "I will start the procedures immediately."

"I assume Diaspad remains below?" Aidan asked.

"Yes, and that is where he will stay until the funeral tomorrow. Oh, I forgot to tell you of Adelaide's funeral, I am sorry." Gody said.

"Tomorrow?" Gillian asked.

"Yes. Mr. Tristamm asked me to tell you Gillian, he will talk with you after the funeral." Gillian nodded.

"Could Diaspad refuse the annulment?" Gillian asked.

"He could, but it would do no good. He confessed to us all the marriage was never consummated." Gody assured her.

CHAPTER 19

▼

The funeral procession issued forth from the village church into the village churchyard. Adelaide's body rested in a wooden casket that sat on a bier draped in a black pall. It was led by the village priest and a few faithful. It seemed a small group considering the size of the village; all assumed that Adelaide was not well known.

At the cemetery, small candles flickered in the mist falling from dark clouds overhead. The graves were heaped with flowers and boughs, while between rows of graves stood people, silent, motionless.

Diaspad stood next to Gody, unshaven, and his features full of shadows. The expression in his bloodshot eyes was cold as he watched Gillian with an unsettling intensity. Gillian stood between Aidan and Lan trying to ignore Diaspad's gaze.

The priest began his prayer. "Good men, as ye all see, here a mirror to us all; a corpse brought to the church. God have mercy on her and bring her into that bliss that shall last forever. Where for each man and woman that is wise, make him ready thereto; for we all shall die and not know how soon." The priest gave a homily sprinkle of holy water; then all departed, leaving the candles flickering in the silence.

Diaspad remained silent; except for the ardent stare he focused on Gillian, during the journey back to castle Aberdour. Aidan made sure to stay close to Gillian lest Diaspad decide to come alive.

Mists blanketed the ground, swirling on currents of air, and then shrouding everything in shades of gray. The mood was somber, no one said much. Gillian chose not to look into the faces of anyone riding in the coach; instead she watched the passing landscape from inside her window as they neared Aberdour.

Beechim greeted everyone at the door and had tea and cakes ready in the parlor. "Sire," Beechim took Gody's cloak, "a letter came for you." Beechim handed him the letter.

"Thank you Beechim." Gody took the letter and followed everyone into the parlor.

Ranulf passed the tea and cakes and poured himself something stronger. Diaspad, still mute, took a seat in the corner. Gillian took a seat on the sofa and began to serve the tea. Lan took a seat next to her; remaining in the same room with Diaspad was something he normally wouldn't have done but did so out of respect.

Gody stood by the fire reading his letter with little emotion. Gillian served Aidan, then Lan.

"Sire, would you like some tea?" Gillian offered.

Gody looked up from his letter. "No thank you, go right ahead." Then returned to the letter.

Gillian poured another cup and stood and walked over to Diaspad. Everyone watched. She offered the cup of tea to Diaspad. He looked at her with no words and slowly reached up his hand and took the cup from her. A slight polite smile played around her lips. The room became quiet at Gillian's courteous gesture. She returned to the sofa as if nothing was out of the ordinary.

"Uncle, what has you so enthralled?" Ranulf asked.

"What?" Gody's attention was broken. "Oh, sorry. It is a letter from king Odden. It seems the princess Eleanor will soon be journeying through our kingdom on her way to her uncle's at La Marche in the south. Her father is requesting an invitation that she might stay with us awhile, for a rest, until her journey continues on to La Marche.

"Ellie, coming here? It has been years. We were but children when she last visited." Ranulf said with a smile.

Gody looked at Aidan as if there was more to the letter than he made mention. Aidan could sense Gody had more to tell him. "When will she be arriving father?"

"By the end of the week if we request. I'll have to send out a letter immediately to king Odden."

"I imagine Ellie is all grown up now." Ranulf commented. "Didn't she give you your first kiss Aidan?" Ranulf laughed. Aidan smirked at Ranulf but did not answer. "She gave me mine. A demanding little thing she was. I remember I had such a crush on her." He laughed in his reverie.

"Excuse me sire," Beechim interrupted, "Mr. Tristamm has arrived."

"Send him in." Aidan said.

Tristamm entered with his permanent comely smile. "I hope I am not disturbing anyone on such a sorrowful day."

"No, not at all." Gody said.

"Won't you have some tea with us Mr. Tristamm." Gillian offered.

"Yes, thank you." Tristamm took a seat in a chair next to the sofa as Gillian poured him a cup of tea.

"Cream and sugar?" Gillian asked.

"Cream please." Gillian poured the cream and handed the cup to Tristamm. "Thank you." He took a tiny sip and smiled at Gillian. "I mentioned to king Gody that I would let all of you know what my findings were from the examination of the departed. That is, if you don't think this is an inappropriate time?"

"No, please tell us what you found." Gody suggested.

"If you insist. Besides from the obvious—the crushed windpipe, bruises on the throat. The only other thing I did find was a lot of skin under the nails, as if she fought back, scratching her assailant."

"I see. Thank you Mr. Tristamm." Gody said.

"Well, if you will excuse me, I must be off. Thank you for the tea." He gave a nod to Gillian.

Gillian and Aidan looked at each other as if the two were exchanging thoughts mentally. Everyone waited until Tristamm had exited before speaking a word.

"Still think I'm the murderer?" Diaspad was the first to speak.

"The undead speaketh." Ranulf remarked before taking a sip of brandy.

"Would anyone like to check my body for claw marks?" Diaspad asked.

No one answered him as everyone's eyes searched each other's.

"He has a point." Gody said. "It seems to me, find the person with claw marks and you find your murderer."

"What do you think Gillian?" Lan asked.

"That sounds like a good place to start to me." Gillian said.

"And since Diaspad is so willing, let's start with him." Ranulf suggested.

Gillian exited the room while Diaspad undressed and was searched, then returned upon him being cleared. "I volunteer to search Gillian." Ranulf said with his hand raised high in the air. "Come Gillian, you can disrobe in my chamber." He grinned.

"Don't be silly Ranulf." Gody scolded. "Aggie can check Gillian for marks, though I am certain she will find none. Gillian gave him a nod of her head for the vote of confidence.

CHAPTER 20

▼

Everyone was checked thoroughly, one by one, for scratch marks from Diaspad to the king himself. No marks were found on anyone in the room, clearing everyone of suspicion.

"Now that we know no one in this room is under suspicion, let us go into dinner and put an end to this day." Gody suggested. "And Diaspad, to be assured the rest of this evening continues and ends in peace, you will be confined to your chamber until further notice. Aggie will bring you something to eat."

"Sent to my room like a child?" Diaspad said with a nasty tone.

"Unless you prefer your quarters of last?" Gody smirked. Diaspad shook his head. "No, I didn't think so. And while you have so much time on your hands and with a clear mind, you can read over the annulment papers I expect you will sign without hesitation or refutation."

Diaspad looked at Gillian with a scornful gaze. Gillian could almost read his thoughts as well. Aidan stepped between the two and escorted Gillian into dinner.

Dinner began in peace just as Gody had wanted it. For the first time since Gillian's arrival at Aberdour, Lan joined them at the dinner table.

"It's nice to have you back at the dinner table Lan, we have missed your company." Gody smiled.

"It is nice to be back. But you do understand my absence?" Lan asked.

Gody nodded. "Yes son, we do."

"You have missed out on a lot of activity." Ranulf said.

"Yes, but we all could have had a lot less of it." Aidan replied.

Lan smiled. "So I heard. I am sorry Gillian for the abuse you have had to endure during your stay here. Aberdour is a happy place, I regret you have not had the chance to experience it in the manner you should have."

Gillian smiled and patted her mouth with her napkin. "Thank you, but I'm sure all that will change soon."

"Yes, the annulment. May I congratulate you early on a wise decision." Lan held up his glass to salute her.

"You may, though the break up of a marriage hardly calls for congratulating." Gillian said.

"Can you really call what you have with Diaspad a marriage?" Lan questioned.

"Lan, your manners!" Gody scolded.

"That is alright." Gillian said to Gody. "I understand Lan to be a man that speaks his mind. And to answer the question—you are right. If it were a marriage I wouldn't have requested an annulment."

"Speaking of freedom—it seems you are soon to be a free woman. Given any thought to suitors?" Ranulf smiled.

Gillian glanced at Aidan, but quickly turned her eyes away before being caught. "No, not really."

"Gillian is sure to find many suitors on her door step."
Lan smiled. "A few at this table no doubt." He laughed.

Gillian blushed, lowering her head with a girlish smile.
Courting was something new to her, something she never
would have imagined she would have to consider.

Ranulf cleared his throat and tapped his water glass
with his knife to draw everyone's attention. "I have an
announcement to make: I do not mind telling everyone
that some time ago I made a proposal to Gillian. I asked
her to be my wife." All eyes were immediately on Gillian.
"She has not given me a final answer, but I want Gillian
and all of you to know I stand by my offer."

"Noted, cousin." Aidan said, with little enthusiasm.

"I think all of you are embarrassing Gillian. These are
private matters. Let's talk of something else." Gody said.

"Thank you, sire." Gillian smiled. Gillian remained
quiet for the rest of the dinner her thoughts focused on
Adelaide's murder rather than her dating status. Aidan
watched her as she rubbed the tip of her finger around and
around the edge of her wineglass. Noticeably somewhere
else.

All retired to the parlor after dinner as usual. The discussion centered on Mr. Tristamm's findings. Gillian was
still quiet, her thoughts obviously putting pieces together.
With Diaspad now ruled out, the trail had to lead else-
where; to someone else within the castle.

"Gillian, share your thoughts with us. You seem to
always be on the right track. You have been very quiet."
Aidan said.

Gillian walked over to the double doors of the parlor
and shut them one at a time for privacy. She joined the rest

of the group and paused for a moment. "I have not meant to be so distant, I have been doing a lot of thinking. I wanted to choose my words before I said anything, I wouldn't want to accuse anyone falsely."

"So you do have someone in mind." Ranulf replied.

"Well, we know we are looking for someone with scratch marks. I'm guessing on the arms and or face. The placement of the bruises on Adelaide's neck would suggest a small hand did the choking."

"A woman?" Asked Lan.

"More than likely or possibly a man with small hands. Nevertheless, scratch marks are the key." Gillian stated. Gillian discreetly cut her eyes at Aidan, a look to let him know she wanted to say more, but to him only.

"Seems simple enough. Find the person with claw marks—find the killer." Ranulf said. "I think an examination of everyone in the castle is our next move, starting with the servants."

"Yes. But we must do this discreetly and quietly, as so not to scare the murderer off." Gody suggested. "In the meantime, I suggest everyone bolt your doors at night until we can bring the murderer to light."

Gillian quietly stepped outside on the veranda as the others discussed how to go about a search delicately. Aidan slowly backed out, trying not to be noticed.

"I see something is on your mind." Aidan said softly.

"Do you remember when we first questioned Igraine?" Gillian asked.

"Yes, in the library after Adelaide's body was found." Aidan said.

"And do you remember how she kept tugging at her sleeves as we were asking her questions?" Gillian asked. "As if she were trying to make sure her wrists could not be seen."

"To be honest, no I didn't notice." Aidan replied as he thought back.

"There's one more thing I noticed but didn't really remember until tonight."

"About that day?" He asked.

"Yes, about Igraine." She said. "As I remember that morning she was wearing something different than when we saw her in the library."

"I have to say, I did not notice that either." He said.

"No offence, but you probably wouldn't being a man. I remember thinking the gray she wore that morning reflected the glower she always wears on her face. When we were in the library she was wearing a dark green dress with lace at the cuff of the sleeves, a dress that one would not normally wear to do daily chores in. I thought how much better the color suited her."

"Forgive me, I don't understand." Aidan smiled.

"Let me explain. The time I saw her that morning and the time we questioned her couldn't have been more than five or six hours. It is rare for a working woman such as Igraine to just change clothes in the middle of the day and into a dress with lace. What would be the reason?" Gillian thought aloud.

"Perhaps she soiled her dress." Aidan said.

"Yes, that is possible. Maybe Aggie might know more. If she did soil her dress, Aggie might know how she did it." Gillian said.

"Did you notice anything else?" Aidan asked.

"No. I did not want to say anything because Lan was in the room. I wouldn't want to falsely accuse his mother." Gillian said.

"I understand." Aidan said.

"If Igraine does become under suspicion, can you think of a motive she might have to kill Adelaide?" Gillian asked.

"No. It is my understanding they had never met until you arrived." Aidan said.

Gillian was silent for a moment. "You told me once that Igraine once worked for Diaspad."

"Do you think there is a connection?" Aidan asked.

"I'm willing to bet there is." Gillian said

CHAPTER 21

▼

The swollen ascendant moon stood perched out over the loch in the black canopy of sky. The first real break of rain in days. Gillian sat up in bed unable to sleep with nothing more than a candle to keep out the dark, the hours between dusk and dawn brought forth a seething horde of images of Diaspad. The thoughts appeared at random of him, as shapeless shadows. A clootie, as Aggie called him, a devil. He appeared in her dreams in assumed bodies that were patchworks of stolen parts—goats' hoofs and cats' claws, dogs' fangs and human faces. Aimlessly evil, he huddled in dark corners waiting for the chance to pinch and claw, to corrupt and maim. Would she ever be free of these images?

Gillian reached across her bed to the nightstand, where the book that Beechim had given her sat. She had forgotten all about it, and now seemed a good time as any to catch up on her reading.

Gillian thumbed through the book to first glance at the sketchings. When she did, a small picture of a girl fell from between the pages. Gillian picked up the picture and held it closer to the candlelight. A sweet smile, she thought. She turned the picture over and read the inscription: Love forever and always, J. Knott.

Gillian assumed the pretty girl was a loved one of Beechim's and placed the photo back between the pages. She would remind him, upon returning the book that the picture was in the book in case he had missed it.

Gillian read a few pages, but found herself too restless for reading. Despite the warnings that all should remain behind locked doors until the murderer was caught, Gillian's restless soul needed some air.

Gillian found herself in the garden, just below her balcony. All was still and quiet, the moon provided enough light for Gillian to feel safe. She took a seat on a bench that overlooked the rest of the garden and breathed in the fresh clean air.

The moon slipped in and out of pale clouds as all slept on. The only thing that stirred was a silver-gray hare almost invisible in the faint light. Gillian watched as it hopped from shadows slowly. When it touched the open ground; it sat up on its haunches and froze, long ears erect. Free the little hare was. How free, she thought, to roam, free to be nothing more than it was.

Gillian put her feet up on the bench and pulled her knees up to her chest as she stared out onto the swaying silhouettes of flowers. Suddenly her tranquility was interrupted by a dark figure stepping onto the garden path.

"Gillian? Is that you?" The voice said, upon discovering her.

"Lan?" She inquired.

He chuckled. "What are you doing out here, all by yourself?"

"I could ask you the same." She said as he sat down beside her.

"I guess I dozed off on the sofa, I haven't had such a heavy meal in some time. Now, what is your story?" He propped his elbow up on the back of the bench.

Gillian smiled. "I couldn't sleep. I thought I would get some air. Clear the cob webs and all."

"You should not be out here all alone. It is too dangerous." Lan said, as if almost scolding her.

"But I am not alone." She smiled. "Not any longer, anyway."

He grinned, his pearly whites glowing in the pale light. He looked into her eyes as if he were thinking of kissing her. "So tell me, lady Darnaway, are you soon to be wedded to Count Ranulf of Aberdour? Or is there still time for other suitor's to make a proposal?"

Gillian laughed. "You sound as if I am up for auction. Why? Are you thinking of proposing?"

"And what if I were?" He smiled.

"I would not think you serious." She laughed.

"Ma che're, you break my heart. Why would you not take me serious?" He grinned.

"I think women fascinate you. We are soft, fragile and endlessly pleasurable creatures. You and Ranulf are a lot alike." She said.

"Are we now?" He said, as he gently brushed her shoulder with his finger.

She grinned. "Yes. Little boys with a new toy, but soon you will grow tired of it and trade it for another."

Lan laughed. "Is that how you see us? You are right about one thing, I do find women, certain women, endlessly pleasurable." His voice deepened and became more serious. "You for instance—coy and seductive, whose silken wrappings I could no more resist exploring than I could stop breathing."

Gillian's breath quickened, as he moved a little closer. "Oh my." She said, remembering to breathe. Gillian put both hands on his chest and slowly pushed him back. "I think you should mind your distance."

Lan laughed. "If you insist. For now, ma che're." Lan stood and offered his hand to Gillian. "Come with me."

"Where are we going?" She asked, before accepting his hand.

"Come, I will show you." Lan smiled. Gillian took his hand and he led her back to the castle doors. "I have just the thing for a sleepless night."

"Oh, and what pray tell is that?" She laughed as he led her into the kitchen.

"Have a seat." Lan pulled out one of the chairs under the wooden kitchen table. The kitchen was large dominated by an enormous fireplace. Gillian caught a glimpse of the iron cauldrons set on tripods and ropes of onion and garlic hanging from blackened beams of the ceiling.

"Do you know what you are doing?" Gillian smiled as she watched Lan rumbling about in the cupboards.

"Trust me. I'm going to fix you one of Aggie's teas to help you sleep." He pulled the tea from the shelf and filled the kettle with water. "Aggie has had to fix it for me on several occasion, I know for a fact it works." He said smiling as he placed a cup and saucer in front of Gillian.

"I will take you at your word." Gillian smiled.

The cry of the tea kettle sounded, startling Gillian. Lan carefully poured the hot water into Gillian's cup then took a seat across from her. "After you drink your tea, I will tuck you in." He grinned.

"I think I can manage." She said stirring her tea with her spoon.

"Yes well, the tea will make you very sleepy. Besides, it is a rather good excuse to be invited in your boudoir. Don't you think?" He said, grinning at her.

Gillian laughed. "You are a naughty boy, aren't you?" She took a sip of tea. "I shall have to ask your mother what you were like as a boy, I imagine a little devil."

"I'm afraid you would have to ask someone other than my mother. My mother has done little more than to give birth to me." Lan said, tracing the worn marks in the table with his finger.

"I'm sorry." Gillian said.

Lan looked up at her. "For what?"

"For you having to feel pain from your mother's abandonment." Gillian lightly touched his hand resting on the tabletop.

Lan smiled at her. "Oh ma che're, you misunderstand. There is no pain. Aggie and the Queen provided me with much love and care. The Queen treated me no different than her own son. When I was a young boy, she would sit me in her lap in an old rocking chair and tell me stories as we looked out at the loch. She made me feel as if I was her son." His eyes were moist as he smiled a sweet smile. "I am very grateful for the love she provided."

"You loved her very much." Gillian said.

Lan nodded. "I never knew a finer woman or person."

"Then I'm sorry Igraine missed out on being a mother to you and that she missed the joy of watching you grow into the gentleman you have become." Gillian beamed a warm smile at him.

Lan took her hand and kissed it. "Drink your tea." Gillian nodded. "Then, I will escort you to your chamber."

As Gillian neared her door, she was beginning to feel the effects of the tea. Lan opened the door for her and took her hand, leading her in. "If you don't mind, I will sleep better tonight if you allow me to make sure your chamber is safe before I leave?"

Gillian nodded. "If it pleases you."

Lan searched around the room, under the bed behind doors and in any other room of the chamber until he was satisfied all was safe. "Everything seems to be safe ma che're." He smiled.

"Thank you for the conversation and the tea. The tea works well, I am getting very sleepy." Gillian said.

"Anytime I can be of service." Gillian waited for him to say goodnight but instead Lan stepped closer and placed his finger under her chin and tilted up her chin and gently bestowed a warm kiss to her lips. Gillian was so sleepy she made little protest, other wise she would have surely done so. Lan grinned then left her chamber, closing the door behind him. Gillian smiled and touched her lips with her fingertips. She secretly enjoyed all the attention.

CHAPTER 22

▼

Gillian approaches Aggie in the corridor of the servant's wing. "Aggie, could you point me in the direction of Beechim's room? I need to return his book to him."

Aggie smiled. "Sure deary, tis that woon thir." She pointed to the door at the end of the hall.

Gillian gave a nod and approached Beechim's door, knocking twice. "Enter." A voice cried out. Gillian opened the door slowly and found Beechim resting in a chair by a fire.

"Oh, lady Darnaway," he stood in surprise, "I had no idea." Beechim said startled.

"Please, please, don't get up." Gillian said. "I hope I am not disturbing you?"

"No, milady. Please come in. Can I do something for you?" Beechim said sitting back down and coughing heavily.

"I think the question is, can I do something for you? Your cough is no better, have you seen a doctor?" Gillian stepped closer to him with concern.

Beechim gave her a warm smile. "I am an old man, this is expected."

"But the doctor could give you something for that cough, at least make you more comfortable." Gillian insisted. "I'm going to ask that you be relieved of your duties at once, you need time to rest and get well."

"Have a seat milady." Gillian took a seat and placed the book in her lap. "I have seen a doctor, and just between me and you, I will not be getting better." Gillian looked at him with sadness. "I am dying." He smiled acceptingly.

"Can anything be done?" Gillian asked.

"No child. I have known it for some time now. I have had a comfortable life, if God calls, I gladly go." He smiled.

"I am sorry Beechim." Gillian said, reaching over and touching his hand.

"I tell you this only because you remind me of my daughter." Gillian smiled. "This remains between us?" He smiled at her.

Gillian nodded. "If you wish."

"Now, what brings you to seek me out today?" Beechim asked before covering his cough with a handkerchief.

"I wanted to return your book to you." Gillian said, placing the book in Beechim's lap.

"But you are welcome to keep it as long as you like, you need not hurry to return it."

"You were kind to offer me the book, I found a photograph of a lovely girl between the pages, and I assumed the book was of some importance to you. Besides, I finished it. It kept me company on a few sleepless nights." Gillian stood and reached for a blanket folded at the end of Beechim's bed. She unfolded the blanket and placed it over Beechim's lap.

"The photograph is one of my daughter." Beechim thumbed through the pages until he came upon the picture. He lifted it from its resting-place and closed the book as he stared at the photograph in reverie. "She was but a

young girl when this was taken, around sixteen I think."
He smiled warmly. "That was long ago. So long ago." His
warmness turned to sadness. "Four years after this photo,
she was dead. She died too young, too soon. Parents are
not supposed to out live their children. It goes against
nature, it does."

Gillian could see the pain in his face. "I'm sorry for
your loss."

He smiled. "She was all I had. I also lost my first grandchild when I lost her."

"Grandchild?" Gillian questioned.

"Yes, she was pregnant with my first grandchild when
she died. It was long ago, but the pain is as if it were yesterday." Tears welled in his eyes. "I look forward to seeing
my family in heaven, to finally be reunited."

Gillian suddenly had a collage of thoughts. Things she
had heard, rumors. The things Ranulf had told her and
the name on the photo. "Can I bring you something?
Some tea, or soup?"

"No, no. I am fine, thank you. Aggie will bring me in
something later. However, there is one thing you may do
for me. That is if it not too much to ask."

Gillian smiled. "Please, what may I do for you?"

"Tomorrow would have been my daughter's birthday, if
I am not able, would you place some flowers on her grave
for me? And make my excuses?" He asked with smiling
eyes.

Gillian knelt down at his side and placed her hand over
his. "I would be honored."

He nodded with a smile. "My days are numbered on
this earth, so I will not waste anymore time or words. You
are a kind woman that deserves much more than life has

offered you. Do not waste anymore of your life. Free yourself and be happy, before it is too late. Take a lesson from
my daughter's wasted life." He smiled. Now, if you don't ·
mind, I think I will take a little nap."

"Yes, of course." Gillian pulled the blanket up over his
arms as he began to drift off to sleep. She leaned over and
gently kissed his forehead. "Sweet dreams." She whispered.

CHAPTER 23

▼

After dinner, all gathered in the parlor as usual for after dinner drinks and what not. Diaspad was allowed out of his chamber, with Gillian's approval, but was not allowed to dine with the others. He agreed to be on his best behavior and was reminded of an empty room in the bowels of the castle if he should forget. He sat in a corner, quiet watching Gillian, motionless.

"I sent a letter to king Odden today, welcoming Princess Eleanor." Gody informed everyone. "She should arrive at the end of the week, I expect." Aggie entered with a small tray of little goodies. "Oh Aggie, you might want to inform Igraine of Princess Eleanor's arrival early."

Aggie looked at him strangely. "Sire, I thoot ya new. Igraine hoz ben goon fer sum days now."

"Gone? When did she leave?" Aidan asked.

Aggie thought back. "Tha day oof Miss Adelaide's funeral."

"Do you know where she went?" Gody asked.

"Nay sire." She looked at Lan. Lan shook his head. "I ded see-yer leevin."

Gillian and Aidan looked at each other. "Did you notice anything strange about Igraine before she left?" Aidan asked.

Aggie was silent and turned her eyes away. "Please Aggie, if you know something you must tell us." Gody said.

Aggie nodded with hesitation. "I woold hat-ta git any woon in trooble withoot all tha facts."

"Just tell us what you know Aggie." Aidan smiled.

Aggie looked at Lan. It was obvious she didn't want to speak in front of him. Lan could see her hesitation. "Aggie, don't worry about offending me. Please feel free to speak."

Aggie took a deep breath and released it slowly. "It waz tha day oof tha funeral, befor it in fact. Igraine cam ta-me and asked fer sum fisyk."

"Fisyk?" Gillian questioned.

"Yes, medicine. Fer her arms. I took a-look see, at-her woons. Loong marks deep woons. I asked how she goot-em. She sad a chicken scratched-her, she ded, when she waz fetchin woon fer dinner."

"A chicken? Did you believe this?" Lan asked.

"Well, I hod no reasun ta doubt-her. At leest noot til I waz told we woold all be questshooned and inspected fer marks. I thoot little oof it til thin."

"But you made no mention of her wounds to any of us." Ranulf spoke.

"I a-sumed she hod tha woonce over lik tha rest oof-us." Aggie said.

"No, in fact Igraine was the only one we didn't get around to taking a look at. I assumed she had gone into town for supplies, but now it is clear she was already gone." Gody said.

"She must have some how caught wind of it, or some-how over heard us talking." Lan said.

"Well, it seems obvious who the killer is now, doesn't it." Ranulf commented. "Sorry Lan, ol' boy. I don't mean to sound insensitive."

"No, I understand. It seems obvious to me as well. Why else would she run off without a word."? Lan said.

"If Igraine did kill Adelaide, what was the motive?" Gillian asked. "Lan, you have known her the longest, and though she was never the mother she should have been, is there something you know that we don't?"

Lan was silent, realizing, by the look on his face, that all secrets must now be revealed. "I have kept quiet for a very long time, why I am not sure. A family based on secrets is a family that is sure to fall apart." Lan poured himself a brandy and took a seat on the sofa. "Father, dear." Lan looked at Diaspad.

"Father?" Some repeated in surprise.

" Yes, Lord Darnaway here is my father. Why don't you tell the story."? Lan said with a sarcastic tone. Silence fell across the room, all eyes turned to Diaspad. He remained silent. "Don't you remember, Father? How you seduced my mother into your twisted ways got her pregnant then abandoned her. That is why she went away, to France. An unmarried woman with a bastard child! Don't you remember when we returned? You wanted nothing to do with her or me; in fact, you paid her to stay away. To keep quiet, so your wife at the time would not find out about us."

"You bastard!" Ranulf stepped forward, ready to pounce on Diaspad. "You never deserved Knottie or Gillian for that matter! You should have been the one to die!"

"Yes, you should have been, maybe then my mother would have finally given up her love for you. She blamed me for you not returning her love and hated anyone that came in contact with you. That was her motive. Adelaide took her place."

Gillian took a seat next to Lan, taking it all in. There was so much she did not know about her husband. She looked at Diaspad seeing what he truly was. "What a cruel man you are. Do you comprehend the severity of the pain you have caused in everyone's life? Do you!" She paused, but did not expect an answer. "How does one turn away one's own flesh and blood? Did you ever stop to think how that must feel to a child? No wonder this man hates the sight of you, I completely understand now. I too hate the sight of you for that alone, never mind the things you have done to me. What a despicable man you are. No, that is wrong, I cannot call you a man. You are not a man, but a devil a mere imitation of a human being."

Ranulf clapped. "Well done Gillian."

Aidan approached Lan and placed his hand on his shoulder. "I am deeply sorry, I had no idea. Mother knew all of this, didn't she?"

Lan nodded. "Yes, and your father. That is why they both have been so good to me. The mother and father I never had." Lan looked up at Aidan and smiled.

Gillian touched Lan's hand. "Fate blessed you with the love of two wonderful people. I would hate to think of the man you might have become if Diaspad had accepted you as his own. Be grateful God saved you from such a fate." Gillian smiled warmly into his eyes. Lan lifted her hand to his lips and kissed it.

Diaspad stood suddenly. "Oh please, save me from such dramatics! Igraine never loved me; she wanted me for the wealth and stature she thought she would gain. And as for you," he pointed to Lan, "granted you were an accident, it was never proven you were of my loins. You could have been anybody's!" Diaspad walked over to the bar and poured himself a stiff drink. "And you my lovely wife, you think you are soon to be free of me?" He took a gulp of brandy. "Never! I'll soon see you dead, than to let you run into the arms of another!"

"How dare you!" Aidan roared. "How dare you even consider such an act!"? Aidan lunged himself at Diaspad. The impact of flesh hitting flesh drove air from Diaspad's lungs, toppling him to the ground. "See that you never touch her again!"

"What? Put a crimp in your plans for *my* wife, does it?" Diaspad smiled a devilish grin. "Good." He brushed his trousers off and tried to stand in a dignified manner.

"Diaspad, why must you continue this torture?" Gody asked.

Diaspad looked at him and smiled. "Because I can."

"Pay him no mind, Gillian, he is only trying to scare you." Ranulf said.

"Gillian is fully aware that I mean what I say. Aren't you *dear?*"

"You are a sick man, Diaspad." Gillian said through gritted teeth.

"Don't you remember my dear? Till death do us part." Diaspad grinned.

"Do you really think any of us would allow you to take Gillian away from Aberdour? After knowing all that we do?" Aidan spoke calmly and self-assured.

"Must I remind you, she is *my* wife. Mine!" Diaspad tapped his finger on his chest.

"As you said, *father,* till death do you part." Lan looked at Diaspad, his eyes full of scorn.

"Should I take that as a threat?" Diaspad sneered.

"Take it how ever you wish. The only way the lady leaves is by her own accord." Lan said firmly. "Gillian, do you wish to return home with Diaspad?" Lan's eyes did not leave Diaspad as he asked her the question.

"No." Gillian replied.

"There is your answer." Lan said simply.

"The law is on my side, I have the right to do with her as I please." Diaspad grinned smugly.

"The law gives you no such right." Aidan sprang toward Diaspad. "Gillian's life does not belong to you!"

"And I say she does. I am her husband." Diaspad quickly answered.

"Husband?" Gillian raised her voice. "When were you ever a husband to me? You obviously do not know the meaning of the word! Have you forgotten our marriage was never consummated? The marriage is null!"

"Found some gumption these days of late, have we? I will allow it, it somehow becomes you." Diaspad grinned. "As far as the consummation, that will change when we return home."

Gillian's face began to flush with anger. "I would sooner die, than allow you to touch me!" She spoke with a fierce contempt.

Diaspad laughed with a snide tone. "Then so be it."

Aidan suddenly pounced over to Diaspad and lifted him with one hand by the throat against the wall. "Listen to me and take heed!" Aidan tightened his grip. "Harm Gillian and I will harm you. Make her cry or touch one hair on her head and I will make you wish you were dead!" Aidan's hand released him. Diaspad caught himself as he fell to the floor. He gritted his teeth as he felt a warm wetness in his pants. Aidan took Gillian by the hand and led her out of the parlor rather swiftly.

Aidan was quiet as he led her out into the garden amongst the explosion of giant yellow flowers, lovely purple vines and lacy trees swaying in the moonbeams.

Gillian and Aidan waded into the flowers lining the path. Even in the dimness of the moonlight he could tell her color was high, but not so much from anger, as he thought, but from the simple pleasure of him holding her hand.

Aidan led her into a lattice-covered gazebo with pretty little flowers spiraling in and out of the small openings of the latticework. A long white bench sat in the middle facing out toward the gardens.

Gillian took a seat with Aidan beside her and watched him in his silence. She relaxed as she took a deep breath and released it. "How quiet the woods are tonight, not a murmur except for the soft purring in the treetops." Still Aidan was quiet. "They remind me of you." She looked at him and smiled.

Aidan smiled. "Forgive me. My thoughts were wandering."

"Where?" Gillian asked.

"Somewhere far away. Somewhere safe." Aidan shifted his body on the bench to face her. "Gillian, if I knew of a place like that, somewhere safe and far away from Diaspad, would you go with me? Somewhere Diaspad would never be able to find you?"

Gillian was taken by his sentiment. "Oh Aidan, you flatter me with such an offer." Gillian smiled and laid her hand on his. "Aidan I could never ask you to do such a task, no matter how romantic and bohemian it sounds.

Have you forgotten you will one day be King?" Gillian laughed a little at the sweet thought.

Aidan smiled. "You must think I am a fool."

"Not at all. That has got to be the best proposition I have ever received." She giggled. "But don't tell Ranulf I said so."

Aidan snickered then became quiet again. "What will you do if Diaspad will not grant you a divorce or sign the annulment paper?"

Gillian sighed. "I can no longer stay married to Diaspad. I will do what ever it takes to be rid of him."

Aidan looked at her but said nothing, he wasn't sure what she meant by that and wasn't sure he really wanted to know. He lifted her hand and kissed it. "I will stand by you with what ever you decide."

She smiled up at him. "Thank you Aidan, you have been a true friend. Your loyalty has been greatly appreciated." Gillian lowered her head choking back the emotion and anger that had torn her. "I am frightfully sorry Aidan." She said, lifting her face with a passionate penitence.

"What ever for?" Aidan asked.

"You have been so kind to me, and I fear I have repaid you only with distress and difficulty." Gillian said.

Aidan snickered. "That is not true milady. I have cherished every moment of our friendship, the good and not so good."

Gillian looked at him and grinned. "Will you do something for me?"

"Anything."

"You are aware that Beechim has not been feeling well?" She asked.

He nodded. "Yes."

"Well, in the event he was not able, he asked if I would put some flowers on his daughter's grave tomorrow. It would have been her birthday, you see. I was wondering if you would go with me?" Gillian asked. "I thought you might know where she is buried."

"Yes, of course I will accompany you. However, I am sorry to say, I do not know where his daughter is buried. Nevertheless, I am sure we could find it together." He smiled.

"Thank you, I will get further directions from Beechim in the morning." She said.

A shuffling breeze sprang up stirring the varieties of fragrances in the garden. The woods were alive with fireflies and the aroma of pine balsam faintly charged the air.

"It's a beautiful night tonight." Aidan commented.

"Yes, I feel it's Spring in my soul." Gillian shut her eyes, lifted her nose, and breathed in the floral air.

Aidan noticed the delicate curve of her throat and could not stop his fingers from caressing the length of her neck with an agony of slowness, as if he were learning every detail of her. Gillian lowered her chin and slowly opened her eyes to look at him. Aidan's finger's never left her skin as he caressed the curve of her bottom lip with his thumb. The two moved closer to each other. The warmth of his breath bathed her; so close she could taste the heat, the masculine strength and the whisper of need that moved her.

His lips brushed hers, dazzling her with his tenderness. Then he tasted her; the rough velvet of his tongue glided along the curve of her mouth. Desire, long denied exploded through Aidan. He silently cursed that he should feel such rage of need for Gillian. He wanted to take her, right there, as he felt his flesh press hard against his belly. To feel her beneath him and hear her soft cries.

A smile came to his lips as Aidan reluctantly pulled his lips from Gillian's. "Again, I must apologize for taking such liberties." He spoke in a whispery voice.

Gillian grinned. "Did you hear me protest?"

Aidan shook his head no; as he watched her lips form words. "I still fully intend to court you properly once Diaspad is out of your life." He said, softly. "That is, if you will allow me." Gillian nodded, shyly.

CHAPTER 24

▼

Gillian was late in dressing for breakfast. Diaspad was not allowed in the dining room and ate his breakfast in his room. Everyone else had already begun breakfast except Gillian, who was running late.

"Princess Eleanor will be arriving any day now." Gody said, before taking a sip of his tea.

"I'm assuming father, there is more to her visit than a mere friendly call." Aidan said. "Before Gillian joins us, why not tell me the rest of the story."

Gody pressed his napkin to his lips. "Alright. Princess Eleanor comes to us with a heavy dower."

"I knew it!" Ranulf exploded. "The princess is on a husband hunt."

"Is this true father?" Aidan asked. "Who is the intended prey?"

"You are cousin." Ranulf laughed.

Aidan looked at him with a smirk. "I hardly think this is a laughing matter, Ranulf."

"Now, now, let's not jump to conclusions. I am not clear on the intentions of the princess' stay, just that the King did make mention of the dower." Gody explained.

"Why else would he do such a thing father? He is waiting for you to offer me up. She is not homeless or penniless. As to marriage, she is quite as likely to accomplish that else-where as here."

"Maybe it is as said, and Ellie is just stopping for a visit." Lan said.

"Let's calm down. No need to get excited till we know more." Gody suggested.

Gillian entered a dreadfully quiet dining room. "Sorry I am so late, I over slept."

She took her seat as she studied everyone's face. "Did I miss something?"

Gody smiled. "No dear, please have some breakfast."

Gillian looked at Aidan, who would only glance up at her. Ranulf was still smiling to himself. Lan kept his eyes on his plate. "Please, it is obvious something is going on. I feel very much out of place."

"Shall I tell her?" Ranulf grinned. Aidan gave him a dirty look. "We were discussing the meaning behind Princess Eleanor's visit. Aidan is not too excited to see our long lost play-mate."

"Really?" Gillian looked at Aidan. "I feel there is more to the story."

Ranulf laughed. "Ellie is on a man hunt, and her sights set on Aidan."

"Really." Gillian looked at Aidan, who now just hap-pened to be looking at her.

"Nothing has been made clear. Why the King chose to mention the dower, is not known." Gody said. "If it be known, the dower is an attractive one. With our wool market growing with an exceeding volume the people are in need of more land. I must admit I cannot help but to think of the people's benefit. Sorry Aidan, I don't mean to sound as if I have already married you off."

"I understand father. You are thinking of your people just as a good King should." Aidan smiled, but it was not a happy smile. Aidan knew as a royal, the people come first, and he must put the people and the countries needs ahead of his own.

After breakfast Gillian paid Beechim a visit. She knocked gently on Beechim's door. "Come."

"Hello, I hope I am not disturbing you." Gillian said smiling.

"No, not at all. I was just writing a letter to a friend." Beechim explained.

"Then I won't keep you from it. How are you feeling today?"

"Better, much better." He coughed uncontrollably. Gillian could tell he was no better, in fact worse. She knew he was trying to hide how he really felt.

"I was about to take some flowers to your daughter's grave, when I realized I had not asked where she lay." Gillian said.

"Her grave sits just under the old giant elm. To the West as you enter. You can't miss it." He smiled.

"Do you mind if I bring Prince Aidan along?" Gillian asked.

"No, as a matter of fact, I think that is a good idea. The both of you should go together. I should have suggested it." He said. "Tell my little lamb I will see her soon enough."

Gillian nodded. "Well then, I will let you get back to your letter. How about I bring up some tea and cakes later and we can have a visit?"

Beechim smiled. "That would be lovely."

Gillian met Aidan outside who was waiting patiently beside the royal carriage. He smiled as she came swiftly out of breath through the front doors. "You need not have hurried so, I would have waited."

She smiled. "Oh, my father taught me that it was impolite to keep a Prince waiting." She said as she climbed into the carriage with the assistance of Aidan's hand.

Down the winding road they traveled, past gardens, fields, houses and green

pastures. Spring had once again come to the land; Gillian looked dreamily out the window of the carriage where big fat yellow and red buds were bursting out in response to the sun's rays.

Every stride of the horses and every turn of the wheels were taking them nearer to

their adventure.

"Aidan, did you know Beechim's daughter?"

"No, he never mentioned her. I always assumed she died when she was a young child." Aidan said.

Gillian paused and thought back to her conversation with Beechim. "But that can not be. I saw a photograph of her when she was sixteen, then Beechim said that she died four years later. That would make her around twenty." Gillian explained.

"I don't understand." Aidan looked puzzled.

"Neither do I. If she were in her twenties would you not have met her at one time or another?" Gillian asked.

"I would think so. That is odd. Beechim did say it was the Aberconway grave yard?" Aidan asked.

Gillian nodded. "Yes, I'm sure of it. He was happy that you were going with me, it seemed important to him." Aidan looked at her, listening intensely. "Oh, I almost forgot, he also mentioned she was with child when she died. That would surely make her married."

"I was not aware of all this. I never knew Beechim had any family. Did he say when she died?" Aidan asked with a look of suspicion.

"No, but I gathered from the way he talked it was some years ago." Gillian said, studying the look on his face.

The carriage pulled up to the iron front gates of the graveyard. Pale pink roses drowsy with fragrance tenderly climbed a stone wall that surrounded the graveyard. Off in the far ground were wind-swept hills slashed by steep wooded valleys alternate with undulating fields that are patchworks of bright yellow, lavender and fresh spring wheat. The village in the distance glowed golden as a ray of sunshine lit up the countryside, then went silver as a thundercloud threatened overhead.

The two entered through rusty gates that squealed in protest. "What name are we looking for?" Aidan asked.

Gillian looked at him and laughed. "How stupid of me. Would you believe I never asked what her first name was? Beechim said, go west from the entrance that she lay under the giant elm. There." Gillian pointed in the direction of the huge tree that sat like a beacon.

"That tree there?" Aidan asked.

"Yes, that is what he said." She answered.

"Are you sure?" Aidan asked again.

"Yes, unless you see another tree that is larger. Why?"

"Come. I'll show you." Aidan said. Aidan took Gillian by the hand and she followed him over the broad tree.

Gillian stood respectfully at the foot of the grave and read the head stone out loud. "Our beloved Jullian Knott

'Knottie', wife and daughter, rest in peace." Gillian and Aidan looked at each other.

"Now, I understand. It all fits." Aidan said.

"Please, fill me in." Gillian suggested.

Aidan smiled. "Beechim's daughter and Diaspad's first wife are one in the same."

"Knottie." Gillian said, taking a seat in the soft grass as she let all of it sink in. "Yes, now I see. J. Knott was inscribed on the photograph." Gillian said, then suddenly placed her hands on her cheeks. "Oh! The child she was carrying…. Beechim's first grandchild, he must hate Diaspad."

Aidan took a seat in the grass next to her. "Diaspad must not know Beechim was Knottie's father. I wonder if anyone knows."

"But why not?" Gillian asked.

"I would imagine Knottie's background was kept a secret so she might marry into a different class." Aidan explained.

"My father and Beechim were trying to do the same thing, I guess, they just chose the wrong man. It's sad really. Now I understand what Beechim meant, he was trying to warn me. I think he must have wanted you to know the truth also, that is why he was so happy to know you were coming along." Gillian smiled.

"Beechim must despise Diaspad as much as the rest of us. He lost a daughter and a grandchild because of Diaspad." Aidan said.

"Aidan, I have never known why Knottie fell down those stairs, only that she did and it was a accident. Do you know the story?" Gillian asked.

Aidan nodded. "Yes, I do."

"Please, can you tell me?" Gillian asked. Aidan looked at her, then gave her a nod, knowing he could not refuse those brown eyes.

"Despite my dislike for Diaspad, I have to say I do believe Knottie's death to be an accident. There was an argument at the top of the stairs, some arms flying about, or something like that, she lost her balance and fell."

"What was the argument about?" Gillian asked.

Aidan paused. "Were you aware that Diaspad is not able to produce children?" .

Gillian shook her head slowly. "But Knottie was with child…Oh!" Gillian gasped. "Oh, now I fully understand. The child was not Diaspad's."

"No, it wasn't." Aidan said, waiting for her to figure it out on her own.

"Then who's…." Gillian gasped again, when suddenly she remembered something Ranulf had told her. She looked at Aidan. All the pieces of the puzzle were now complete. Aidan smiled. He could tell by the look on her face she knew. "Ranulf was the father of Knottie's child. Ranulf once told me of a woman he once loved named Jullian, and that she died." She said to Aidan, he nodded yes. "I see why Ranulf has such contempt for Diaspad. Ranulf lost a child and his lady love." Gillian looked at Knottie's grave and smiled with tears in her eyes. "Diaspad has caused so much grief to so many."

"That is why you must get away from him. The sooner, the better. Even if he should refuse to grant you a divorce or annulment you must not return to Cardoness with him. Here I can protect you and see that you are safe." Aidan said. A crash of thunder sounded overhead then released a few drops to the earth. A tiny raindrop landed on Gillian's nose. Aidan tenderly wiped the raindrop away with his finger. "I think it is time for us to go." He smiled.

Gillian quickly placed the flowers on Knottie's grave and sweetly whispered a birthday wish. She strangely felt a special bond with Knottie and knew that if she were alive Gillian would have liked her.

CHAPTER 25

▼

The night was gusty; a hurrying night… even the clouds racing in the sky were in a hurry and the moonlight that seeped through them was in a hurry to flood the world. Aberdour lay dark under a canopy of black dismal clouds heavy with rain. The rain outside slackened and grew soft. The high wind blustered around the castle and roared in the chimney; sounding wild, cold and stormy.

Aidan and Gillian entered the dining room just in time for dinner. "I see we made it just in time." Aidan said, as he escorted Gillian to her chair.

"Sorry we are late everyone." Gillian said, placing her napkin in her lap.

"I was getting worried, with the storm and all." Gody replied.

"Where were you two anyway?" Ranulf asked. "You're lucky I'm not a jealous man." He smiled.

Aidan looked at Gillian before he answered. "We will tell you after dinner."

"Sounds very mysterious." Lan said.

"Not really. However, there are some telling secrets to be told." Aidan explained.

Aggie entered the dining room looking pale and troubled. "Sire, may I hove-a-wood."

Gody looked at Aggie who was clearly disturbed. "Aggie? What is it? You're as pale as a ghost."

"Sire, I thin ya better cume with me." Aggie said with tears in her eyes.

"Alright." Gody said. "Can you tell me more?"

"It's…it's Beechim sire. Please cume." Aggie said wiping her tears.

Everyone including Gody rushed up stairs to Beechim's room. Gillian entered first, given her experience. Beechim lie peacefully on his bed with a serene smile with his hands resting on his chest. Everyone gathered around the bed, looking on as Gillian bent over him and took his pulse. She released his wrist and shook her head. "I am afraid he is gone." She said softly.

"It is my fault, I had no idea he was so sick. I assumed it was a bad cold." Gody said.

"No. It is no one's fault." Gillian said. "Beechim had been sick for some time now. He asked if I would keep it a secret, he did not want anyone to worry about him."

"What is this in his breast pocket?" Lan questioned as he pointed to a piece of paper purposely stuck half way in his pocket.

"Go ahead, take it out and read it." Gillian said.

Lan pulled the piece of paper out of Beechim's pocket, unfolded it and began to read. "Dearest Gillian…" Lan paused and looked at her. "Maybe che're, you should read this?"

"No, please, you read it." Gillian smiled. Lan gave her a nod and continued.

"Dearest Gillian, by the time you receive this letter I will have gone on. Tell everyone to grieve not for me, for I have had a long and prosperous life; I look forward to going home. Today as you lay flowers on my dear sweet Knottie's grave, I hope that you now know the truth and understand the things I tried to warn you about.

Dear sweet angel, forgive me for the sin I committed there on God's earth, but know I did it for you. To keep you from suffering the same fate as my dear departed and to keep the ones that love you from suffering a life without you, as I did without Knottie.

As my last act on earth I can only think of redemption. However, not for me, for the people I care for and for who have showed me true friendship. Salvation I give to all of you, so you might not suffer any longer.

Gillian, you have been a true angel in my last hours; for the sharing of your kind gentle heart the most grateful gift I can think to give you is your own salvation. So that you might learn to live, love and be loved. Be happy child, for our time here is limited. Beechim."

Gillian began to cry. Ranulf stepped closer and put his arm around her to comfort her. Gody offered her his white linen handkerchief from his breast pocket. Gillian wiped her tears as Ranulf cradled her in his arms.

"He is at peace now, there is nothing more we can do for him. Why don't we all go down to the parlor."? Aidan suggested.

All were quiet as they entered the parlor. Gillian took a seat on the sofa, Ranulf still devotionally attending her.

Lan took a seat next to Gillian. "Here, ma che're." He handed her the letter from Beechim. "The letter is written to you, you should keep it." Gillian smiled and accepted the letter. "One day it will bring you a smile when you are in need."

Gody stood mournful next to the fire. "I am speechless. I do not know what to say. I wish that I knew sooner of his illness."

"It is alright father, we are all in shock." Aidan replied.

"This is the way Beechim wanted it." Gillian said, now better composed. "He wanted to do his duties as long as he was able. He took pride in that." She smiled.

"Gillian, if it is not too personal, what did Beechim mean when he talked of salvation for us all?" Aidan asked.

Gillian paused. "I do not know, Aidan. That puzzled me too."

"He mentioned Knottie." Ranulf said. "What does all this have to do with her?"

Gillian and Aidan looked at each other again. "Gillian, why don't you begin." Aidan suggested.

Gillian nodded. All eyes watched and waited for her to speak. "To start from the beginning, Beechim had given me a book to read and inside the pages I found a photograph of a young girl, it was signed J. Knott. At the time I just assumed it was a loved one and mentioned the photo upon returning the book. He told me the photo was of his daughter and that she died with child some years ago. He asked if I would place some flowers on her grave today, for it would have been her birthday, in the event he was too ill.

I asked Aidan to accompany me; in the event he might know where she was buried. However, Aidan had assumed his daughter died as a child. To make a long story short, when we arrived at the grave it turned out to be the grave of Jullian Knott, Knottie." Gillian paused while the others thought about what she had told them. Ranulf put his head in his hands and became silent. "Knottie, Diaspad's first wife was also Beechim's daughter."

Ranulf raised his head. "Does Diaspad know all this?"

"No, no one knew." Gillian said. "We assumed Beechim kept the identity of his daughter a secret so she might marry upper class."

"Ha!" Ranulf scoffed. "Upper class, my ass."

"Ranulf! Mind your tongue!" Gody scolded.

"Forgive me Gillian." Ranulf said.

"Well, his intentions for his daughter were innocent. He had no way of knowing he was marrying her off to a monster." Aidan said. "The same as Gillian's father."

Ranulf stood and walked over to the fire, staring into its flames. Gillian watched him; she knew he was in pain. He had made no mention of his involvement with Knottie or the child she was carrying, his child.

Gillian stood and joined Ranulf, she placed her hand warmly on his back. He looked up from the flames to find Gillian smiling in an understanding way. "You know." He said softly, where only she could hear, his voice trembling.

Gillian nodded, still smiling. "But only Aidan and I." She said softly.

"Now you understand why I hate him with such passion." Ranulf gritted his teeth. With a burst of emotion, he stormed out onto the veranda.

"What is that about?" Gody asked. Aidan knew, but said nothing. Gody took a seat in one of the large leather chairs. "We were all very fond of Knottie." Gody said to Gillian. "This has brought up some difficult feelings for us all, Ranulf as well I guess. He cared deeply for her, as we all did."

"I think I will go and see if Ranulf is alright." Gillian said. Gillian entered the veranda and stood behind Ranulf watching him watch the rain. "Ranulf, are you alright? Would you prefer to be alone?" She asked in a sweet voice.

He turned around and said, "no," rather quickly as if he were afraid she would leave. Gillian walked over to him. "I am sorry Gillian. I am sorry you had to find out the way you did. I should have told you. Being that I did propose marriage, there should be no secrets." Ranulf lowered his head.

Gillian lifted his chin with her finger and smiled into his eyes. "You must not blame yourself. You were only trying to keep me from any further pain. I know that."

Ranulf looked deeply into her eyes. "You are truly an angel, just as Beechim said." He grabbed her shoulders and pulled her into his chest. His lips crushed down on top of hers in a suffocating kiss. Aidan was pouring his father a drink when he happened to look out the glass doors and see Gillian and Ranulf kissing.

Gillian managed to put her hands on Ranulf's chest and wedge a space between them. "Ranulf, I understand you are upset…"

"Forgive me Gillian. I knew your soft sweet lips could ease my pain, and they have." He smiled.

"Let's go in, I will fix you a drink." Gillian suggested.

The two entered the parlor; Gillian stopped to pour Ranulf a glass of wine and brought it to him. Gillian could feel Aidan's eyes upon her and assumed his concern was for Ranulf.

Gillian walked over to Aidan while the others talked. "Ranulf is alright. I think he had a lot of feelings to overwhelm him at once."

Aidan smiled but he could not help from feeling a bit jealous. "Yes well, I am sure you knew just what to say to comfort him." He could not harbor jealous feelings for long, for he knew truly where Gillian's feelings toward Ranulf stood. As well as Ranulf's tricks to gain sympathy and liberties a lady might not ordinarily give.

Annie entered the parlor a bit flustered. "Sire, might I have a word?" She asked Gody.

"Yes Annie, what is it?"

"Sire, I took Lord Darnaway's dinner tray up to him, as usual. But he would not answer the door when I knocked." Annie explained. "Sire, I must say, I do not like what is happening here with Beechim now having died. I have much fear. And now Lord Darnaway does not answer."

"Calm yourself girl. I am sure Lord Darnaway is just fine. When did you last see him?" Gody asked.

"This morning sire. I delivered his breakfast tray." Annie paused. "Forgive me sire, I am mistaken. I did take the tray to the door, but it was Beechim who met me at Milord's door and knocked."

"Beechim?" Aidan asked.

"Yes sire. He took the tray from me and said he would attend to Lord Darnaway. I heard Lord Darnaway open the door as I was leaving." Annie explained.

"Well then, it is odd that Beechim should find the strength to manage such a feat before his death, but I am sure he is fine." Gody tried to comfort her. "Rest your fears child, we will check on him later." Annie nodded with a faint smile and excused herself.

"Yes, curled up with a bottle no doubt." Ranulf remarked. "I'm sure he's drunker than a brewer's fart by now." Gody gave him a hard look.

"Do you not fine it strange of Beechim to do such a thing when only this morning Gillian visited him practically on his death bed, then later in the day we find him passed away?" Lan broke his silence.

"Maybe Beechim was trying to complete one last duty. We all know how devoted he was." Gillian offered an answer.

"Yes, this is true." Gody said.

Lan gulped down the last of his whiskey and stood with a long stretch. " Well if you will excuse me, I think I will retire." Lan approached Gillian and took her hand. "Sweet dreams, ma che're." He tenderly kissed her hand.

"Goodnight Lan." She smiled. "I think the rain has stopped, maybe I will take a walk before retiring. Goodnight all."

"I will escort you Gillian, you should not be out alone." Aidan said. Gillian smiled with a nod.

Gillian and Aidan left the parlor to walk in the garden. Gody and Ranulf remained in the parlor finishing their drinks.

"Ranulf, what do you say you and I go and check in on Diaspad?" Gody suggested.

"Concerned uncle?" Ranulf smirked.

CHAPTER 26

▼

The storm had passed. The lightning flickered on the horizon now and the pounding rain had diminished leaving traces shining on the stones of the garden walk. The air was fresh and cool after the storm, like just washed linen.

Aidan's hand warmed to the sweet curve of the small of Gillian's back as they walked through the dripping foliage and rain soaked flowers. Gillian looked up into the night's sky. The twinkling stars struggled to be seen through the passing of the clouds.

"Would you like to sit in the gazebo?" Aidan asked.

Gillian smiled, remembering their kiss. "If you like."

Aidan took her hand and guided her up the gazebo steps where they both took a seat. "Are you alright?" He asked with concerned. "You have had to deal with more than your share of death lately."

His concern touched her. "I was at first upset with losing Beechim, we were becoming friends and friends are always hard to loose." Gillian smiled. "But I think back to the last time I talked with him. Despite his horrible cough he seemed content. Happy if you will. He was genuinely looking forward to being with his family again. I now find it hard to feel sad, for I know he is happy. To grieve for my loss seems very selfish."

A pale moon looked down from a bank of dark purple clouds. Aidan looked up to see the moon smiling down at them. "Yes, I understand. He must have been very lonely without his family around. I know I would be. How wonderful you are to see death in such a beautiful way."

Gillian laughed, smiling into his eyes. From a distance music suddenly began to play, from the woods nearby. Gillian stood and peered out into the darkness in the direction of the music. "Where is it coming from?" Gillian asked.

"There is a clearing in the woods. Some of the villagers have celebrations there. They think it is magical. I have heard tales of lovers going there to profess their love." He smiled. "Would you like to go?"

"Out there? But it is so dark, what if we get lost?" Gillian laughed.

"We will just follow the music." Aidan said simply. "Come." He held out his hand. Gillian smiled and slipped her hand in his.

The shrill wail of bagpipes filled the dark night as Aidan's heart soared in the direction of the music. He led her through the woods making sure to hold tight her hand. As they neared the music grew louder and a bright firelight could be seen.

"Are you sure we are welcome?" Gillian asked.

"Trust me. Besides, this is still part of Aberdour." He said pulling her into the clearing amongst the people laughing and dancing. "It has been some time since I have danced, but I think I still remember how. May I have this honor?" Aidan bowed and held out his hand.

Gillian laughed and took his hand. Together they joined the couples spinning and twirling about in the forest glade.

She looked at him, laughing. "You are a fine dancer, sire. You haven't forgotten a step."

Aidan laughed and drew her closer. Her breasts brushed against his chest, something he could not ignore. Gillian's face flushed with heat. He lifted her up and spun her around and around. Their eyes linked together, no words were spoken. The place was indeed magical. Aidan felt as if he were looking into magical mirror, seeing a part of himself reflected. His other half. A part of himself he knew he could not live without. Gillian's smile was so bright it lit up the night, brighter than the summer sun. He had never witnessed such joy in her face, in her entire being.

The primal need to take her, to make her his, shuddered through him and left him shaking in his knees. Many couples embraced under the guise of dancing, but a few canny eyes and shrewd smiles were cast their way. Old women smiled and whispered behind their hands. They were having a glorious time and their jovial voices and gayer laughter echoed up and down the glade. Excitement hung around Gillian like a garment; it shone in her eyes and kindled in every perfect feature of her face. Aidan was in wonderment of her spirit unleashed. Gillian danced around the fire, like a lighthearted sprite, through the shadows frolicking amongst the fireflies.

The music stopped, Aidan held on to Gillian's waist, the two completely out of breath. Gillian could not stop smiling. "Let's sit down." Aidan suggested. He led her over to a small clearing away from all the excitement and took a seat on the grass. Breathless, Gillian collapsed smiling next to Aidan.

"I can't remember when I last danced as much." She said laughing.

Aidan looked down at her smiling into her eyes. "Your laugh is magical. I have never heard it so free."

Gillian's laughter stopped, replaced with a warm smile. She thought about what Aidan had just said. "Free." She said aloud. "That is how I feel, right now, with you." She paused and looked into his eyes. "Odd, I don't feel scared anymore. When we were out there dancing, I felt a lovely burst of utter indifference. It was divine! A divine emptiness that followed the desertion of all fear." Aidan's green eyes fixed themselves unwaveringly on hers. He smiled. His breath caught in his throat at her shocking beauty. God had not known what he was doing when he made woman so beautiful that strong men feel weak before them. "Why do you look at me that way?" Gillian asked grinning.

"I never saw you more beautiful. You are lit from within." He smiled. "I wish you could see your face. Being out from under Diaspad, away from his watchful eye, where he can not find you that is what has made you feel free."

"He doesn't exist. Not here, at this moment anyway. Even if it is just for a little while, it is nice to pretend." Gillian looked up above her and smiled. "Listen to the trees talking in their sleep, what nice dreams they must have. It would be lovely to sleep in a cherry tree, don't you think? All white with bloom, to sit and watch the sunset stream through the woods?"

Aidan beamed down at her and it seemed nothing mattered. There was only the two of them at that moment under a cherry tree swelled with blooms. He caught her off guard when he suddenly leaned forward and kissed her.

There was a painful urgency to his kiss, sweet and warm like honey. Why did he have to be so irresistible?

CHAPTER 27

▼

Aidan and Gillian returned to the castle. There was no one in sight and all seemed deserted. Shadows fell all around from the towering gray walls, and beyond them the thunder began to roar in the far distance. All was silent and desolate except for the fire blazing in the hearths and the crackling and spitting offered proof that life still went on.

Aidan walked Gillian to her chambers and said goodnight. A smile lingered on his lips as he approached his own chambers his thoughts still on Gillian. Aidan opened the door to find Ranulf and Gody waiting for him in his sitting room. "Is something wrong?"

"Yes Aidan, I am afraid there is." Gody said standing to his feet.

"Is it good news or bad? It is hard to tell with Ranulf's smile and your scour." Aidan said before poking the fire.

Gody threw a stern look at Ranulf. "Son, I'm afraid Annie's fears were justified."

Aidan looked up immediately. "What do you mean father?"

Ranulf stood, smiling and poured him a drink. "He means the old bastard is dead."

"Ranulf! Show some respect, for God's sake." Gody scolded.

"Dead, how? When?" Aidan asked taking a seat.

"Who cares? I say we go and wake Gillian and celebrate! May I be the first to raise my glass in a toast."? Ranulf said, raising his brandy snifter high above his head.

"I will have none of that Ranulf! Control yourself, please! No, I order you!" Gody said furious with him.

"Alright uncle. I will do my celebrating when I am alone."

"Thank you." Gody said. "Now, to answer your question Aidan, when you and Gillian left, Ranulf and I went up to Diaspad's chamber. The door was locked and he did not answer, I had Aggie search for a key. When we opened the door, we found him dead."

"A gruesome sight, cousin. He looked as if he had stared the devil himself in the face. Died of fright if you ask me." Ranulf replied.

"No one did, Ranulf. We do not know how he died. We waited for you here to catch you alone. I wasn't sure how Gillian would take the news, with Beechim just passing away and all." Gody said, mournfully.

"I understand father. But she will undoubtedly have to be told." Aidan said.

Ranulf stepped closer to Aidan. "Bring to mind a few new possibilities, hey cousin?" He whispered where only Aidan could hear. Aidan gave him a cross look.

" I am aware that Gillian could no doubt shed some light on the cause of Diaspad's death, but I believe it would be most improper to ask." Gody replied.

"Gillian is stronger than any of us could imagine, but I do see your point father." Aidan said. "Let's wait and tell her the news in the morning after she has had a good nights rest, then leave it up to her."

Gody poured himself a drink and stood in front of the hearth. "Aberdour sure has had her share of tragedy lately. I am almost fearful of allowing the princess to visit."

"What do we know so far? We know that Igraine killed Adelaide and her motive for doing so. Beechim has died from a long bout with illness and now Diaspad." Aidan replied.

"When it comes to wanting Diaspad dead, I'm afraid we all are under suspicion. But I can not see where Ellie would come to any danger." Ranulf said. "And I am looking so to seeing her. Aren't you cousin?" Ranulf asked, with a sly smirk on his lips. Aidan cut his eyes at Ranulf. Ranulf knew now that Gillian would be free to marry and with Aidan paired off with princess Ellie that would give him even more opportunity to win Gillian's heart.

"Father, what about Gillian?" Aidan asked with a look of concern. "Now that she is a widow, can she not claim Darnaway estate?"

"Yes, there is no one to keep her from it now." Gody replied. "But Gillian is more than welcomed to stay on as ward."

Aidan smiled. "I'm sure that will bring her much comfort."

"Comfort? The news of Diaspad's death alone should bring her comfort." Ranulf said, before gulping the last of his brandy.

"Ranulf the days of her abuse may be over and granted Gillian may not have loved Diaspad the way a woman loves a man but do you really expect her to celebrate? To be as joyous as you?" Aidan commented.

"Yes! Why not. She no longer has to put up with that horrible waste of flesh." Ranulf said, propping his feet on the table in front of him.

"Well then, cousin, you do not know the woman you claim you want to marry." Aidan placed his empty glass down on the table. "Now if you two will excuse me, I am going to retire."

"Come Ranulf, let us retire as well." Gody suggested as he walked toward the door. "Tomorrow is no doubt to be a long day."

CHAPTER 28

▼

Gillian came gliding into breakfast fresh and bright as a yellow daisy despite the dreariness of the day outside. "Good morn all." She said with a beaming smile. "Am I late again?" She asked smiling. "I can not seem to wake up early when it is raining."

Other than the normal greetings, no one said much of anything else and they all found it hard to meet her gaze.

"You look beautiful this morning Gillian." Ranulf said with a smile.

"Thank you Ranulf, I was beginning to wonder if I had lost all my feminine wails." Gillian snickered.

Suddenly Lan entered all dripping wet. A towel hung around his neck with which he dried the droplets of water from his face. "Che're, I just heard." Lan took Gillian's hand and kissed it. Gillian was totally in the dark about what he meant. "I do not know what to say, I am happy for you and too for you I am sad."

Gillian looked around at all the stunned faces looking back at her. "Won't someone tell me what is going on?

"Oh ma che're, you do not know?" Lan looked around at the others.

Aidan shook his head. "We were about to tell her."

"Yes, I'm afraid we were taking our time about it."
Gody said.

Gillian looked at Aidan. "Tell me what?" She waited for
a reply. Lan took her hand again, this time for support.

Aidan took a deep breath then released it slowly and
looked into her eyes. "Diaspad is dead." Aidan paused to
let his words sink in.

Gillian became suddenly quiet and shook her head
slowly from side to side. "No. Is this a joke?" Aidan shook
his head. "How?"

"We are not sure. He was found in his chambers."
Aidan answered.

For a moment or two she sat breathless hardly able to
believe her ears. Then her senses and voice came back to
her, while a crushing weight of responsibility seemed in an
instant to be lifted from her soul.

Gillian sat still as a plaster figurine, never to soften. "I
must see his body." She spoke calmly.

"My dear, this time might not be such a good idea. The
way he died…it is not a pleasant sight." Gody tried to
change her mind.

"That makes no difference. I have to see his body. I
have to know for myself that he is dead. Do you understand?" Gillian expressed her emotion to Gody. He smiled
and gave her a nod. Gillian looked at Aidan with a plea for
understanding in her eyes.

Aidan faintly smiled. "If that is what you wish."

Aidan and Gody escorted Gillian upstairs, while Lan
and Ranulf waited down stairs in the parlor. Aidan opened
the chamber door and waited for Gillian to enter first.

Gillian quickly caught the trace of something in the air, the smell of decay. Foul smells were there; a bitter almond scent lingered amidst the smell of decomposing flesh.

The body of Diaspad lay on the floor among the breakfast dishes. Gillian walked slowly over to the body and scanned the area surrounding it.

"We left things just as we found them." Gody said.

Diaspad's pale eyes were unclosed, yet unmistakingly dead. His mouth was frozen in an agonized grimace, his body convulsed position. Was he really dead? At first, Gillian was afraid to get too close; afraid he might reach out and grab her by the ankle. Alternatively, that he might sit up at any moment, a cruel joke.

Aidan lightly placed his hand on her shoulder to remind her he was near if she should have need of him. Gillian reached up and placed her hand on top of his. "Do you smell that odor? The bitter almond aroma, I mean?"

"Yes," Aidan said, "What do you make of it?"

"Cyanide. It is unmistakable. Look how red his skin appears. Cyanide turns the blood and tissues of the body cherry red." Gillian explained.

"Yes, now I recognize the smell. I could not identify it at first, but then I remembered back when I was a boy and how Beechim would mix the cyanide as a rodenticide." Aidan said, remembering.

Suddenly they all looked at each other as if someone had just told them a revealing secret. At that instant they had remembered Beechim's letter.

Gillian took a seat in a chair as she looked at Aidan. "Could it be?"

Aidan nodded. "It all makes sense. If you are sure it is cyanide, I do not think anyone would doubt your opinion. Beechim had access to the cyanide and in his letter did mention an act of salvation that would end all your suffering."

Gillian nodded. "Beechim did bring Diaspad his breakfast tray."

"And by the looks of it, it is apparent that was his last meal." Gody said, looking at the strewn food and plates on the floor.

Gillian took another look at Diaspad's tormented body. The ghastly monster that had been for so long a phantom to drive her mad, that kept her under a cloud of doom was no longer. Darkness had been one of her names but not the one she answered to, not any longer.

"Have you seen all that you need to see?" Aidan asked Gillian. She nodded. "Come, let's go down to the parlor."

"You two go ahead. I will call for the guards to take Diaspad's body to the cellar until Mr. Tristamm can collect him." Gody said.

Aidan and Gillian entered the parlor where Lan and Ranulf awaited the news of the cause of death. Gillian was quite, still somewhat in shock. Lan poured Gillian a brandy and handed it to her. "I realize it is early che're but you look as if you could use this." Gillian offered him a smile and took the brandy from his hand.

"Well what is the verdict?" Ranulf asked.

"Gillian says the cause of death is cyanide poisoning." Aidan said.

"Cyanide? As in rodent kill?" Ranulf asked.

"Yes." Aidan said.

"How and who?" Ranulf asked.

Aidan looked at Gillian, and she at him. "We suspect Beechim." Aidan said.

"Beechim? That poor old sick man? He's dead." Ranulf scoffed.

Aidan nodded. "Do you remember Annie having said that Beechim approached her and took in the breakfast tray himself? And think about what was in Beechim's letter."

Ranulf nodded and sat down. "Who would have thought that old man would be capable."

"He blamed Diaspad for the death of his daughter and grandchild, as I do." Lan said. "Do you not blame him as well Ranulf? What of your lady love, of your Jullian? Could you not kill him for that?" Ranulf looked at him, surprised that he knew of his relationship with Jullian Knott. Lan smiled. "Yes, we all knew of your love for her."

"The truth can do no harm now." Ranulf said admittingly. "And yes, I see your point. I too could have killed him. What a clever thing to do. Cyanide, rodent kill for a rat, how befitting. Ironic, don't you think?" Ranulf paused in silence. "Why such a horrible expression and distortion?" Ranulf wondered.

Gillian raised her head to speak. "After ingestion a person can breathe but oxygen is not absorbed. Asphyxiation is slow and the victim strangles to death because the cyanide blocks air, resulting in convulsions and death."

"Painful death is it?" Ranulf asked.

"I imagine it is not pleasant." Gillian answered.

"Again, how befitting." Ranulf replied. "I'm sorry Gillian, I don't mean to sound cold. If you tell me I am insulting your husband's memory then I will keep quiet."

"I understand your anger Ranulf. I imagine most see Diaspad's death as just punishment. And maybe it was. Maybe that is why God chose such a horrible death for him." Gillian said. She was quiet as she walked over to Lan and placed a gentle hand on his arm. "It is you I am concerned about."

"Me, ma che're?" Lan looked surprised. "You were aware of my feelings for him."

"Yes, I know you hated him, but now there will never be a chance for forgiveness or reconciliation. You will never have the chance to know your father, if for any reason in the future you might have wanted." Gillian smiled.

Lan took her hand and kissed it. "No ma ami, all the chances for those things had long past. He would have never changed enough to make me want to know him, he had no heart. You on the other hand, have more heart than anyone I have known in quite some time. I thank you for thinking of me, but your worries would just be a waste." He flashed his pearly whites.

Gody entered the parlor and walked directly over to Gillian and took her hand. "All is taken care of. I sent word to Tristamm who should arrive soon. I don't want you to worry about anything." He said patting her hand. "You are still among family and we will help you get through all of this."

Gillian smiled. "Thank you milord." Gillian felt an inexpressible relief, a soothing conviction and security. "I wish the funeral to be held as soon as possible."

"Yes, I think that to be wise." Gody smiled.

CHAPTER 29

A day thick with gray mist, hanging stillness and the long regular breathing of the fog horn far out away at the point, can bring such intensity, such an awareness of everything. Sweet in that silence is the awareness, from the passing of a bird in the mist to the measured strike of ones own heart.

The curtains were drawn in the library where Gillian sat alone after Diaspad and Beechim's funeral. It being an overcast day the room was quite dark, which suited her. She was full of remorse and guilt that the darkness seemed appropriate. Gillian sat in the winged chair and closed her eyes, thinking of Aidan. And then something happened. It was as if a curtain had been swept aside, and there came to her a feeling of renewal, of freedom, of resurrection. As one rises from the grave, so did her soul rise. She came into a burst of light that electrified her after the long darkness that had held her. She would not close her eyes to the brightness, for she knew with whom her heart belonged.

Aidan entered the library without a word and took a seat next to Gillian. He was quiet for a moment then spoke in a soft voice. "Gillian, is there anything I can do for you?"

Gillian raised her head and gave him a faint smile. "You can tell me why it is that I can not cry. I have been up here for hours and still I cannot grieve. You must think me heartless."

Aidan softly chuckled. "Is that why you have hid yourself in this dark room all day?"

"I feel so ashamed Aidan. I can not show my face." Gillian turned her face away from him.

Aidan reached over and with his hand turned her eyes back to meet his gaze. "Gillian, I do not think you heartless. You are anything but. Diaspad caused you much pain for far too long, it is no wonder you do not grieve for the death of your tormentor." He smiled into her eyes. "No one will condemn you for not shedding tears."

Gillian lowered her head. "I feel such a feeling of relief from his death. As if my spirit is weightless."

"And so you should." Aidan said. Gillian lifted her head and looked into his eyes. "Let your spirit soar, if that is what it wants to do. Don't worry, I will not let you go too far." He smiled. Gillian returned the smile, relieved he understood. "Come, you must be famished. Everyone is already down stairs."

"I do not have much of an appetite." Gillian said.

"You must try to eat something. Keep up your strength." Aidan said. Gillian nodded and allowed Aidan to escort her downstairs to dinner.

Gillian and Aidan entered the dining room where the others had already began to dine. "Gillian, my dear, please have a bite to eat, you look a bit peaked." Gody said.

Gillian took her seat after greeting Lan and Ranulf. Quietly she placed her napkin in her lap then took a sip of her water without raising her eyes to meet anyone.

"How are you ma che're, you do look a bit pale." Lan asked with a gentle pat to her hand.

Gillian looked at him and smiled. "I am fine, thank you. I believe I am mentally fatigued. I think I will retire early tonight."

"That is probably a good idea. You can start fresh in the morning." Gody suggested.

"A new life, hey Gillian. A fresh beginning without Diaspad." Ranulf replied.

"Ranulf! It is ill to speak of the dead without respect." Gody scolded.

"Sorry uncle, just stating fact." Ranulf said. "Forgive me Gillian?" Ranulf looked at her with puppy dog eyes.

Gillian smiled and let out a little giggle. "Of course Ranulf."

"So uncle, how long does Gillian have to wait before she can marry again?" Ranulf asked before taking a sip of wine.

Gody gave him a look of surprise. "Getting ahead of yourself aren't you son? The man has not been in the grave a whole day."

Aidan leaned toward Ranulf. "Why not give the lady time to heal before you start hounding her."

"If you all will excuse me, I need some fresh air." Gillian said, patting her mouth with her napkin. Stern looks were cast in Ranulf's direction.

Gillian stood from her chair. "Please, be seated." She said to all the men rising to their feet. She headed for the door as Ranulf grabbed her arm gently to pull her to his side. "Did I give you offence Gillian?" He asked in the same puppy dog manner.

Gillian smiled and bent forward to kiss him on the forehead. "No Ranulf, you would never do such a thing."

"Shall I go with you?" Ranulf asked.

Gillian patted him on the shoulder. "Finish your dinner, I will be fine."

Aidan wanted to go with her but he could feel she was in need of some space.

Gillian retired up to her chambers to undress and slip into anything comforting but the black morning dress that would now become her uniform. She opened the doors that led out onto her private balcony; the breeze was in a hurry to flood the room.

The wind was somehow fresher now, cool and crisp with a sense of renewal. The night could now seem friendly, no more cowering from shadows. A knock came at the door, Gillian expected Aggie with her tea.

"Come in." She called out from the balcony.

Aidan entered and looked around the room for Gillian. His eyes stopped on an exquisite silhouette standing on the balcony in the darkness. Aidan stood silent, he could tell by the passion rising inside him that he should not be there.

"Gillian." He said softly.

Gillian turned around suddenly. She smiled then walked toward him, forgetting the sheerness of her gown. She crossed the room careless of the chilly air that cut around her bare shoulders as keen as a knife. "Aidan. I was expecting Aggie. I asked her to make me one of her teas to help me sleep."

Aidan lowered his eyes, trying not to notice he could almost see right through Gillian's gown. "Then I am disturbing you." He said almost apologetically.

"No. Not at all." Gillian suddenly realized her manner of dress from the way Aidan refused to look directly at her. Without making any mention of it, she gathered her robe up from the chair and slipped it on.

"I saw that your light was still on, I just wanted to make sure you were alright." Aidan said, now returning his eyes to her.

Gillian smiled. She stepped closer and brushed his cheek with her hand. "You are so sweet to think of me. I am fine, just could not sleep. My soul seems restless."

"Restless?" Aidan asked.

"Yes, a strange feeling. I feel like I don't know what to do with myself. What do I do? Where is it that I fit in?" Gillian walked back over to the balcony doors and leaned up against the casement looking out.

Aidan followed her, watching her. "What is it you want to do?"

"I don't know. Now that I have my freedom, should I leave? Should I start a life anew?" Gillian looked at Aidan.

"You must do what you must, but I for one would not want to see you go." Aidan stepped closer. "You are free here at Aberdour as much as anyplace else. In addition, as far as your place, you are a member of the royal family. You always have a place here at court." Aidan took her hand and pulled it close to his heart. "Gillian take what ever time you need to be alone with yourself, discover the person inside. Learn what it is like to live without fear. Spring is a time for rebirth, so it should be with you as well." He pulled her hand up to his lips and gently kissed it.

Aggie entered with Gillian's tea. "Oh thir ya ar dear. Sire, canna git-ja anythin?"

"Thank you Aggie, no. Here, let me help you with that." Aidan took the tray from Aggie and sat it down on a nearby table.

"Thank you Aggie." Gillian said, closing the balcony doors behind her.

"Now, ya drink this and git inta bed, it will hep ya rest." Aggie smiled and headed for the door. "Mind that ya donna stay too loong sire, tha lass neds-er rest."

"Yes mame." Aidan smiled and gave her a bow of his head.

"Stay, please, while I drink my tea?" Gillian asked.

"If you wish." Aidan said.

"Come, sit with me by the fire." Gillian took his hand and led him over to the fireplace where they both sat on the floor. She took a sip of her tea and looked at Aidan. "Why are you so quiet?"

He smiled. "It is not always easy to just sit and look into your eyes. Especially when we are alone, in this room, in front of this fire and when you are wearing so little."

"I will take that as a compliment." Gillian grinned.

"You should. Now, I see that you are almost finished with your tea, so I will bid you a good night." Aidan took her hand and kissed it, forcing himself to part her company.

CHAPTER 30

▼

Princess Eleanor arrived late in the day with four knights of ripe judgment accompanying her. King Gody, prince Aidan, Gillian and Ranulf stood in the front bailey or courtyard awaiting the royal carriage to come to a halt.

The carriage came to a stop and after what seemed like a long time the princess materialized. Gody was first to take her hand and welcome her to Aberdour. Her blonde hair was coiled very closely about her small erect head. Her blue eyes might have belonged to an impish sprite in any fairy tale. She wore a dress of simple blue velvet against fair skin. She was not beautiful according to ordinary standards, but there was a charm about her, an alluring quality. She moved with natural grace and it was obvious the lady was well bred.

Gillian felt very plain in her black mourning frock as she was introduced to the princess. Nevertheless, Gillian offered her a smile and curtsied with the utmost respect.

King Gody and the princess entered the castle first, the rest followed. The servants scurried to unload the luggage from the weighted carriage. Never in all Gillian's life had she seen so many bags for such a small woman.

Gody escorted the princess into the parlor, where she preceded to remove her cloak and gloves and hand them to a maid. "Well Ranulf, I must say, you have not changed much. A bit taller, but still the same smile." The princess laughed.

"Oh, but you have changed Ellie! You filled out in all the right places." Ranulf let out a big laugh.

"And Aidan, dear sweet Aidan, my...to borrow Ranulf's words...my how you filled out." The princess beamed a smile at him. "What nice broad shoulders you have." She took a seat still smiling at Aidan.

"It is nice to see you again Ellie." Aidan politely said.

"Did you have a pleasant journey your highness?" Gillian purposely meant to break the princesses gaze on Aidan with her question.

She turned to look at Gillian as if she had forgotten Gillian was in the room. "It was as well as could be expected. You must forgive me; I am just awful with names. Now what was your name again dear?"

"Lady Darnaway." Aidan immediately spoke up.

The princess held her head high. "Yes, Darnaway." She said, as if it made little importance. "I expected to see Lan here." She turned her inquiry toward Gody.

"Lan would have been here to greet you as well, but he had to go into town. You will see him at dinner." Gody smiled. "Would you like to retire to your chambers to re-fresh yourself before dinner?"

"Yes, I would your highness. It was a long journey." She smiled graciously.

"Come with me, Aggie can show you to your chambers." Gody said.

Ranulf was quick to grab the princess's hand. "Until later." He pressed his lips to her hand. She smiled, and then followed Gody out of the parlor.

"I see you are not wasting any time." Aidan said, quietly.

"What is wrong with you? You hardly spoke a word to her." Ranulf scolded. "How rude, cousin."

"Rude? How would you feel if you were looked at as a prized cow?" Aidan threw his hand up. "Never mind, don't answer that."

"He's right Ranulf." Gillian spoke up. "I thought at any moment she was going to part his lips and check his teeth." Gillian said with earnest, and then realized she protested too much.

The two men looked at her and smiled. "Gillian," Ranulf put his hands on his hips, "if I didn't know any better I would think you were jealous." He put on a big grin.

"Jealous?!" She scanned both of their faces. "I was merely commenting on the ladies boldness."

Aidan was flattered at her out burst. Ranulf walked over to Aidan and put his arm around his shoulder. "You know cousin," he said to Aidan while grinning at Gillian, "I think our lovely lady Darnaway here has gotten use to being the only lady of the house and now another woman is stepping on her toes."

Gillian huffed at Ranulf. "I welcome the presence of another woman in this castle."

"Ranulf, stop teasing Gillian." Aidan said with a smile.

"Well, if you two will excuse me, I am going to dress for dinner." Gillian tried to sound annoyed, but the controlled smile on her face gave her away.

Gillian entered the parlor dressed in black, a different dress, but black all the same. The men were in a discussion about land and the growth of the populace while waiting for the princess.

"Gillian, you look lovely as ever." Gody commented.

"Thank you sire." Gillian smiled with a bow of her head. "I see the princess has not joined us."

"She is royalty, I am sure she will be fashionably late." Ranulf smirked.

"One of the many quirks of the blue bloods." Lan commented. "No offence to present company."

"So, just how long are we suppose to wait on her highness?" Aidan asked with an annoyed tone.

"I am sure she will be down soon." Gody said.

With having said that, the princess emerged in a sapphire blue gown, which her ample snow-white bosom swelled forth like snowcapped mountains. Ranulf sprang forward like a jackrabbit toward the princess.

"Ellie, you look exquisite." Ranulf took her gloved hand and kissed it.

Aidan and Gillian tried to hold back their laughter. Lan stepped forward and waited his turn.

"Lan!" Ellie smiled. "What a handsome lad you turned out to be."

"Enchan`te." Lan leaned down and placed a slow kiss on Ellie's glove. By the look on her face the heat from his lips must have penetrated right through the glove.

Aidan constantly remained at a distance from the princess, it was evident he wanted no part of the proposed union. Gody gave Aidan a stern look. He knew exactly what his father meant. Aidan calmly walked over to the princess and offered his arm. "Shall we go in to dinner."?

Lan took Gillian's hand, smiling and placed it on his arm. "Please allow me to escort you Madame."

Everyone gathered in the dinning room and began to be seated.

"I don't know how we are placed, but I believe I will sit between Aidan and Ranulf." The princess said.

Ranulf was quick to help her with her chair and happily took a seat next to her. "I was wondering if the stars were on my side tonight." He said to Ellie.

Ellie leaned over and spoke in a low voice. "They're not."

Dinner had begun. Gillian was rather quiet allowing the princess to monopolize the conversation. And so she did for the remainder of dinner. Gillian ate her dinner, listening and politely smiling when it warranted.

Lan noticed Gillian's silence and leaned over to whisper to her. "Are you alright che're?"

"Yes, fine." Gillian said in a soft voice but somehow caught Ellie's attention.

Ellie looked directly at Gillian and must have thought her silence was a sign of meekness. "My dear, do you often favor black?" She didn't give Gillian a chance to answer. "Some women can wear black well, but I find it is often a very drab color, reminds me of death." She giggled.

Aidan quickly spoke. "The lady Darnaway *is* in mourning."

For the first time in what seemed like hours, Ellie was silent. "Oh, well…you must forgive me. I did not know."

Gillian gave her a faint smile with a nod of her head. Gody explained. "I am sorry Eleanor, we should have told you. We kept our silence as so to move on with our lives. We have had some tragedies at Aberdour one being the death of Gillian's husband. Forgive me for not making this known earlier."

Eleanor looked flustered. "If I had known, I surely…"

"Please, don't worry yourself, it is quite alright." Gillian assured her.

"We are all still recovering from some terrible tragedies." Gody said. "Please forgive our somberness."

"Only if the Lady Darnaway will forgive my outburst." Ellie looked at Gillian and waited for her answer.

Gillian looked her straight in the eye. "Yes, of course, your highness." Gillian gave her a slight bow of her head.

"Now that is out of the way, do you have any children Lady Darnaway?" Ellie asked then took a sip of water.

Gillian looked at her, surprised by Ellie's sudden interest in her. "No I do not." She smiled.

"Well, you are still young and pretty, maybe the next time." She said, without even looking at Gillian and taking a bite of food. "Lord Darnaway, did he have any children?" At the mention of that name everyone sat in silent apprehension, as if it alone might bring horror and mayhem into the room. Ellie looked up from her plate when no answer came. "Did I say something wrong?"

Gillian was first to speak up. "No. No children." Gillian gave Lan a little pat on his leg under the table.

Ellie wiped her mouth with her napkin. "Well, I don't think I could possibly eat another bite."

"Why don't we retire to the parlor?" Gody suggested. "And you can tell me what your father has been up to Eleanor."

Aidan politely escorted Ellie into the parlor as the others followed. Lan stoked the fire as Ranulf poured some sherry in the glasses. Gillian played hostess and helped serve.

Gody listened attentively while Ellie rattled on about her father and her life in her kingdom. Lan quietly pulled Gillian out onto the veranda. No one noticed but Aidan, who kept an inconspicuous eye on Gillian.

"Is the night air too cool for you che're?" Lan asked.

"No, I'm fine, but why did we sneak away. Didn't you find the princess's story intriguing?" Gillian giggled.

Lan smiled. "Hardly. I just wanted to know why you did not mention I was Diaspad's son. I have nothing to hide."

Gillian took a sip of her sherry. "I know. But I don't trust her Lan. We know very little about her. Why should she know all the details? I did not want to give her anything to make her look down on you. You know as well as I, Diaspad's reputation. There are those who think the apple doesn't fall far from the tree you know."

Lan smiled. "My sweet che're, you are kind to care so. Careful, I may get the impression you are sweet on me." He teased.

CHAPTER 31

▼

A week had passed with the company of Princess Eleanor still present at Aberdour. Gillian chose to stay as far from the princess as possible. The known fact that the princess had her sights set on Aidan was just too painful.

Gillian was out in the far end of the flower garden when Aidan joined her. The wind was filling the pine trees and the grove was alive with robins. Plump little fellows strutting along the path.

"I am sorry that we have not had much time together lately." Aidan said softly.

Gillian continued cutting flowers to arrange in a vase. She gathered them and gently placed them in a basket. "And where is the princess?"

"She went into town for some shopping." Aidan said.

"She did not want you to accompany her?" Gillian still did not look at him.

"Yes, but I had hoped for a chance to spend some time with you." Gillian watched him touch one of the blooms with a gentle finger, tracing its soft delicate velvet curves. She was aware of a strong jealousy, envious of the flower. He raised his eyes to meet hers, observing her mouth. "Amongst these flowers I can't help but to be reminded of your lips. So soft, and red."

Gillian held her breath. She marveled at his ability to move her with his words. She wanted very much to respond to him, but knew she must not. "I need to put these into some water."

"Here, let me help you." Aidan took the basket of flowers from her hand and carried them into the castle for her.

They entered the kitchen where Aggie was snapping peas for dinner. "Let me git-ya a vase for tha flowers."

Gillian took the vase, filled it with water and began to arrange the flowers as Aidan watched. "I think I will put these in the parlor." She said to Aidan with a smile. "Come, help me find a spot for them." The two entered the parlor as Gillian's eyes searched the room for the right place. "How about the piano?" Gillian placed the flowers on the piano and took a step back.

Aidan grabbed her arm and swung her around. "Let me take you to dinner this evening. I want to have you entirely to myself." He pulled her close and wrapped his arms around her waist.

Gillian closed her eyes and allowed herself the pleasure of feeling his strong arms wrapped around her. Slowly she pushed him back. "You know that is not possible. You forget I am still in morning. What would people think?"

"To hell with everyone, Gillian!" Aidan said with ferocity.

"Shh!" Gillian placed her finger to his lips. "And besides, I doubt if the princess would let you out of her sight for that amount of time." She smirked with some jealousy. Aidan grabbed her and pulled her into his body, she didn't struggle. His senses were flooded with the sight of her. He pressed his mouth on hers with a ravenous hunger. Her body molded into his as his hand slid down her back pulling her bottom into his groin.

Suddenly they parted when a voice called out from the entrance hall. "Aidan! Aidan, you must come and see what I bought." Ellie yelled out. She entered the parlor where Aidan and Gillian stood. "Oh, there you are." She said throwing her cloak over a chair. "I picked up some lovely things."

"If you will excuse me, I'm going to see if Aggie needs any help." Gillian gave the two a bow of her head.

"Are you short on servants?" Ellie laughed.

"No, Gillian likes to help out in the kitchen." Aidan said.

"How quaint." Ellie replied.

Ranulf entered with a bounce in his step. "Hello all, it is a beautiful day why aren't you out enjoying it?"

"I myself, I have just returned from doing some shopping." Ellie said.

Ranulf strolled over to the vase of flowers and took in their fragrance. "I see Gillian has begun to fill the castle with flowers."

Ellie forced a smile. "And what doesn't our lady Darnaway do?"

"Gillian has many talents. Is that not right, cousin?"" Ranulf smiled singing her praises.

"Do I detect a tone of fondness in your voice?" Ellie asked.

"We are all fond of Gillian." Aidan said, looking at Ranulf.

Ellie watched the two as they starred at each other for a moment. "Yes, well I'm off to unpack the new things I bought." The two men both gave her a bow of their heads.

Ranulf waited until Ellie was out of sight. "You know cousin, you could be a bit warmer."

"If you were in my position you would feel the same." Aidan expressed.

"Your position? Oh yes, you have it so bad." Ranulf mocked. "Look around you cousin. You are a future king with riches abound. You can have and do anything you want."

"Anything but marry for love." Aidan said, and then left the room.

Gillian made her way back outside to enjoy what was left of the glorious day. She walked down by the stables to where Lan was attending to some horses. "Hello!" He called out. Gillian smiled and gave him a wave. He quickly finished and joined her.

"Am I intruding?" Gillian asked.

"Never." He said smiling as he placed his hand in the small on her back and led her over to a bench. "Sit and talk with me." He sunk his tall frame into the bench next to her with a very masculine grace that she couldn't help but to admire. "Walking alone today are you?"

Gillian smiled. "I prefer my own company from time to time. I don't need an escort, I'm a big girl now, or haven't you noticed."

"Oh yes, che're, I cannot help but to notice." He grinned. Gillian looked at him trying to determine the weight of his remark. "I must warn you, today I have an uncontrollable urge to flirt with a beautiful woman, a compulsion you are undoubtedly aware. And you che're, are the most beautiful woman I have seen today." Gillian blushed with a smile.

Gillian laughed. "Being that you have been at the stable all day, I will try to take that as a compliment."

"Are you and the princess getting along?"

"I wouldn't call it that. I find her cold." Gillian said.

"Women hate you for your pretty face, you know this, yes?" Gillian looked at him. "You look angelic," he grinned, "you with your veil of auburn hair and sweet face and huge dark eyes." His voice was tender. "I was wrong about you at first. You seemed an innocent child, quiet, shy and so…"

"Say it. Weak? Naivete?" Gillian interrupted.

"No. Just unseasoned. But now I see you like a gentle flower, waiting for the first sign of Spring to bloom." He smiled. "Mother Nature has given you all the knowledge within you, you just have to release it." Gillian looked shocked. "You forget, I've sampled that fire you are so determined to hide." Gillian's mouth gaped open then snapped shut. He glanced at her mouth then returned to her gaze with a look that was anything but subtle. "There is a fire burning within you, lucky is the man that unleashes it."

Gillian was momentarily rendered speechless as she looked at him. "You are too bold."

Lan laughed. "Yes, but I speak the truth che're. And you know it."

Gillian stood and looked at Lan. "It is getting late, I must go and dress for dinner."

Lan took her by the hand and held on to keep her from walking away. Gillian refused to look at him, trying to seem offended. "Look at me."

"No." If I do you will undoubtedly melt my resolve. Gillian hid her smile. Lan smiled and let go of her hand.

CHAPTER 32

▼

"Tell me Ranulf," Ellie said, "tell me about Lady Darnaway."

Ranulf sat his glass on the table in front of him. "What is it you want to know?"

"For a grieving widow, I have scarcely seen her grieve. Was it a good marriage?"

Ellie waited for him to answer.

"Well, you could say they had a religious problem." Ranulf smirked.

"What do you mean, religious problem?"

"He thought he was God, and she strongly disagreed." Ranulf picked up his glass and emptied it into his mouth. "He was a bastard, she is good to be rid of him."

"I understand Lord Darnaway to have been a wealthy and prosperous gentleman." Ellie said with a suspicious smirk.

"Yes, he was a member of the royal family." Ranulf replied.

"Yes, and what a great opportunity for a young woman of simple means." Ellie said looking at Ranulf.

"Are you implying that Gillian married for money?" Ranulf asked with surprise.

"Well Ranulf, she wouldn't be the first woman to realize a good opportunity when she sees one."

"No. Gillian is nothing like that." He protested. "She doesn't care about money or riches. She is nothing like the aristocracy. Gillian does not put on airs, she does not have to. You call her simple? Yes, I guess she is, but in a good way, one that you nor I could ever comprehend."

Ellie smirked. "You indeed are fond of her."

"Yes, I admit I am." Ranulf stood to pour himself another drink.

"Dare I say you are in love with her?" Ellie fished.

Ranulf took a sip and smiled. "Everyone is in love with Gillian."

Gillian entered the parlor. "Did I hear my name?" She beamed a smile at Ranulf.

"I was just singing your praises my dear." Ranulf poured Gillian a glass of wine and handed it to her.

Gillian took the glass and sat down in front of Ellie. "I'm afraid Ranulf is sometimes too lavish with his compliments." She smiled at Ellie.

Ellie forced a smile. "I'm sure you are worthy Lady Darnaway." Ellie turned her attention to Ranulf. "What could be keeping Aidan?" Ranulf shrugged his shoulders. "You must know, Lady Darnaway." Ellie said with a hint of spite.

"No. I'm sure I do not." Gillian said with the same tone.

Gody and Lan entered together with Aidan not far behind. "There all of you are!" Ranulf said. "I think the ladies were afraid they were going to have me all to themselves."

"You should be so lucky, cousin." Aidan laughed. Aidan walked over to Gillian and took her hand. "Gillian," he kissed her hand, "you look beautiful as always." Gillian smiled and gave him a nod. He stepped toward Ellie.

"Princess." He took her hand and kissed it. She waited for a compliment, but none came.

"Tell me your highness, did you enjoy shopping in our town?" Gillian asked, taking Ellie's attention from Aidan.

"Yes, I did. It has grown since my last visit. You will have to come up to my chambers later and see what I bought." Ellie said, with a little too much sweetness.

Gillian smiled. "I would be honored." Everyone was quiet as they watched the two exchange pleasantries.

Gody walked over to Gillian and whispered something in her ear. She immediately got up and followed Gody out the parlor doors. "You wanted to speak with me sire?"

"Gillian dear, I just received a letter about Diaspad's estate. I was discussing it with Aidan and Lan, that is why we were so late coming down."

"The estate?"

"You know as Diaspad's widow the entire estate comes to you." Gody reminded her.

"Yes. I guess I have not given it much thought. The look on your face tells me there is more?" Gillian asked.

Gody nodded. "You are aware of Diaspad's drinking habit. Well it seems that he left a sizable debt. The pub owner wishes to discuss the matter with you immediately. I am sure that this matter can be worked out; I sent word that you would arrive in town tomorrow. Aidan and Lan will accompany you. They will help you get all your affairs in order." Gody patted her on the hand.

"Thank you sire." Gillian said, and then kissed him on the cheek. He offered his hand to escort her back inside.

"Shall we all go in to dinner?" Gody said as they entered and walked through the parlor into the dining room.

CHAPTER 33

▼

After dinner, Ellie requested that Aidan escort her on an evening promenade through the gardens. Aidan agreed to do so with some reluctance. The night was cool and clear with a host of stars twinkling above against a black backdrop of sky.

"Normally I don't care for long walks. It is dreadful, nipped fingers and toes. But I'm sure I will be warm enough with you." Ellie said, snuggling against Aidan's arm. Aidan did not say much, but offered her a smile.

"Would you like to sit in the gazebo?" Aidan asked.

"Yes, that would be nice." Ellie said.

Aidan escorted her down through the masses of flowers to the gazebo. "Do you think you will be warm enough?" Aidan asked out of politeness.

"I am sure I will as long as I stand next to you." She beamed a girlish smile at him. "It is lovely out here, you must bring me here during the day."

"If you wish." Aidan said, with little enthusiasm.

Ellie's eyes glittered. They were bold and fixed on Aidan. She ran her tongue along the crimson of her lips and her smile was a challenge. She was trying very hard to emanate a sort of come-hither sexiness and occasionally brushing up against him as if by accident.

"Do you find me attractive Aidan?" She asked as she ran her finger along the length of his arm.

"You are very pretty Ellie." Aidan said.

"Then why have you not tried to kiss me?" She asked moving closer to press her breast against his arm.

"I would never take such liberties with a woman I barely knew." He said politely.

"But we are old friends. Besides, I give you permission." She pressed her body even closer. Aidan was pushed back against a support beam. He knew if he did not kiss her she would be greatly offended. He lowered his head and gave her a light kiss that was anything but passionate. Ellie opened her eyes. "Come now, I've had more heart-felt kisses from my father." She giggled. "I won't break if you were to put your arms around me. You can kiss me without fear of frightening me."

Aidan felt pressured, but knew he must kiss her with some emotion. He took her in his arms and soon felt the warm heat of his mouth on hers. Her lips parted and she drew the velvet of his tongue deep inside. Aidan's thoughts quickly shifted to Gillian. He pretended it was her in his arms. He suddenly felt her fingers seeking the laces of his pants. She slid her hand down his belly to his taut flesh that quivered and leapt beneath her seeking fingers. He pulled his lips from hers. She now closed her hand around him, making it hard for him to push her away. Her fingers barely encircled his veined flesh to glide from warm satin tip down the length of him. Aidan held his breath trying to keep his control from slipping.

"Ellie," he managed a breath to speak her name. "You shouldn't."

"Why, does it not feel good?" She whispered. "I have many talents I'm sure you would find pleasurable."

"Yes, I'm sure." He said breathless. "Please Ellie." He found strength and forced her back. "I can't…you must not."

"I want to pleasure you." She said, going for his pants again.

"No, Ellie please." He took her by the shoulders.

"I thought you found me attractive?" She said, confused.

"I do. But that does not mean I wish to take you into my bed." Aidan said, fastening his pants.

"Does my touch not please you?" Ellie looked bewildered.

"Yes it does. That is not it." Aidan did not want to tell her the reason was Gillian. He could share his heart with no other woman. "I have too much respect for you to treat you as a passing whore. These things require a certain amount of time. This is too soon."

"Time you say, I understand. You indeed are a gentleman." She giggled. "Alright, I will move slower, if you prefer."

When Aidan and Ellie returned, everyone was still in the parlor. Gillian was anxious for Aidan's return from his walk with Ellie. Aidan entered, his clothes still a little disheveled. Gillian noticed this immediately as well as the faint blush of lipstick on his lips. Ellie still clung to Aidan's arm making sure Gillian took note.

"Have a nice stroll did you?" Ranulf asked.

Ellie giggled like a schoolgirl. "Very nice."

Aidan looked at Gillian who had not taken her eyes off the two of them since they entered the parlor. Aidan quickly turned his eyes away from Gillian.

Lan walked over to Aidan and pulled him away from Ellie. Discreetly, he handed Aidan his handkerchief and pointed to the lipstick remaining on Aidan's mouth. Aidan had not realized, and knew Gillian must have noticed the lipstick. Aidan turned his back to everyone and wiped his mouth, slipping the handkerchief into his pocket.

Lan placed his arm around Aidan to whisper in his ear. "She has put her mark upon you mon ami." He smiled. Aidan knew he had some explaining to do.

Ellie began to flit around the room. "The gardens are lovely. Aidan insist upon showing them to me in the day time." Gillian remained quiet. Aidan watched her face for changes. "I do not normally take walks in the sun. It is so bad for my delicate skin I must be very careful." Ellie looked at Gillian. "You are lucky, you don't have that problem Lady Darnaway. It must be a comfort not to have to worry about the sun on ones skin."

Gillian smiled and gritted her teeth. "There are more important things to worry about. I think women spend too much time worrying about their looks."

Ellie laughed. "A lady can never be too concerned about her looks, her presence. Just as one can never be too rich."

"I believe knowledge is more attractive on a person and more so for a woman. Beauty fades." Gillian said.

"The only things a woman needs to learn are things that would please a husband." Ellie said.

"Nonsense!" Gillian replied.

"I agree. Gillian's learning should be an example to us all." Gody spoke up.

"You are right father," Aidan said, "without Gillian's knowledge, I doubt if the past events would have had as many answers or even been solved." Ellie looked at Aidan as if he should have agreed with her views.

"Yes well, how fortunate you all were to have Lady Darnaway here." Ellie replied in an undertone of peevish displeasure, looking at Gillian.

Silence overcame the room. Gillian stood to excuse herself. "Well if all of you will excuse me, I am going to retire early so that I will be well rested for our trip into Aberconway tomorrow."

Aidan was first to kiss her hand and bid her goodnight. Ellie watched, studying their faces.

"I think I will turn in as well." Lan said. "Come ma che're, I will walk you to your chamber on my way out." Lan escorted Gillian to her chamber door and opened it for her as he stood in the threshold. "You get a good nights sleep ma che're. And don't worry about tomorrow, we will take good care of you." Gillian smiled, kissed him on the cheek and said goodnight.

CHAPTER 34

▼

The Spring air was cool as the three began their journey for Aberconway. The interior of the carriage was dark as they settled into the seats. The morning light casts dim shadows across the carriage as they made their way down the road. Gillian sat across from Aidan, she could feel his steady gaze upon her as she stared at the passing scenery.

"You are very quiet Gillian." Aidan said, taking her attention away from the landscape.

She looked at him. "Sorry, I do not mean to be." She took a deep breath. "I must be honest and say that I am not looking forward to returning to Cardoness, to that house."

"But it all belongs to you now." Lan said.

"It means nothing to me. A horrible reminder of the past." She said.

"You must remember, it is all in the past. Nothing can harm you now. I would never allow it." Aidan said. Gillian offered him a smile.

"Aidan is right, mon ami. We are with you." Lan said, patting her hand.

"I don't want you to worry about any debts Gillian. I will take care of them all." Aidan assured her.

"No Aidan. I cannot allow you to do such a thing. They were Diaspad's debts. He treated you horribly, you owe him nothing." Gillian protested.

"It is not Diaspad I worry about. His debts are now yours. It would be no great sacrifice. Allow me to pay off the debt, then you can sell what was left to you." Aidan pleaded.

"Yes ma che're. At least you would have some money for yourself. You deserve that much." Lan said.

"No. I will take care of it myself. I am tired of always being indebted to someone. Do you understand?"

Aidan and Lan nodded. "Yes, I understand ma che're."

"But I can always use your friendship." Gillian smiled.

"That you will always have." Aidan said. "Have you given any further thought as to what you would like to do with the estate and the contents of the house?"

"I only want what was mine from inside the house. The rest I have no want for it, I guess I will sell it." Gillian said.

"I thought you might. I took the liberty of contacting a solicitor in town that can handle those matters for you." Aidan said.

"Oh thank you. Yes that would be of help. He would negotiate a fair price?" Gillian asked.

"Yes. I know him well; he is a trustworthy man. His name is Mr. Duncan and will assist you with all your legal matters." Aidan explained.

Gillian smiled. "You are a good friend Aidan to think ahead for me."

"It is my pleasure." Aidan bowed his head to her.

The carriage came to a halt just outside a wooden gate that was the entrance to Cardoness, the Darnaway estate.

The house could be seen from the front gate, sitting back
from the road. Lan exited the carriage first, then Aidan.
Gillian took pause and stared out the window with great
hesitation. Aidan held out his hand through the open door
of the carriage. "It will be alright, we are with you. Come,
take my hand." Gillian slowly slipped her hand in his. She
took a deep breath when her foot touched earth. She
looked up at Aidan for assurance. He smiled and gave her
a nod.

"I will go in first ma che're." Lan offered. Lan walked
up the path and up the stairs to the front doors. He slowly
opened the doors and entered where a housekeeper
greeted him. The royal family had hired someone to take
care of the house in the Darnaway's absence.

Gillian stood at the bottom of the steps looking up at
the house. "It's funny, I remember it bigger, more menacing." Gillian began up the steps toward Lan where he
waited in the doorway. She walked through and stood just
inside the front doors. A chill came over her as she walked
further into the house. "Nothing has changed." She said as
she peeked through each room.

"Except now it all belongs to you." Lan said.

"Only because Diaspad is dead. I feel no attachment
what so ever. I cannot recall one pleasant memory to have
any fondness for this house. It is just a house, full of
things, nothing more." Gillian said looking around. She
began to realize her fear and apprehension was leaving her.
"There is nothing here. I thought I would feel a horrible
presence of some sorts. But there is no life here, this house
is dead, just as Diaspad is dead."

"Are you sure there is nothing here that you want?" Lan
asked.

"No, nothing. Nothing but my father's medical books." Gillian said.

Aidan started up the staircase. "Which room was yours? We will pack your books for you."

"My old room is not in the house." Gillian said.

Aidan started back down. "I don't understand. Not in the house?"

"Come, I will show you. I have an old trunk we can put the books in." Gillian led them through the house and out of the kitchen door. Down some steps and around to the side of the house.

"But this is a storage shed." Lan said, after seeing where she was leading them.

Gillian led them to the door, which she pushed open with some force. Aidan entered first, then Gillian and Lan. Aidan and Lan were surprised to see the conditions that Gillian was forced to live in.

Aidan was quiet for a moment before he could speak. The room was heartbreakingly impoverished with its simple furnishings and dirt floor. "Gillian, this is where you lived?" Gillian nodded. Aidan became quiet again.

"Che're, there are huge cracks in the walls and ceiling. Tell me the time you have spent away has warred upon this place?" Gillian shook her head no. She then began to pack her books in the empty trunk. "How did you manage? Surely during winter months you slept in the house?"

Gillian smiled. "If it got too cold, I slept in the barn. You would be surprised at the generosity of cows. They are not discriminating about bedfellows." Gillian noticed Aidan was very quiet and in a stupor. "Aidan? Are you alright?"

Aidan came too at the mention of his name. "I'm sorry, what did you say?"

"I asked if you were alright?"

Aidan smiled. "Yes, I am fine." He did not want Gillian to know just how his heart was breaking for her. He found the conditions she lived in appalling. Just one more reason for him to hate and curse Diaspad. Curse him as he lay rotting in his grave.

"Well that is everything." Gillian said as she shut the trunk.

"What of your clothes?" Lan asked. "Do you not want them?"

"I have none. This is everything I own here in this trunk. Please, can we go now?"

"Yes. Of course." Aidan said. "I feel that we should stop to see the solicitor to make sure all paper work is in order."

Gillian was silent on the way to Mr. Duncan's office. She had taken one last look at the house from the carriage window and felt no loss. That life had seemed so many years in the past. Things were so different now, she was different.

Mr. Duncan who welcomed them all into his office met the carriage. He was a stout man with blue eyes, red cheeks and gray thinning hair. He was well dressed, well mannered and seemed to waddle from side to side when he walked. "Welcome, welcome! Ah! This must be the lovely Lady Darnaway I have heard so much about." He gleamed a smile at Gillian.

"It is nice to meet you sir. I hear great things about you." Gillian smiled. "I am told you are a fair man."

"I like to think so." He grinned. "Come, please be seated and tell me what I can do for you."

"I have no need for Cardoness estate or the contents of the house. I wish to sell it." Gillian explained.

"Well, if that is what you wish. You are aware Diaspad left some due debts?" Duncan asked.

"Yes sir, I am. And I wish to pay them immediately."

"Are you aware that your husband left sizable debts?" Duncan asked.

"When you say 'sizable' what do you mean exactly?" Gillian asked.

"Maybe you would prefer I discuss this with Prince Aidan." He offered.

"No, Mr. Duncan. I prefer that you discuss it with me!" Gillian became annoyed. "Is it not my debt we are discussing?"

"Yes milady. I did not want to tarnish your memory of your dear departed. Men sometimes participate in activities that wives do not always approve of…"

"Please Mr. Duncan, treat me as if I were one of your male clients. Do not keep me in the dark simply because of my gender." Gillian explained.

Duncan looked at Aidan who gave him a nod to continue. "Well, I have gone over your husbands papers and it seemed not only did he have a debt due to drinking, but he also had a gambling debt."

"That is no surprise to me sir." Gillian said.

"It seems that the pub owner is asking for money immediately for the drinking debt." Duncan explained. "There is a matter of one more thing that I only discovered just this morning." Duncan paused.

"Please Sir, don't keep us in suspense." Gillian urged.

"I'm afraid the gambling debt is much larger than I had anticipated." Again, he paused. "It seems that the pub owner not only holds the drinking debt but the gambling one as well."

"How much larger?" Gillian asked.

"The pub owner is holding the deed to the land as collateral until the debt is paid. It seems that Diaspad gave it to him to hold until he could come up with the money. Apparently, he did not live long enough to pay off that debt and take back the deed."

Gillian looked at Aidan who did not look happy about the news. "Please Sir, what does all this mean?" Gillian asked.

"I'm afraid Milady that the house or its contents can not be sold without the deed. The house rests on the land and the deed rests in another's hands." Duncan explained.

"But how can I pay off the debt if I am not allowed the sell the house and its contents? I assume the sell of the contents will pay the balance?"

"Oh yes, and then some." Duncan said.

"Then I would like the remainder of the monies to go to Lan." Gillian instructed.

"No ma che're. You can not mean what you say." Lan protested.

"Lan, you are the rightful heir. Diaspad took so much from you, it is only fair." Gillian explained.

"But Milady," Duncan spoke abruptly. "That would leave you with very little, if any. In good conscience I cannot advise this. It would leave you impoverished at best."

"Oh but you are wrong dear Sir." Gillian smiled and place one hand on Aidan's and the other on Lan's. "I am wealthy beyond any man's dreams or woman's as the case would warrant."

"If this is what you wish." Duncan said with great dis-approval.

"What can we do then Duncan?" Aidan asked.

"I can try to talk with the pub owner on your behalf and see if we can come to a settlement. Or Milady might except the generosity of her friends to pay off the debt, a loan if you will, until the sell of the Estate."

" No. I would like an itemized statement if you don't mind of everything that I own." Gillian instructed. "And in the meanwhile, I shall pay this pub owner a visit. I'm sure he is a reasonable man."

"Yes, of course. Milady is astute." Duncan said. "But are you sure you would not prefer me to intervene?"

"No. Not at this time, I must learn to fight my own battles." Gillian said. "I have changed my mind. When the matter of all debts are clear, I wish for the house to serve some purpose. The house needs life. Let it be used as a hospital. With the populace growing, I'm sure it will be of use."

"Milady is generous as well as proficient." Duncan smiled. "And what about the livestock?" Duncan asked.

"The horses were sold off some years ago. What remains of the livestock are a few cows and chickens. Do what you will with them, I have no need for them." Gillian said. "There are some sacks of grain, a hundred-weight or so in the barn. I would like that distributed out to the needy."

"As you wish Milady. I will take care of everything and be in touch with you." Duncan said.

"And I, you." Gillian stood. "Thank you Mr. Duncan it was a pleasure to meet you and do business with you."

Gillian offered her hand. Duncan immediately took her hand and kissed it.

"The pleasure was all mine Milady. I will be in touch." Duncan smiled and placed his hands behind his back. "I wish you luck with the pub owner." He yelled out as the three were entering the carriage

CHAPTER 35

▼

Lan entered the pub first and found seats for his friends while inquiring about the owner from a barmaid. Lan returned to Gillian and Aidan. "The girl is going to find the owner a Mr. McNair."

Gillian looked around the cold dank room, seeing for the first time where Diaspad spent most of his time. The place was like him, cold, dark and unfriendly, she imagined that was why he liked it so.

A tall burly man came out from the back. The barmaid pointed to the table where Gillian, Aidan and Lan sat. He approached the table, wiping his hands on a white towel. Gillian noticed the man's big bushy eyebrows rise with surprise when he saw Aidan.

"Your highness, forgive me, the girl did not tell me it was you who waited." The man bowed his head. "You honor me with your presence."

"You are Mr. McNair?" Aidan asked.

"Yes, I am the owner." He said with a confusing look.

"This is the Lady Darnaway." Aidan introduced. "I believe she has some business to discuss with you."

The man's heavily browed eyes popped open. "Diaspad Darnaway?" Gillian nodded. "I am honored to meet you Lady Darnaway, I knew your husband well."

"Yes, I'm sure you did. That is why I am here. Is there a place where we can discuss matters in private?" Gillian asked.

"Oh yes, Milady. Please come into my private quarters." McNair led the three into the back of the pub where him and his son lived. "My home is meek but comfortable. Please sit." He motioned with his hand to a dining room table and chairs. Lan pulled the chair out for Gillian as the rest seated themselves. The home was quaint but clean and cozy.

Gillian glanced around the room noticing a few personal items sitting about the room. Gillian smiled. "You have a nice home Mr. McNair."

"Milady is very kind. Please, tell me what I can do for you." He smiled.

"My husband has been recently deceased."

"I was not aware. I am sorry for your loss." McNair said.

"Thank you. I am aware of my husband's debts. Sizable debts that he owed you. These debts are now mine and I wish to pay them off." Gillian explained.

"Yes Milady I understand." McNair gave his full attention.

"But you see I have a problem." Gillian paused.

"Yes milady?"

"You hold the deed to the land. And without the deed I cannot sell off any of the Estate." Gillian waited for a reply.

"Yes, I see your predicament. However, I am sure Milady can understand that the deed is the only item proving the debt. I gave your husband ample time to come up with the money. It was only because of our friendship that I allowed the debt to go unpaid for as long as I did. Maybe if you could come up with half the money, I would be willing to wait a bit longer for the rest."

Gillian paused and took a deep breath. Aidan remained quiet and let her conduct the business as she wished. "Mr. McNair, let me be clear. Diaspad left me no money only the Estate. The fact that I have clothes on my back and food in my belly is sheerly by the grace and goodness of his highness and his family. If you do not release the deed to me, then I am afraid we are at a standstill. Neither of us wins. You have a deed to land you do not own and I have land and no deed." Gillian made her point and was quiet. From the next room a muffled moan was heard.

"Maybe we can do business. My son has an injured leg and the new doctor has not arrived, I am told it will be a few days. I fear my son will loose his leg without the proper attention. Your highness, if you would see it your way to call upon your personal physician then the deed is yours." McNair said.

"I am sorry to say, we use the same doctor as the village. Only in dire circumstances do we ever send for a doctor outside the village. But I'm afraid even if I were to do that, it still would take some time." Aidan explained, then suddenly smiled "Look no further, here is your healer." Aidan placed his hand on Gillian's shoulder.

"Yes, Gillian is an excellent healer." Lan boasted.

McNair looked worried. "No offence, Milady. Your highness, she is but a woman. A noble woman, what does she know of medicine, of healing?"

Aidan placed his hand on McNair's shoulder. "Everything. I assure you Lady Darnaway's skills are quite capable. If I did not believe this with all my heart, I would not have suggested it."

"Very well your highness. I trust your judgment." McNair said with some reluctance. "Come, follow me."

Gillian followed him into the young man's dimly lit room. "Please, I need more light." Another oil lamp was brought in. Gillian could see the young man sleeping in his bed. Gillian placed her hand gently upon his chest. She could feel the slow steady beat of his heart. "What is his name?"

"Will."

Gillian moved the cover that lay over young Will's leg. "How old is he?"

"Eighteen. He is a good worker. I have been at a disadvantage with him laid up like that." McNair explained.

"What caused his wound?" Aidan asked.

"A farming tool. Five days ago. I cleaned the wound the best I could. He has been in a lot of pain. I gave him some valerian to help him sleep." McNair said.

"Well it seems you are a better nurse maid than you thought Mr. McNair." Gillian smiled at him. "The wound looks as if you did a fine job cleaning it." McNair seemed to relax a bit. "Now, I will need a few items, will you get them for me?" He nodded. Gillian gave him a list of things and he left the room.

"Can you save the leg?" Aidan asked Gillian.

"Yes, I believe so. He is young and strong, I think he will be just fine." Gillian said. Gillian pulled up a chair to the young man's bedside, just as McNair returned with all the items Gillian had requested. Gillian began to work quickly covering the open wound with a poultice soaked in a concoction of horsetail and comfrey. Gillian explained while she worked. "The horsetail will prevent the wound from turning bad, while the comfrey will hasten the healing." Then Gillian was silent as she said a little prayer over Will.

McNair was looking worried again. "Are you sure this conjuring will do him no harm?"" He directed his question at Aidan.

"With Lady Darnaway's exemplary skills I assure you, your son is in no danger." Aidan said.

"I am uneasy with her standing over him in that strange trance." McNair did not say quietly.

Gillian turned and looked at him. "Trance? Yes this ritual is ancient, known for thousands of years now. It is called prayer. Surely you do not think your son in danger because I prayed over him. You are familiar with the practice?"

"Forgive me Milady. I did not think it was common in ones that call themselves healers. I am not accustom to seeing women in this role."

"Sir, healing and medicine share the same outcome. When one is absent you rely on the other. It makes no difference if the practitioner is male or female only the results. Now, the patient needs his rest. I suggest everyone leave. I will stay with him tonight." Gillian shooed everyone out with a wave of her hands.

"Gillian are you sure that is a good idea?" Aidan asked.

"I'm sure I will be quite safe. I will return in the morning once I'm sure the boy is healing properly." Gillian smiled.

"I do not feel right leaving you here. Alone I mean." Aidan said.

"She won't be." Lan spoke up. "I will stay with her." He turned and faced Gillian. "And I will hear no argument from you." Lan pointed his finger at Gillian with a smile.

"I would feel more at ease knowing someone is with her tonight." Aidan said. He wanted Gillian to return with him. She would seem so far away, her not being under the same roof as he.

"Go now, I'm sure the Princess is wondering why I have kept you for as long as I have." Gillian said. Aidan turned to leave after saying his good-byes. Gillian could not help but to notice he looked liked a shunned puppy.

Gillian and Lan returned to the young man's bedside and tried to make themselves comfortable. Lan sat looking at Gillian and smiling.

"What?" Gillian asked.

"That remark you made about the Princess. That must have stung ma che're. You have to know he did not want to return to her." Lan smirked.

"I did not mean for it to sound that way. I will apologize tomorrow." Gillian folded her arms across her chest and slumped back resting her head on the wall. She watched young Will as he slept a peaceful sleep and thought about Aidan.

Lan stood and stretched. "I will go and see if Mr. McNair could find us something to eat ma che're." Gillian smiled with a nod.

The young man began to stir and awoke. Gillian sat up in her chair and waited for his eyes to focus better. "Are you an angel?" He asked. "Or have I perhaps ventured in the other direction?" Gillian giggled. "Although you are far too lovely to be a devil."

Gillian offered him a smile. "I am neither milord. My name is Gillian, I have been tending to your leg."

"Have you taken my leg? I no longer feel the pain." Will asked.

"I am glad you feel no pain and no, you still have your leg. I thought it would serve you better to keep it." Gillian lifted the cover to show him. "See." He slowly raised then fell back on his pillow in relief. "Rest now, I am here if you have need of me."

He smiled a sleepy smile. "I can rest with no worries, now that an angel guards my bed." Gillian watched as he drifted off to sleep.

Lan pulled his chair closer to Gillian's. "Gillian, we must speak of the offer you made, of the money."

"My mind is made on that matter, even your charms cannot sway me." Gillian smiled.

Lan took her hand and pulled it to his chest. "Then share it with me."

"Share it?"

"Yes, marry me and we will share it together." Lan grinned.

Gillian was taken by surprise. "Lan, I don't know what to say."

"Say nothing now, just promise me you will consider it?" Lan asked. Gillian nodded.

CHAPTER 36

▼

Gillian and Lan found their way back to the castle by late afternoon. The two entered and found everyone relaxing in the parlor. "Oh good!" Ranulf exclaimed when Gillian and Lan entered. "There you two are. Now Aidan can stop pacing the floor." He said laughing.

"I was simply worried, I knew they were to be back by this morning." He said a little embarrassed.

"Sorry to make you worry. Mr. McNair gave me the deed and we took it over to Mr. Duncan's office so he could get started with all the paperwork." Gillian smiled and took a seat next to Aidan on the sofa. "Nice of you to worry so." She said in a soft voice to Aidan.

"Well good, then all your affairs are underway." Gody said.

Princess Ellie glided into the room. "Ah, lady Darnaway I see you have returned. Aidan has told us that again your little talents came in handy. How nice. That must make you feel needed." Gillian gave her a half smile. "Aidan has done nothing but sing your praises...*all* morning." She said in her typical undertone of displeasure.

"Thank you, the young man is healing fine and should be on his feet in no time." Gillian said looking sternly at Ellie.

"Well, on that note…. I have some horses that I am sure have missed me." Lan walked over to Gillian and took her hand. "It has been a pleasure spending the night with you ma che're." Lan said with a smile as he left the room.

"Hmm. He looked happy." Ranulf said jokingly. Aidan cut his eyes at him, but said nothing. "It is nice to have you back Gillian, you have surely been missed. Without your genteel essence this homestead has been at a loss. No offence Ellie."

Gillian stood to her feet with laughter. "Ranulf you sound as if I have been away for a very long time."

"It seems that way. For some of us more than others." Ranulf looked at Aidan.

Gillian placed a sweet kiss on Ranulf's cheek. "Thank you for noticing my absence. It is nice to be missed. Now, if you all will excuse me, I would like to freshen up and relax with a cup of Aggie's tea."

Aidan watched Gillian's every step out of the room; once she was out of his sight; he turned his attention back to the room noticing Ellie's eyes watching him.

Aidan knocked at Gillian's door with the cup of hot tea she had asked Aggie to bring. He waited for some time and when she did not answer he slowly opened the door and called out her name. He assumed she was in the bath and set the cup of tea on the table next to the window. He stood quietly looking out the window while he waited for her.

"Aidan?" He turned to see Gillian standing in the doorway of the bath. He had not heard her open the door. It was the use of his name that struck him, breathless and intimate upon her lips.

"Gillian, I know I am intruding. I needed to talk to you." He said softly.

Gillian smiled. "No, that is alright, I needed to talk with you also."

"You did? Please tell me what it is you want to say." Aidan asked.

"I wanted to apologize for the remark I made before you left yesterday, about you and Ellie. It did not come out of my mouth the right way. I am sorry if my words hurt you." Gillian stepped closer and placed her hand gently on Aidan's cheek.

Aidan gently moved her hand from his cheek to his lips and gave her palm a slow warm kiss. "I missed you Gillian. One day, one night without seeing your lovely face or hearing your sweet voice was an eternity."

Gillian smiled, trying to hold back her emotions. "Well now, I must go away more often." She tried to lighten the mood.

"I am serious Gillian." Aidan said, pulling her into him and wrapping his arms around her. His grip was unyielding, his senses flooded with the sight of her neck and breast of her slightly loosened robe. "You try a man's control."

He loved her for herself alone, with an intensity that burned away lesser things. He loved her and wanted her. She looked deep within his eyes and stretched out her arms folding them around his neck. "I did not want too, but I missed you as well." Gillian pushed some space between them. "I should be ashamed. Ashamed for thinking of you when my thoughts should have been with the young man." She smiled and turned away from him.

Aidan grabbed her arm and spun her into him once again kissing her, kissing her hard and passionately. Gillian melted then managed some strength to severe their lips. "You are not mine to love." She backed away; her gaze did not leave his eyes.

"Whose am I? Ellie's?" Aidan asked.

"I had one night to think. To put everything in perspective. We are all aware the Princess is here to win your heart. This is what your father wants and what the people need. How can you deny either of the two? You know as well as I, you must marry the Princess." Gillian looked heart broken.

"Is this what you want? What about you? Will you marry Ranulf or Lan because father wishes it? What about what you want, what I want? Does that not mean anything?" Aidan asked.

"Yes of course it does. Nevertheless, you know as well as I, sometimes we must do what is best. We do not always get to pick and choose. You are of royal blood, you of all people must understand that." Gillian lowered her eyes. She could not look at him.

"Look at me Gillian and tell me you could be happy married to someone else and live under the same roof." Aidan paused. She could not look at him or answer. "Could you live with the thought of another woman in my bed?" Aidan suddenly got her attention with his question. Gillian did not answer, she was silent as she walked over to her dressing table and sat down. Aidan moved up behind her and watched her reflection in the mirror. Her breast rose and fell rapidly with each breath. He laid his hands on her shoulders. She closed her eyes; all resistance began to melt with his touch. He lowered his lips to her ear and took her lobe into his warm mouth.

She fought within herself. "No Aidan, stop." She stood to walk away from him. He caught her and spun her around, pushing her against the wall. His warm breath brushed her cheek. "Please Aidan." She sighed. He turned her face up with his finger, her lips parted and he kissed her pushing her mouth wider with his tongue. The roar in her head drowned out rational thought. She swallowed hard when his lips left hers. She lowered her eyes, her gaze drifting down to his mouth. "Please do not do that again." She said, breathless.

"My God, your beautiful. I have such need of you." He softly groaned. The sound he made was primeval like some ancient creature in agony. Her innocence, her trusting behavior was all that protected her from his mounting hunger. He backed away slowly, staring at her, then left the room.

CHAPTER 37

▼

Aidan watched longingly from the library window as Gillian was wandering happily in the far end of the garden, waist deep among flowers, singing to herself, with a wreath of lilies on her head as if she were some wild spite. The robins were singing exuberant vespers in the high treetops filling the golden air with their jubilant voices. The beautiful world of blossoms had lost none of its power to please Gillian and thrill her heart. Life still called to her with many insistent voices. Gillian lay down in the grass as brown swallows sailed overhead. She lay amidst the flowers and her breathing, deep and rhythmic. A touch of ruby flushed her cheeks, and she was reminded of the legend of the sleeping princess who could only wake when the right man kissed her.

"Aidan!" Ellie raised her voice snatching Aidan's attention away from the window and the beauty outside of it. "Have you heard a word I said?"

"I am sorry Ellie, you were saying?" Aidan tried to give her his attention.

Ellie walked over to the window. "What is outside this window that has you so preoccupied?"

"The gardens are lovely this time of year." He said.

Ellie took a long look outside the window and saw Gillian lying on the grass. She said nothing and took Aidan's hand, pulling him away from the window's view. She took both of his hands and placed them on her breast, holding them there. "Aidan, I could make you very happy. I have many talents if you would just let me show you."

"Yes, I am sure Ellie." Aidan said, trying not to offend her.

"I could take your mind off of what's out that window if you let me." She pressed his hands harder on her chest. "I have seen the way you look at Lady Darnaway. She is a pretty thing, but cannot give you what I can. She is young and inexperienced. Not to mention, she is not of royal blood. Her title comes from marriage alone. I have seen the way all the men in this castle look at her. The way they lavish compliments on her. I assure you it's just a passing fancy." Ellie lifted one of her hands and placed it on his crotch, squeezing gently. "Ask any man in confidence and they will tell you, they want a Lady on their arm and a whore in their bed."

Aidan tried to fight his hunger but couldn't help but to feel aroused. Too long without the companionship of a woman he rationalized. "Ellie, please."

"Please don't push me away again Aidan. Let me come to your room tonight." Ellie put her head closer to his, brushing his lips with hers. He could no longer hold her off. His lips crushed hers in a ravenous kiss that was nothing but sheer lust. She groped and pawed at him, if they had been anywhere but the library, she would have ripped the clothes right off him. Ellie slid her hand in his trousers, grabbing his taut flesh. "I can feel you have some like for me." She whispered. "I assure you that feeling will grow, just like the one in your trousers has." Her lips found his again, the two feeding off each other with a savage hunger. Aidan came up for air, raising his head to see Gillian standing in the doorway, motionless, frozen. Their eyes locked for what seemed like an eternity. His green eyes fixed themselves unwavering on hers. Gillian backed away, slowly. Aidan took small steps toward her; Ellie grabbed his arm pulling him back. Gillian bolted from sight. He called out her name; his heart sunk deep in his chest.

"It is for the best." Ellie said, with a smirk of happiness. It couldn't have been more perfect if she had planned it, she thought.

Gillian found herself outside of Lan's cottage. Her feet just seemed to carry her there, she didn't know why. She knocked softly and waited. "Come in Che're."

Gillian opened the door slowly. She didn't see Lan at first. "How did you know it was me?" She asked, waiting for her eyes to adjust to the dim light of the cottage.

"Your knock is soft, feminine." His voice revealed himself sitting in the bath. "You are the only female I know that would come to call."

Gillian lowered her eyes as soon as she noticed he was in the bath. "I am intruding, I'm sorry. I will come back another time."

"No. Please, come and sit." He pointed to a chair near his tub.

"I think I should go." She said, turning for the door.

He laughed. "Do I make you nervous?"

"No, of course not." She tried to act like she had seen many men naked in their bath.

"Then why do you act like a timid girl?" He teased. Gillian turned around and took a seat in the chair that Lan had offered, trying to prove a point. "Tell me che're, what do I owe the honor of your visit?"

"I wanted to talk to you." She said averting her eyes, without making it seem like she was.

"Wash my back and talk, I will listen." He said holding out a sponge for her.

Gillian swallowed hard and hesitated. "What, over there?"

Lan smiled, trying not to laugh at her. "This is where my back is, no?"

Gillian stood and tried to compose herself. She told herself that there was nothing wrong with washing his back. She could turn her head or overt her eyes if need be. Gillian took the sponge, dipped it in the water and gently began to wash his back. She admired the glistening water running down his smooth golden flesh.

"What is it you wanted to talk to me about?" Lan's voice shook her from her thoughts.

"Oh." She quickly finished, handed the sponge back to him and took a seat back in the chair. "I was curious about something." Suddenly, Lan stood and stepped out of the tub without warning. Gillian's mouth fell open, time stood still. His scent rose like sweet incense, like smoke from candles just snuffed. Heart pounding under the skin of his smooth chest. Tight belly glistened with droplets of water. His skin was the color of copper, light and defining. She could hardly breath. She had never truly looked at a naked man before, always choosing to avert her eyes, as any decent woman should.

Lan took a towel from the back of a chair and wrapped it around his waist. "Yes, go on cher`e."

"I want to know something about men from a man's point of view." She paused, trying to ignore the fact that a half naked man was standing right in front of her. "What do men want? In a woman I mean?"

"Ah." Lan smiled. "Well, I think men look for a woman that is nice, caring, warm hearted, with some amount of intelligence and being attractive does not hurt."

"No, that is not what I mean." Gillian paused. She stood and paced a bit about the room. "You know, it would be much easier to talk to you if you were dressed."

Lan smiled. "As you wish." Gillian turned her head as he slipped on a pair of pants. "Is this better, che're?" Gillian turned around and gave him a nod, although his chest was still bare. "Now, you were saying..."

"What kind of a woman does a man prefer, experienced or inexperienced?" Gillian asked.

"Oh, I see." Lan laughed. "I think it depends on the man."

"You for instance?" Gillian probed.

Lan grinned devilishly. "I do not have a preference." He paused and stepped closer to Gillian. "If an inexperienced woman were to give herself to me, I would honor the fact that she saved herself for me. However, an experienced woman, not a whore mind you, also has its benefits. Do you understand? Then there is the question, is the man marrying this woman or merely keeping her for a mistress."

Gillian nodded. "And what type of man do you think Aidan to be?"

"Ah I see," He paused, smiling, "I can not speak for Aidan, but I know him to be open hearted and accepting." Lan said. "That is what this is really about."

"I am sorry Lan, I have no right to ask these questions of you, being that you proposed marriage to me. I should not have come. I hope I have not offended you."

Lan took Gillian's hand and pressed his lips against it. "Che're, when I proposed to you I was aware of your feelings for Aidan." Gillian looked surprised. "You are really asking me if Aidan would prefer you a virgin or not. I can not answer that." He smiled. "On my own behalf, I will take you which either way you come to me. And if one day you decide you would like to become an experience woman, I would gladly tutor you." He grinned. "Waving all fees of course." She could not help but be sadly attracted to him. Most would have slapped his face and been justified in doing so. But she could not bring herself to perform such a symbolic hypocrisy.

Gillian thought back to Aidan and Ellie caught in their embrace and the pain it caused her. It would be easy to let that pain turn to revenge, to make Aidan suffer the way she was suffering. It would be very easy to allow Lan to take liberties no man ever had.

Gillian's face lifted to his, her lips softly parted. He pulled her close and kissed her deeply. He loosened her hair and pulled his fingers through the silken strands. Their lips parted, he held his breath as Gillian looked up from his chest to his face. He watched her dark eyes shimmering with intense concentration as she battled her conscience. She pushed him back just enough to severe the current of passion. She backed slowly, clumsily away, like a hunted animal caught in the deadly sights of an invisible stalker. "Lan, your touch pleases me very much, and makes it hard for me to say this but, I cannot allow you to make love to me, it would not be for the right reason." She backed toward the door, her hand fumbling for the door handle.

"Che're." Lan could see the pain in her eyes.

"No, please do not speak. You will no doubt say something sweet or charming and I will have an even harder time walking out this door. And I am, walking out this door." She forced her feet to move. "Right now." Gillian opened the door, while still staring at him and backed herself through the threshold.

CHAPTER 38

▼

The evening meal was quiet and uncomfortable for some. Ellie seemed to revel in the silence as if she had just won a difficult feat. Gillian chose not to reveal any hurt feelings, no matter how much Aidan seemed to ogle at Gillian, looking for some sign. Gillian had hid herself away from Aidan until dinnertime to avoid a confrontation. Lest she have to hear from him about a 'man's needs' and all.

"You know, I feel as if I have missed out on something." . Ranulf remarked, noticing the change in atmosphere at . the table. "Anyone want to fill me in?" All ignored him.

Ellie started up a conversation about Spring and up coming events, making a point to touch Aidan and whisper in his ear as much as possible. Gillian pretended not to notice and tried to turn her attention to Lan. Lan could feel Gillian was uncomfortable and played along giving her his undivided attention.

Ellie giggled girlishly making sure Gillian saw her kiss Aidan on the cheek now and then. Gillian's discomfort suddenly heightened.

"Did you enjoy your afternoon in the gardens Lady Darnaway?" Ellie asked Gillian.

"Yes, I did." Gillian answered only out of politeness. "Did you enjoy your afternoon in the library?" Gillian asked with extreme composure, pouring herself a second glass of wine.

Ellie paused before answering. "Why yes, very much. Aidan recommended some very nice books for me. He seems to know my taste so well." She giggled and brushed Aidan's hand.

Aidan kept an eye on Gillian's face. "Really, I wasn't aware there were any *picture books* in the library." Gillian heard her own words come very strong and determined. She marveled at herself, how one can hear ones own voice in their head.

Everyone stopped and stared in awe at Gillian. Ranulf almost choked on his wine at her remark and loved it. Gillian appeared calm, but Aidan could feel the tension of a powerful emotion radiating from her.

Ellie, utterly embarrassed, gasped for words. "Well! I never!"

Gillian let out one big laugh. "I find that hard to believe!" She downed the glass of wine. Everything in the room stopped as if she had just suggested they all disrobe and wallow in the frumenty pudding. She had had about enough of the Princess. Gillian stood to her feet. "If you will excuse me." She said while refilling her wine glass.

"Are you alright my dear?" Gody asked, concerned. He had never heard her speak in such a manner.

Gillian smiled. "Yes, I have not felt this good in a long while. It is rather stuffy in here, I think I will get some air."

The gentlemen stood. Aidan looked very concerned, he wanted so badly to go to her.

"I will go with you." Lan offered, putting his arm around her waist to escort her out to the veranda.

Gillian took in a deep breath. "Thank you for coming with me." She smiled.

"Would you like to tell me what all that was about? I have never seen you so defiant che're." He laughed.

"Do you think I should go apologize?" Her eyes were downcast, her long black eye lashes fanning her cheeks.

Lan put a finger under her chin and lifted her face to meet his eyes. "No, I do not. But you can tell me what happened to get you so riled up."

"I do not know what I am doing. I don't know how to act, how I should feel. I am new at this. I did not mean to bring you into any of this. I do not want you to think I am toying with your emotions." Gillian looked at him as if she were waiting for some answers. She took a deep breath and let it out slowly. "I saw the Princess and Aidan embraced in a kiss."

"Ahh, I see. There are many innocent reasons why he might have kissed her." Lan tried to rationalize.

Gillian looked at him with disbelief and a smirk. "Her hand was in his trousers."

Lan just looked at her, not knowing how to rationalize that. "It is my fault really." Gillian said. "I have pushed him into her arms. I may be …. unseasoned, but I know a man can only be put off so many times."

"Look at me Gillian. Do you love him?" Lan asked pulling her near.

"Yes. But though no one has used the words marriage, I know he is expected to marry her. That is what is best, is it not?" She looked up at him.

"In my opinion, the kingdom will survive without the Princess's dower. But Aidan will not, if he marries one he does not love." Lan said.

"He has told me as much." She said.

"You do not believe him?" He asked.

"I do not want to be responsible for any suffering of the people. I would never want him to resent me."

"But you would allow him to suffer?" Lan asked.

"Does not the needs of the many out weigh the want or needs of one? Who is to say he would not forget me in time. I have known many marriages to begin without love and later turn into love and fondness with time. It is his duty to put country and people first." Gillian said with conviction

Lan smiled. "Do you believe this yourself or are you trying to convince me you do?" He took her hand and kissed it. "It will all work out, you will see. Of course, you could always marry me. My offer still stands." Gillian smiled at him.

Gody stepped out onto the veranda. "Gillian, would you excuse us, I would like to talk with Lan." He smiled.

"Yes, of course your highness." Gillian returned the smile and entered the parlor.

"What did you want to speak to me about Sire." Lan asked.

"I am worried about Gillian, is she alright?" Gody asked.

Lan chuckled. "She is fine. She just gave Ellie a dose of her own medicine. It was due."

"You are aware I would prefer this marriage to take place between Ellie and Aidan?" Gody asked.

"Yes Sire, I am. I am also aware that you secretly wish for Gillian to be wed to Ranulf. But have you considered the consequences?" Lan asked.

"I am aware that Gillian and Aidan are fond of each other. But I believe in time Aidan will realize that this is what is best for the land." Gody said. "I would never push Gillian to marry against her will.

"Can I speak freely Sire?" Lan asked.

"Yes, please do my son."

"I have proposed marriage to Gillian. I would gladly marry her and do my best to make her happy. You must know she would be happier with me rather than Ranulf. I ask you Sire, do you know your son's own heart? His heart and Gillian's are as one, that will not change. If Aidan were forced to marry Ellie, and I to marry Gillian, then I would have to take her far away. I would not see her hurt everyday of her life, knowing the man she loves is married to another." Lan said.

"Lan, you are like my son, this is your home. It would break my heart to see you go, and Gillian as well." Gody said with sincerity.

"As for Gillian, she may protest but she will do what ever you ask of her. She loves you and honors you that much. What is best for the land? That there be more of it, or that their future king rule happy, honest and wise?" Lan said.

Gillian entered the parlor just as everyone else for an after dinner drink. Ranulf was first to meet Gillian. "Gillian, my faire lady."

"Hullo Ranulf, would you be so kind as to pour me another glass of wine?" Gillian never drank more than one glass, she was now on her fourth and the effects were starting to show.

Ranulf leaped over to the wine. "Your wish is my command."

Ellie sat on the sofa, silent, trying to regain a semblance of control. Aidan stood in front of the fire. "Gillian, I think you have had enough." Aidan said.

Ellie sneered. "She's drunk as a lord."

Gillian turned and looked at Ellie. "Drunk, no your highness. Tipsy, maybe." She laughed.

Aidan smiled at Gillian, finding it impossible to do otherwise. "Why don't you sit down and relax Gillian."

"I do not wish to sit. Do you wish to sit Ranulf?" Gillian giggled.

"No, I do not. Let us dance!" Ranulf said, grabbing Gillian about the waist.

Gillian laughed. "There is no music."

"Of course there is." Ranulf began to hum Liebesleid as he twirled Gillian around the room. Gillian burst with laughter. Aidan smiled as he was reminded of the time him and Gillian found themselves at a celebration in the forest. He remembered her laughter and the glow on her face.

Ellie looked at Aidan as he watched the two, silently cursing the smile on his face. Lan and Gody entered after hearing the noise from inside.

Gillian placed her hand over her cheek. Her face was flushed and she couldn't stop laughing. "I think we need to stop." She said breathless.

"If you insist." Ranulf stopped twirling Gillian and helped her over to the sofa. "How about it Ellie?" He held out his hand.

Ellie gave him a look of sheer absurdity. "Don't be so infantile, it is your least attractive quality Ranulf."

"Is that a no?" Ranulf smirked.

"Maybe the Princess does not like to dance." Gillian said.

Ellie looked at her and curled her mouth into a slight smile, that was neither gentle nor amused, but somehow depreciating. "I like to dance just fine. At a dance with music."

"Aidan is a wonderful dancer." Gillian said while smiling at Aidan. "Did you know that, Princess?" Gillian looked at Ellie and waited for her answer.

"No." Ellie said with little emotion.

"I imagine there is very little that Aidan does not do well. Wouldn't you agree Princess?" Gillian said smiling at Aidan. Ellie said nothing but there was a curious scrutinizing quality in her gaze—a deliberate summing up.

Aidan bowed his head to Gillian, but tried not to show too much emotion.

"Don't worry Aidan, judging the look on some faces, I shall turn and jeer at you directly." Gillian said teasingly.

"Jeer as much as you like." Aidan said with a grin.

"How rude." Ellie said, but Gillian ignored her.

Lan poured himself a drink and joined Aidan next to the fire. "Rudeness is an art really, like everything else; some people are just more finished at it than others. Personally, I prefer the open rudeness to the veiled variety." He smirked at Ellie.

Aidan stood in front of the hearth, craving and despising its heat. He needed to be cold. Cold and composed to be able to deny his feelings.

"Gillian, your glass appears to be empty, let me remedy that predicament for you." Ranulf approached her with bottle in hand.

"I believe Gillian has had enough, Ranulf." Aidan spoke with some authority.

"Don't be silly." Gillian said, holding her empty glass up in the air.

"Ranulf." Aidan said calmly but with a tone that could shatter stone. Ranulf looked at Aidan and knew he was serious.

"Yes, well, maybe Aidan is right Gillian." Ranulf said, cowardly.

"Party pooper." Gillian said to Aidan.

"That I might be, but you will thank me in the morning." Aidan said.

"I think someone needs to help Gillian to her chambers and to bed." Gody said.

"I don't need any help." Gillian said, trying to stand and just as suddenly found herself back on the sofa. "Alright, maybe I need a little help."

"I will volunteer for this unpleasant task of taking her up to bed, undressing her and tucking her into bed." Ranulf too quickly donated his service.

"Yes, I'm sure you will." Aidan looked at him sternly.

"I'll ring for Aggie." Gody suggested.

"No need father, Aggie retired early for bed. Besides it's easier if I just carry her up." Aidan said.

"Yes, how convenient." Ellie said, under her breath.

"Please, stop making such a fuss over me." Gillian said.

Aidan walked over to Gillian and scooped her up in his arms. "See, it is not a problem." He said smiling at her. Ellie wanted to say something to change his mind, but knew the point was mute.

Effortlessly, Aidan reached Gillian's chambers. He pushed open the door with his foot then laid her on the bed. "I am really not sleepy." Gillian said.

"You will be." Aidan answered as he shut the chamber door.

"Are you going to tuck me in?" Gillian asked with a little flirtation in her voice.

Aidan smiled. "Careful, you should not give me any ideas being in your condition." Aidan took a blanket from the foot of the bed and covered her with it.

"Then how about a bedtime story." She giggled. "Sit." She patted the space on the bed next to her.

Aidan sat down. The pain in him was sharp, almost unbearable. "I am lonely Gillian. I am lonely beyond a man's endurance." He said, lighting a candle next to the bed..

Gillian reached up and touched his cheek, then looked at the candle. "When I was young, my mother made candles and would pass them out among the unfortunate, so that they would always have a light to guide them. She made me a small candle to sit by my bed at night. And she told me there would never be darkness to fear as long as I had that little candle. She told me that inside each person a tiny light burned, like the flame of a candle and that we were all connected through our tiny light." Gillian took his hand and smiled. "I will always be a candle for you Aidan, you will never be alone."

Aidan pulled her hand up to his lips and kissed it. "I want more than just your friendship Gillian. I want you to be my wife." He said reaching out and pulling her into his embrace.

"The Princess can offer you so much more. Her dower is worth more than I could ever offer." Gillian said, not wanting to let go.

"No, you are wrong. I want you Gillian. For yourself. For your mind and heart as much as your beauty." He kissed her, but not with a fiery passion this time, but lovingly. Slowly he released her and laid her to rest on her pillow. He placed his finger gently over her lips to stop her from speaking. "Get some sleep." He stood and left the room.

Aidan didn't bother returning to the parlor; no doubt, Ellie would be waiting on him. He did not care to hear her remarks. He just wanted to retire to his chambers with his thoughts.

Aidan met Ranulf in the corridor just outside his room. "Come up for air so soon?" Ranulf teased Aidan.

"I hate to ask Ranulf, but I'm sure you will tell me what you are referring to anyway." Aidan waited.

"I did not think you would be leaving the lovely ladies chambers so soon?" Ranulf hinted.

"Ranulf, only you would take advantage of the lady's condition." Aidan said nothing more and entered his room.

"True, so true." Ranulf smiled as Aidan slammed the door in his face. "I guess this means you don't want to share any intimate details." Ranulf said through the closed doors.

CHAPTER 39

▼

The next morning Gillian awoke just before lunchtime. She hadn't realized she had slept for so long. However, despite all the wine from last night she awoke fresh. Gillian opened a window and breathed in the fresh air. In the courtyard below, a child of one of the servants with a voice of an angel chanted a rhyme. "Glamoryam...the golden apple of the sun...Isabelle de Clare faire O faire!"

Gillian took one last deep breath of air before dressing. She could smell the rain way off in the horizon. The clouds were not yet threatening rain, but she knew they would before nightfall.

As Gillian came down the stairs, she could see the others entering the dining room for lunch. Lan was straggling in the corridor.

"Psst!" Gillian tried to get Lan's attention. Lan paused. "Psst!" he heard even louder. He turned around to see Gillian at the foot of the stairs motioning him over to her. He smiled; sensing what the worried look on her face was about.

"Sleeping beauty awakes." Lan smiled.

"Please tell me I didn't do or say anything that I might have to apologize for today." Gillian studied the look on his face.

Lan took the opportunity to tease her. The look on his face turned serious. "I am not sure if you want to go in there che're."

Gillian had a look of sheer terror. "Alright, go ahead and tell me what I did."

"Oh ma che're, the things you said! I do not know where to begin. And when you...well, we were all shocked!"

Gillian covered her face with her hands. "Oh dear Lord, what have I done."?

Lan could no longer hold back his laughter. Gillian uncovered her face and realized he was playing a trick on her.

"Oh how cruel." She laughed.

"I am sorry ma che're, I could not resist. You did nothing to be ashamed of last night." He grinned. "Come, I will take you into the dinning room."

Gillian and Lan entered and took their seats. "Ah Gillian, how are you feeling today?" Gody asked.

"Well, your highness. Quite well." She looked at Aidan and smiled. Aidan returned the smile, although not sure of what to make of it.

"No headache Gillian?" Ranulf asked.

"No, believe it or not. Actually, I feel rather refreshed." Gillian smiled.

"Well then, I guess wine has an opposite effect on you. Most would need something to clear out the cobwebs." Ranulf laughed. "Maybe you should drink more often."

"I think I will leave the indulging to you Ranulf." Gillian smiled. "And if I said or did anything to offend anyone, please accept my apologies."

"Stop worrying child and eat something, you did nothing wrong." Gody smiled warmly at her.

"I think I will go riding after lunch." Gillian said, pouring herself a glass of water.

"It looks as if it might rain, do you think you should?" Aidan asked.

"I think the rain will hold off for a while." She smiled at him. "I will be alright, but I will be sure to take my cloak just in case." Gillian smiled again. "Would you like to join me?" Gillian's invite threw him off. Ellie spoke up before Aidan could answer.

"Aidan promised to take me on a walk near the loch." Ellie said, cuddling up to Aidan's arm.

"Yes. I did." Aidan answered not looking forward to it at all. "Some other time?"

"Yes, of course." Gillian answered.

"Ranulf, why don't you join Gillian, it's been sometime since you went riding." Gody suggested.

"As honored as I would be to spend the afternoon with such a beautiful lady, I'm afraid the wine from last night has had adverse effects on my head. I don't dare go near anything that moves today." Ranulf said. "Sorry Gillian."

"Don't be silly. I am perfectly capable of going riding by myself." She smiled. "I have done so on many occasion and Lan can attest to my riding know how."

"Yes, Gillian does know her way around a horse." Lan said, reaching for the bread.

"Of course she does." Ellie said with sarcasm.

"Do you ride much at home Princess?" Gillian asked, choosing to ignore Ellie's sarcasm.

"No. I am not very fond of horses, I'm afraid. Smelly beast." Ellie exclaimed.

"No, you wouldn't be the kind to appreciate the magnificence of a such a creature." Gillian said, rather a matter of factly.

"Well, on that note....I will excuse myself and go and saddle your horse for you Gillian. It is rather cool in here all of a sudden." Lan said.

"Thank you Lan, I will be down shortly." Gillian said.

Gillian rode along a winding path on horseback. A crow hovered overhead, carving designs in the air. The air was fresh and alive and smelled of pending rain. Gillian had a delicious feeling of alertness, a change of heart. Though only a short time ago she refused to allow any commitment of real feeling for Aidan to be known; for some strange reason it didn't matter now. She did truly love Aidan and he loved her. During the night she had a realization. If she were to give herself to any man it would have to be the one she loved. Though she never expected to win him, at least she could share his love for whatever time allowed.

Gillian had grown tired of trying to do what was expected of her. She had never loved before and suddenly realized this could be her last chance to experience true love. She no longer wanted to push Aidan away and certainly felt no loyalties toward the Princess. Ellie may have him for the rest of his life, but Gillian wanted at least one night.

Gillian stopped to rest her horse. She gave him a pat and bent over to whisper in his ear. "Life should be as simple and free as this." A loud thunderclap sounded overhead. "Well I guess it is time to turn back now boy, come on."

Gillian arrived back at the barn just as the rain began to fall lightly on Aberdour. She felt such a weight had been lifted off her heart with her decision. Lan took the reins as Gillian slid from the horse.

"Did you enjoy your ride, che're?"

"Yes, as always and as always it was too short." Gillian said, pulling the hood of her cloak over her head. "Have you seen Aidan?"

"No, che're, but since it has begun to rain I imagine they are inside. I do not think the Princess would allow herself to be caught in the rain." Lan laughed.

Gillian ran up to the castle just before the heavy rain had begun. She shook off the rain and hung her cloak up on a hook near the door.

Aggie met her. "Dreadful rain, canna git ya a sput a tee?"

"No thank you Aggie, but you can tell me if you have seen Aidan." Gillian asked.

"Aye, they jost cum in they ded. Oop chongin thir wet cluths I magin."

"Thank you Aggie." Gillian said as she made her way up the stairs for Aidan's chambers.

Gillian knocked on the door to the first room of Aidan's chambers, which was the sitting room. There was no answer, so she entered. She reached to knock on the bedroom doors, but found it was slightly ajar. Gillian took a deep breath, ready to tell him all about her change of heart. She pushed the door open and entered the bed-room. Aidan was nowhere in sight, but Ellie's clothes lay at the threshold. Gillian took a step closer to the bed and could now clearly see Ellie in the bed under the covers. Gillian froze in her steps when her eyes met Ellie's.

"Gillian, you should have knocked." Ellie said, trying to look embarrassed.

"I did." Gillian answered.

"Oh, well I didn't hear you. You do have a way of enter-ing at the most inopportune moment." Ellie said, holding the sheets over her breast.

"Yes, don't I. Excuse me." Gillian left the room.

Aidan came out from the bath drying his hair with a towel. He did not know Ellie was there and was surprised to find her in his bed. "Ellie, what are you doing?"

"What does it look like? Come here, I have something to show you." She grinned a devilish grin.

"I think I will stay where I am. I heard voices. Were you talking to someone?" Aidan asked, standing by the fire.

"No one of importance." Ellie patted the empty space beside her. "I grow cold, come warm me."

"I suggest if you are cold, you put some clothes on." Aidan walked over to her things, picked them up and threw them on the bed. Aidan noticed that now the rain was pouring heavily. He wondered if Gillian had made it back safely. "You may dress in privacy, I have something to attend to." Aidan said, leaving the room.

"I wonder what that could be." Ellie said, after he had left the room. She gave his pillow a hard punch.

Aidan went into the parlor where his father was sitting reading. "Father, have you seen Gillian?"

"Only briefly. She seemed in a hurry about something." He said, glancing up from his book.

"I was worried she had not made it back before the rain." Aidan said.

"Well she did, so you can stop worrying, my son." Gody returned to his book.

Dinner came and went and still no Gillian. Aidan was beside himself with worry and confusion. Gillian did send a message through Lan that she would be skipping the evening meal. She did join them after dinner in the parlor. She was not up to sitting through dinner face to face with Ellie and Aidan. But she wasn't about to let Ellie get the best of her either.

"Gillian, are you alright my dear?" Gody rushed to her side.

"Yes, fine. I had one of those headaches; I thought it best to sleep it off with a nap. I am perfectly fine now." She smiled.

Aidan watched her every move; something was not right with her. She avoided his gaze. Ellie beamed with satisfaction.

"Did you get caught in the rain while riding?" Aidan asked.

"No." Gillian said, with a short answer without looking at Aidan directly.

Aidan was determined to meet her gaze. "Did you have a nice ride?" Aidan asked stepping directly in front of her.

Gillian looked straight into his eyes. "Yes." She answered firmly. Aidan studied her eyes; he could tell she was angry with him. "Did you have a nice *walk*?" She stressed the word 'walk' through gritted teeth.

Softly he spoke where only she could hear. "I would have enjoyed myself more had I been with you."

Gillian gave him a stern look. "I seriously doubt that." Gillian joined Lan by the fire. Aidan was puzzled, but knew it must have to do with the smile on Ellie's face.

Aidan stood next to Ranulf to have a word with him. "I need a favor." Aidan whispered to Ranulf. "Can you manage to capture Ellie's attention for a few moments?"

"I think I could sway her with my charms long enough to take her eyes off of you." Ranulf said. Ranulf took a seat next to Ellie as Aidan slid up beside Gillian. "Tell me Ellie, tell me about your life at court." There was one thing he knew, the Princess loved to talk about herself.

Aidan took Gillian by the arm and slowly pulled her out of sight through the shadows out onto the veranda. "Why am I out here?" Gillian asked with her arms folded across her chest.

"Have I wronged you somehow? Did I miss something?" Aidan asked.

"Alright, if you must know." Gillian unfolded her arms. "I came to your chambers today, after my ride. Do you want to guess what I saw or should I give you the details?"

Aidan rubbed his face in distress. "Ellie. You saw Ellie in my bed." He started to grin at her. "You are jealous."

Gillian huffed at him and turned her back. "That is not the point."

"I can explain. It really wasn't what you think. I was in the bath and when I came out she was in my bed. I didn't even know she was in the room. I handed her her clothes and left to find you."

Gillian turned around slowly. "And that is all there was to it? That is the whole truth?"

Aidan pulled her into the shadows and pushed her gently up against the wall. "I have no reason to lie." Gillian slid her hands around his neck and pulled his lips to hers. She kissed him passionately then released him. Aidan looked deep in her eyes searching for a reason. She pulled him close again and kissed him even deeper. She released him and gave him a coy little smile.

Gillian left Aidan to rejoin the others, without a word said. Aidan remained behind, not in any shape at the moment to make an appearance. He needed a moment to cool down.

Gillian slid back in place next to Lan in front of the fire. The Princess was still ranting about herself and had not noticed Gillian or Aidan's absence.

"Everything alright ma che're?" Lan whispered. Gillian answered with a nod as she noticed Aidan creeping back in from the veranda.

He had almost made it. "Aidan! What on earth are you doing outside? Don't you know there is a storm raging as we speak." Ellie interrupted her own story.

"I needed some fresh air." Aidan answered.

"In the middle of my story?" Ellie became all a fluster.

"Forgive me Ellie, please continue." Aidan gave her a bow of his head.

"I hardly see the point now, besides I lost my train of thought." Ellie sat back on the sofa and pouted.

"Well, I need a drink, join me Aidan." Ranulf suggested. Aidan followed. "Lord man, does she ever shut up?" He whispered. "Do you know what you are getting yourself into?"

"It is not by choice I assure you." Aidan answered.

"I think I will turn in early tonight, goodnight all." Gillian said.

"More sleep? I hope this is not a sign of laziness Lady Darnaway." Ellie said with a sharp tone.

"One can never get enough beauty sleep." Gillian smiled. "Maybe you should try it." Everyone couldn't help but to snicker. Gillian made sure to give Aidan a little smile as she left the room.

CHAPTER 40

▼

The night seemed interminable and the rumble of thunder shook the very foundations of the castle. The rain the storm had brought clawed at the windows like a cold creature seeking warmth. All of Aberdour lay in silence; nothing was heard but the torrents of rain pounding the ground.

The emptiness of the night was an indissoluble cold settling over Gillian. Not even the fire in the hearth was warming. The storm outside raged on, she knew sleep would not come easily tonight. Gillian slipped into her slippers and made her way to Aidan's chambers.

A slight sound caught Aidan's attention; he turned his eyes in the direction of the door. It was a woman or at least the dark silhouette of a woman. But not merely a woman, a magnificent woman, he knew at once it was Gillian.

A fire burned in the hearth taking the chill from the damp stone walls. Candles were lit, casting pools of golden light across the room. Aidan stood before the fire having just bathed, wearing only his trousers. Golden light gleamed across the muscles of his shoulders and chest. Gillian wanted to touch him, to learn the contours of him. Her fingers burned with longing as she curled her hand into a fist. Her feet froze in the place where she stood.

Aidan slowly approached her. He took her hand and drew her inside. Gillian stood in the spill of candlelight; she held a mix of yearning and trepidation on her face.

"You are trembling." He opened his arms and she stepped into them. Aidan led her over by the fire.

If she had been naïve and innocent just moments ago, her wanton passion now was growing, ignoring the convictions she clung to. Gillian reached up and touched his face. Droplets of water sprinkled his honey colored mane.

Aidan slowly bent his head, found her lips and began to kiss her with a fierce hunger that had suddenly unleashed itself. Instead of pushing him away, she found herself yielding to his hunger. The warm insistent pressure of his mouth parted her lips, sending currents of fire throughout her body. A melting sweetness spread through her, then she went limp against him. Without taking his lips from hers, Aidan moved Gillian backward to the bed. He slowly slid her dressing gown off her shoulders. Gillian let it slide from her body along with her innocence. He parted from her mouth long enough to untie the bodice on her gown. She felt his velvety fingers slide against her arms. His arms lifted her onto the bed. Gillian heard Aidan's breath quicken as he drank in the sight of her naked body.

Gillian reclined against the silken pillows of the bed, she covertly watched Aidan unfasten his trousers and slip out of them. She was in awe of his broad shoulders and chest tapering into a slender waist. His penis was hard and erect like an obedient soldier, rising from a nest of dark golden hair.

At last he was going to take her. She wanted him, but his size and girth caused a shiver of apprehension. "How beautiful you are." Gillian heard her voice say aloud.

Aidan joined her on the bed and took Gillian into his arms. She tasted the sweetness of his mouth, felt the length and hardness of his body naked against hers. Lying within the warmth and strength of his arms, she found it impossible to restrain from the mounting need of him. When she felt his large warm hand cup the soft peak of her breast, she gasped as if a flash of lightning had shot through her. The touch of his hands, the pressure of his body, the feeling of being gently controlled by him created in Gillian sensations that she had not known existed, and was powerless to deny. His lips traveled slowly down the creamy column of her neck to kiss the white mounds of her breast, his tongue caressing back and forth over each nipple.

Gillian's arms went around the back of his neck; her fingers laced themselves in the softness of his long golden hair as she pressed his head deeper into her bosom. Aidan lifted his head to gaze down at her; his eyes heavy-lidded with passion had deepened to emerald. She could feel his hardness against her thigh, like a rock.

"I will do nothing against your will. Do you want me to stop?" He said in a breathless voice.

"No, if you stop I will die." She murmured. Aidan's hand moved lowered between her thighs. Her legs parted with a will of their own, and when he stroked her, the shock of pleasure was so intense she wanted to scream. Gillian did not know where to put her hands, but the urge to touch him overwhelmed her. She ran her hand searchingly down the taut flesh of his stomach to his plumage of thick hair. She reached his hardness and gently closed her fingers around him. A sound of suffering came from his throat. "Make love to me my Prince."

Aidan rose up over her and she felt a flood of juices between her legs. He knelt over her and slowly entered her. Gillian arched her back and let out a moan as she opened herself to him. She cried out in pleasure. He forced himself deeper and she felt him bathed in her juices. She moaned in time with his movements and then suddenly he drew himself out. Gillian gasped and drew her hands up to his face pulling his lips to hers. He smothered her with kisses.

"I have wanted you for so long." Aidan drove into her again and she felt herself explode with a quivering pleasure. Aidan gave a moan of relief and she felt him come with a last thrusting motion.

Gillian lay against his chest. He cradled her, and never stopped kissing her. Gillian knew clearly, as clearly as she knew she was in Aidan's embrace that she had never been so alive as she was now. The sight of him, his being there with her had brought her to a fire in life she had never known.

CHAPTER 41

▼

Aidan and Gillian were late making their way down to breakfast. The others had already begun. "There you two are. We started without you." Gody said.

"That is alright father." Aidan said.

Gillian and Aidan glanced at each other as they seated themselves. The both of them were quiet, trying to hide the smiles that played around their lips.

Ranulf studied their faces. "How odd for the two of you to sleep late on the same morning." He smirked. Ellie stopped eating and looked at Ranulf.

Gillian made another glance in Aidan's direction before speaking. "I'm afraid I couldn't sleep last night. I was up most of the night reading." She said before taking a sip of her tea.

Ranulf looked at Aidan. "And what is your excuse dear cousin?" He smiled.

Aidan gave him a stern look, which Ranulf ignored. "I wasn't aware I needed one. Dear cousin." Ranulf looked at him with a know-it-all grin.

Ellie was now suspicious thanks to Ranulf, and began to watch the two of them as well.

Ranulf turned his attention to Gillian. "There is something different about you

This morning Gillian." He rested his finger on his chin while he concentrated on her face.

"Yes, it's called lack of sleep." Gillian said.

"No, that's not it." Ranulf said, still puzzled.

"Oh leave her alone, Ranulf." Gody said. "Let her eat her breakfast in peace."

"Yes, I agree with Ranulf." Ellie said. "There is something different about you."

"Nonsense, I told you it is from lack of sleep." Gillian exclaimed.

"Well it doesn't look as if the rain is going to let up anytime soon. You might as well try to get some more sleep ma che're." Lan said, before wiping his mouth with his napkin. "If you will excuse me now, I have work to do."

Gillian was silent in thought. Aidan watched her fingers unconsciously caress the curve of her water glass. A shudder of desire ran through him remembering her touch on his skin. Gillian looked up, her eyes fusing with Aidan's. There were no words between them, nor did there have to be. Anyone who might have noticed would have seen but a single look, a single trembling breath, and a single desire. In their silence Aidan found peace, a sense of balance. He could not define it yet it was so.

The sky was clustered thick with clouds scudding over the sky and the only sound was the steadiness of the rain falling down and tapping at the windows. The wind danced about the treetops like a whirling waltz. The evening dragged on with a somnolent mood hanging about the parlor due to the weather. Gillian sat in the library curled up in a chair with a book. Everyone else sat in the parlor sipping brandy by the fire joined in light conversation. Gody came to attention when Aggie entered and introduced a guest.

"Sire Mr. Duncan iz ear ta see ya."

"Please, show him in Aggie." Gody said.

Duncan entered splattered with rain. "Good evening all."

"Duncan what brings you out in this weather?" Gody asked.

"I had some surprising news that I just found and had to share it immediately. Is the Lady Darnaway home?" Duncan asked.

"Yes. But I'm not sure where she is at the moment." Gody answered. "You look as if you are about to burst with information."

"Yes, it feels that way. I could not waste a moment or sit on this information until the rain passed."

"Ranulf pour Mr. Duncan a brandy." Gody suggested. "Please have a seat and warm yourself by the fire."

"Here you are Duncan. This will knock the chill off." Ranulf said handing him the brandy.

"I'll get Aggie to find Gillian while you sip your brandy." Gody said.

Ellie was very curious to what Duncan had to tell Gillian. It had to be of good news from the look on his face. "I believe Lady Darnaway is napping." Ellie inched her way a little closer to Mr. Duncan. "I'm afraid Lady Darnaway did not get much sleep last night. The poor dear." She said to Duncan. "You know how us women need our beauty sleep." Ellie let out a giggle. "Why don't you tell us the news and let Lady Darnaway get her much needed sleep."

"Ellie, I don't think that is a good idea." Aidan warned.

"Why? All of you are her family. If it is bad news don't you think it would be better if she heard it from you?" Ellie persuaded.

"Well I can tell you it isn't bad news." Duncan smiled. "Maybe the Princess is right. It would be a nice surprise and it might mean more coming from all of you."

"Alright Duncan out with it." Gody said.

"It seems that Lord Diaspad owned more than just the Darnaway Estate." He paused. "I researched further and found he also owned land under an assumed name." Duncan paused again.

"So what are you saying?" Aidan asked.

"Lord Darnaway was a wealthy land owner. Very wealthy! I don't know exactly how he came about so much but legally it is all his and I have the deed proving it."

"How wealthy?" Aidan asked.

"400 acres. Which now all belongs to Lady Darnaway." Duncan smiled.

Ellie gasped, she knew it was much more than her father was offering in her dower. Her eyes followed Aidan as he poured himself another brandy.

Ranulf clapped his hands together. "Who would have thought our Gillian is a wealthy heiress." Ellie looked at Ranulf and sneered.

"Well now, I have delivered my news I leave all of you to tell Lady Darnaway anyway you wish. I'm sure she will be very happy." Duncan said his good-byes as he was walking out of the parlor. Gillian who was just down the hall in the library heard his voice. She recognized his voice and assumed he must have been calling on her. With book in hand, Gillian quietly made her way down the hall to the parlor. But before she entered, she saw Aidan holding Ellie's hand. Gillian stood in the shadows unseen as she watched Aidan and Ellie speaking privately. She could not see Ellie's face but could see the tender expression on Aidan's face. Then he tenderly kissed her hand and smiled warmly at her. Gillian held her book tight against her chest and ducked back further into the shadows when Ellie turned to leave the room. Ellie walked right pass Gillian without seeing her. Gillian was so well hidden she never got a good look at Ellie's face as she whisked by.

The men waited until Ellie was out of sight. Gody took the Brandy and poured them all another drink. Gillian watched from the dimness. "Well there looks as if there is going to be a wedding!" Gody said, holding up his glass.

"Here, here! It's about time." Ranulf said. Ranulf said as he patted Aidan on the back.

Gillian's heart sunk low in her chest. She pieced it all together in her mind. Mr. Duncan must have been there to settle the transfer of Ellie's dower. Aidan holding Ellie's hand in a private moment. Now the talk of a wedding. The dreaded day had arrived.

Her pain was unbearable sucking the breath from her lungs. She wanted to cry out, to release the pain but it knotted up inside her strangling her voice. She could bare it no longer. Gillian leaped from the shadows and ran out the garden doors, dropping the book she was clutching. The wind pulled at Gillian's hair and whipped it across her face. She ran down the gardens steps into the pouring rain not knowing where she was going.

Aidan left the parlor and was startled by the sudden banging of the garden door from the wind. He walked over to close it and saw a book lying on the floor. He reached for the door handle and peered out into the garden. From a sudden flash of lightning he saw the figure of a woman running down the hill near the barn. He knew at once it was Gillian. Without a second thought he ran after her.

The wind howled and ripped the leaves from the trees, scattering them to the ground. Aidan looked up at the rolling sky, closing his eyes against the rain. "Gillian!" He called out to her, but she didn't stop. He caught up with her and grabbed her arm.

"Leave me alone Aidan!" She said standing before him in the rain, in her wet now transparent dress.

"Come out of the rain." He took her by the arm, trying to pull her toward the shelter of the barn.

"Go back to your celebration! To your bride to be!" She jerked her arm free.

Aidan smiled. "No Gillian you don't understand. I don't know what you saw or heard, but it was wrong." Gillian stopped fighting him to listen. "It is our wedding that we were toasting."

"But I saw you talking with Ellie, holding her hand." Gillian wiped the rain from her eyes.

"Yes, I was telling her I could not marry her. That I loved you and wanted you for my bride." He smiled.

"I don't understand. How can that be."?

"Duncan found another deed to land no one knew about. 400 acres. You're a wealthy woman!" Aidan said, putting his hands on her shoulders. "Did you hear me Gillian? Ellie can no longer stand between us."

"Kiss me." Gillian pleaded. Her eyes drifted down to his lips. Aidan took her in his arms and kissed her deeply.

"Come with me out of the rain." Aidan said, taking Gillian by the hand and leading her into the barn.

They escaped into the dry barn that was lit from a single oil lamp. "Where are you taking me?" Gillian asked.

"Somewhere we can be alone." Aidan started up a latter that led to the loft filled with hay.

"Up there?" Gillian stood at the first step of the latter looking up.

"Yes, I assure you it is safe and quite cozy." Aidan said from top of the loft.

Gillian climbed cautiously up the latter. She reached the top and looked around in what dim light there was. Aidan spread a blanket out on a loose pile of hay, before plopping himself down. "Come, join me." He said reaching out his hand.

Gillian smiled as she took his hand. Aidan pulled her down on top of him with one jerk. His thumbs gently stroked down her cheeks wiping the rain from her face. His lips closed over hers. Gillian tasted the urgency of his mouth stealing her breath away. She gasped when his kiss ended; then again she gasped at the warmth of his mouth on her throat. "From this moment on we will never be separated." He whispered against her skin.

Gillian pulled his shirt open, placing her hand on his hard chest, her fingertips pressing his hard nipple. "I am yours my love." Aidan rolled the both of them over. He pinned Gillian underneath him. She could feel the prickles of the hay through the blanket. His mouth crushed down on hers, thrusting his tongue between her lips. Gillian's tingle turned into a sharp ache of need creating a blaze between her thighs. She unfastened Aidan's trousers and slid her hand down his hard stomach to his magnificent hard penis and gently eased her fingers around it. She felt it throb against her palm as she stroked and coaxed him gently. A prisoner of his senses, he let out a soft moan. She released him to push his trousers from his hips to feel his hardness against her. Aidan delicately slid her undergarments from her hips. His fingers lovingly caressed her silken flesh. Her body shuddered at the intensity of his pleasing fingers. "I want you Aidan." She said closing her fingers around his pulsating flesh. She drew him to her wetness and she felt his hard flesh thrust inside her. She arched her back to take all of him. She clasped her hands on his buttocks, pulling him in to her.

Their bodies came together; retreating then came together again with even more urgency. Ripples of pure pleasure swept through her. His engorged flesh with its pulsing veins slicked with her wetness moved deep inside her. Her aching sex was filled. At last she cried out in relief and felt him come with a last driving motion. He gave a soft cry and held her close.

Gillian lay beside Aidan nestled in his warm embrace. She buried her face in his sweet smelling hair. Then he kissed her lovingly. He lifted her chin with his finger to meet his eyes. "Be my future Queen, my wife?"

Gillian smiled warmly. "Yes my Prince, my salvation."

ABOUT THE AUTHOR

Mechel Cisco is an artist who paints with a romantic vision and chose to put the visions into words. She fell in love with Bronte's story of Heathcliff and Catherine and was hooked on romances from that point on.